# In A Cream Packard

### Edward R Hackemer

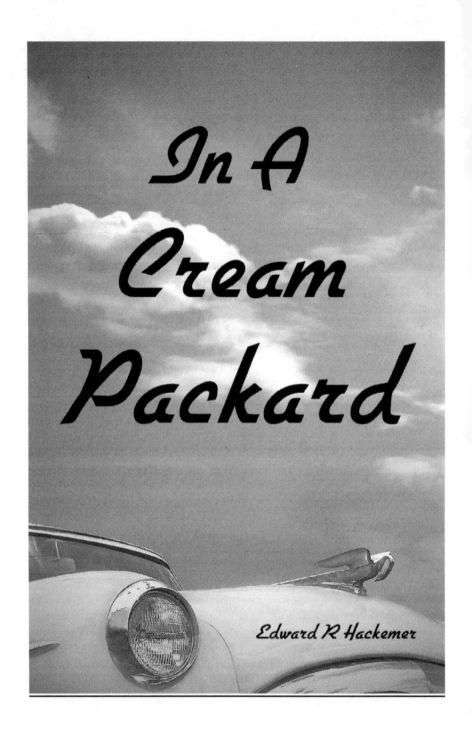

In A

Cream

Packard

Edward R Hackemer

# In A Cream Packard

*(Book 1 - Throckmorton Family Novels)*

~ a novel by Edward R Hackemer ~

Hardcover ISBN: 9798792787889

ISBN-13: 978-1482662801

ISBN-10: 1482662809

# Acknowledgements and Credits

My proofer, Edny.
My editor & pen pal, Letitia.
My reader, You.
The writers, lyricists, musicians, and singers.
The Pirkle Woods, Georgia Packard Parkers.

Cover photo & design:  © 2014 Edward R Hackemer
Location: Ball Ground, Georgia, USA
Longitude: 34.3482381
Latitude: -84.3798456
Above sea level: 1154 ft
Subject: 1954 Packard Patrician
May 3, 2012

# TITLES BY THIS AUTHOR

Tᴏᴏ Sᴏᴏ TᴏᴏᴏᴏMᴏᴏTᴏN NᴏᴏᴏᴏS:

## Sangria Sunsets
*(Book 6 in the series © 2017)*
ISBN-13: 978-1542615945

## The Flying Phaeton
*(Book 5 in the series © 2015)*
ISBN-13: 978-1518707858

## Dollar To Doughnut
*(Book 4 in the series © 2014)*
ISBN-13: 978-1505245110

## A Bridge To Cross
*(Book 3 in the series © 2014)*
ISBN-13: 978-1494972820

## The Katydid Effect
*(Book 2 in the series © 2013)*
ISBN-13: 978-1482669831

## In A Cream Packard
*(Book 1 in the series © 2011-13)*
ISBN-13: 978-1482662801

## PLUS

Tʜᴇ Tᴡᴏ Tʀᴜꜰꜰᴀᴜᴛ Tᴀʟᴇs:

## Phryné Isn't French
*(Book 1 in the series © 2018)*
ISBN-13:978-1975926397

## Phryné Crossing
*(Book 2 in the series © 2020)*
ISBN-13:979-8581963524

Aɴᴅ Tᴡᴏ Cʜᴜɴᴋs ᴏꜰ Rᴇʟᴀᴛɪᴠᴇ Aɴᴄᴇsᴛʀʏ:

## Fables Foibles & Follies
*(A quirky anthology © 2019)*
ISBN-13: 978-1790613717

## Cobble Tales
*(Sussex Stories © 2022)*
ISBN-13: 979-8364639899

*Titles are available in Hardcover, Paperback or Kindle® format.*

Visit the author's Facebook, Goodreads, or Amazon page.

v

# CONTENTS

# THE FINE PRINT

Sincere effort has been taken to ensure that this novel contains the straight stuff for 1954. Please realize that most of this story is fictional except the parts that are factual. The needle was changed to protect the record and only the record. Lingo used in the text is contemporary to the timeline. Regular folk didn't use politically correct language too much in 1954 because they weren't woke up or instructed right.

Most characters in this book are fictional. But any resemblance in the description or name to any real person, living or dead is purely coincidental and unintentional. Any name specific identification, dialogue, expressed or implied, comments or opinions used by any character or characterizations in this book are used solely for descriptive and entertainment purposes. Snowflakes can melt no matter what Arthur Mometer reads.

Brand named products or services (whether actual or fictitious) mentioned in this book are the trademark of their respective owners (past or present) and are used solely for descriptive purposes. The reader should feel free to turn the volume down when the commercial is on and check for availability in your zip code before ordering.

Any lyrics or music mentioned in this book are the intellectual property of individual copyright holders and are referenced only for descriptive purposes. The reader is encouraged to purchase the music, listen and begin to tap his or her foot enthusiastically.

Retail, government, service, or religious institutions mentioned in this book, whether actual or fictitious, are not included as an endorsement of their products, services, or ideology. They are recounted solely for descriptive purposes and not simply an attempt to be ostentatiously opinionated.

# PREFACE: 1954

This is a story of the way they were and the strong forces that effected changes to their world.

Here are a few words taken from the context of a speech by President Dwight D. Eisenhower in Cadillac Square, downtown Detroit, Michigan, on October 29, 1954:

*"We are pushing ahead with a great road program, a road program that will take this Nation out of its antiquated shackles of secondary roads all over this country and give us the types of highways that we need for this great mass of motor vehicles."*

The following story is about a road trip taken in the late spring of 1954 traveling south on US Route 23; the fabled two-lane highway that runs from Mackinaw City, Michigan to Jacksonville, Florida. It's a road trip through time; a road trip started by two people that met by chance and completed by two people who have grown their love. It's a nostalgic look at the sights, sounds and elements of a way of life that drove America's love affair with the automobile and the two-lane highway.

*In A Cream Packard* chronicles the life experiences of a young couple traveling south on the Hillbilly Highway in 1954.

# 1. WISCONSIN

*Falling In Love Again*

**Tuesday, May 25, 1954, US RT 10, Appleton, Wisconsin, 6:03 PM**

Twenty-six-year-old Alexander Nicholas Throckmorton wheeled his new cream yellow Packard Patrician 400 into the gravel parking lot. Small stones clicked against the inside of the wheel wells and little puffs of dust rose up from the white-wall tires into the crisp evening air. He parked the large car close to the entrance and breathed a sigh of relief. It had been a long day, he was tired, and his eyes itched from the birch and alder pollen. The chill of spring had set in, and was perched among the brown branches of the budding maples. Although the first green colors of spring were already popping the aspens, it seemed that winter was stubbornly hanging on and reluctant to leave the Fox River Valley of Wisconsin.

*Maxine's Roadside Rest* was neatly lettered in hunter green enamel on the white clapboard siding. *Home Style Breakfast, Lunch, and Dinner* was right underneath. A modest neon sign that read: *EAT* was flickering red, and on its last watts, sat just above the door and its small rain roof. It was making an electric buzzing, snapping and cracking sound. Three wooden steps led to the boardwalk porch where an old, weathered grey wood and wrought iron bench sat to one side. Individual porch lights with single bulbs were burning on either side of the screened wooden storm door. On the far side of the parking lot was a dirty grey Mack, hooked to an empty hog trailer and coughing at idle. It was parked alongside a much newer and quieter green Kenworth with a flatbed load of milled lumber. Alexander had decided to try this country diner when he drove past it yesterday. His logic was: *any place a truck driver eats,*

1

*the food just has to be good.* He was not only tired, but hungry as well.

Three cars were parked along the front of the building: a 1946 Chevrolet pickup, and a shiny black 1952 Hudson Hornet. A weatherworn, dinged-up, grey 1936 Ford Coupe set apart from the others. Ever since he was a kid growing up on the north side of Detroit, he admired the styling of '36 Fords. That model presented a nicely rounded form, a superbly curved rear end, and teardrop headlights proudly mounted on the front fenders. Years ago, his father had told him that the headlamps of a '36 Ford lit up the world like Betty Grable could light up a dark room. He never forgot that. Years later, he understood exactly what his father meant.

The door squeaked loudly as it opened and banged shut behind him. He spotted two disheveled truckers at the counter and an elderly couple tucked away at a corner table. They hardly gave notice to the tall stranger dressed in a dark brown sport coat, brown slacks, and white silk scarf. Two waitresses stood behind the counter talking and paying polite attention to the two drivers. One was a large middle-aged woman wearing a bib apron, glasses too small for her face, with graying hair pulled back and twisted into a tight bun. The other was much younger, much closer to his age and wore her softly curled auburn hair at shoulder-length. He appreciated that she was wonderfully easy on the eyes.

Alexander sat at a table near the door. Blue gingham tieback curtains hung on the windows, exactly matching the trim tablecloths. Small vases with flowers gave each table a 'welcome home' look. There were twelve or so handcrafted potholders and some crocheted doilies hanging behind the counter with small, white paper price tags attached. The place was very orderly, and he felt justified with his decision to try this little diner. His eyes went all around the room one more time and stopped yet again on the young redhead. This time, she noticed him, smiled and nodded. Their eyes met and locked for a few seconds, before she shifted her glance, walked

2

out from behind the counter, and into the dining room. With each step, her blue-grey uniform flowed and gently swayed over and around her youthful figure. Alexander noticed there was a pronounced weightlessness going on deep inside him, and he recognized it to be more than hunger alone: *I can't be that worn-out or road-weary.* He watched every move the young woman made on her way to his table. His mind was traveling and spinning faster than the world around him; lost in a wondrous daydream. He could not recall looking at a menu, but he did remember ordering *coffee black, country-fried pork chops, green beans, and some conversation* from the chestnut-haired waitress. Standing beside his table, holding onto her order pad, she gave the stranger a delicate smile along with an inquisitive glance.

The young woman was surprised at the daring suggestion hidden within his dinner order. She held onto her smile, and asked curiously, "And what exactly do you mean by *some conversation*, sir?" She shifted her weight to her left foot, pushed her hip in the same direction, and displayed coquettish confidence.

He was looking straight into her emerald-green eyes. They seemed to be the exact center of the maelstrom that had complete control of him. Somehow, he found the courage and conviction to mirror the conversation right back at her with a question of his own: "What's your name, young lady?"

"Maryanne," she replied with assurance, "but I answer to Annie."

Her tone turned to teasing curiosity, "Now, tell me, what kind of dinner order was that?"

"Well, I'll explain my order: coffee black, country pork chops, green beans and some conversation with a young lady named *Annie* ... and a piece of apple pie."

His comment stirred cautious interest, and she felt a flush come to her cheeks. Her scalp tingled from the hairline of her brow to the back of her neck, and she became aware of something happening. She carefully wrote his order onto the

3

little book, and audaciously managed to ask the following question: "And what do you answer to?"

"Alexander … Alex," he smiled.  His glance went over the curled locks of delicate, dusky red hair on her shoulders, down and over her breasts, around her waistline and hips, pronounced by her apron strings, and quickly down her calves to the two-inch-heeled tan pumps.  Her hand with the order book and pencil was boldly perched on her left hip.  She was smiling back, her nose slightly wrinkled between her eyebrows, and pushing those few freckles closer and tighter together.  Alex gazed straight into her green eyes again, and knew he never before saw such a color.  They were such a deep, dense emerald green, he sat bemused.

"Alrighty then," she said, feeling the rush returning to her cheeks, "I'll bring your coffee straightaway.  Your meal will be out soon, don't you know."  There was a lilt in her voice accompanied with a distinct Upper-Midwest twang.  That caught his attention, and it made him remarkably more aware of her presence.

She walked across the small dining room to the counter, knowing that the stranger named Alex was watching her every move, and nervously wondered if the seams on the back of her stockings were straight.  Annie handed the order slip through the kitchen window and announced, "Order in, Bert!"  Walking along the back of the counter, she gave her boss Maxine a bright smile, like the ones shared between schoolgirls, and asked in an unusually low, rather shaky voice, "Hey, Maxie, can I take a short break?"

Maxine whispered, "Sure.  Five minutes.  Then we start to close, right?"

"Right.  Thanks, Maxie."  Annie said those words as she walked over to the coffee station.  Her thoughts were racing and churning around like pink cotton candy twirling onto a stick at the Outagamie County Fair.  She wondered what brought this good-looking, well-dressed stranger to this particular roadside diner in central Wisconsin?  An unfamiliar

4

force was urging her on. She experienced a tingle down her spine and a brief involuntary shudder before she quickly gathered herself. Annie let out a breath, grabbed the pot, and poured the fresh coffee. Looking at the black brew swirling into the cup, she thought of the dark wavy hair of her new customer. It was a stark contrast to his white silk scarf. She could not otherwise explain away her thoughts.

Again, he was watching her every move as she brought the coffee to the table, set it down, and folded her arms. She was standing tableside, right in front of this man named Alex. She paused for a quick breath, reached deep inside for a little more courage and asked, "Are you new in town, visiting, or here on business?" She knew he was not local with a tan like that.

Alex brought the thick white china mug to his lips, blew onto the hot coffee, took a sip and solemnly said, "Well ... Annie ... it's all three rolled into one package. I'm new to town, just visiting, and on business."

Her words ran together, "Oh, alrighty, then. I see. Okay if I sit down with you? Just until your dinner comes out the window. It should be out soon. The cook's fast and I have a five-minute break coming." She cringed as she rambled and thought, *How brassy can you get! Good golly, girl! Learn to talk!*

On impulse, without waiting for a response or invitation, she surprised herself and sat down across from the stranger. Her mind was racing in all directions as their eyes met and locked yet again. Trying to catch up to the moment, she wondered how he would react, and where the developing conversation could take them. Alex's demeanor was reassuring and unwavering, his dark brown eyes calming the young woman. He reached inside his jacket, brought out a pack of *Lucky Strike*, lit one, and offered the pack to Annie. She slightly moved her head and whispered, "No thanks."

He started his story, slowly at first, "Three months ago I was discharged from the Navy after my six-year hitch and I started working on airplane engines off-base in Pensacola, Florida.

5

About a month ago, I bought a house and some land on the GI Bill. Really, it's just a small, non-working farm outside of town. Then a week ago Saturday, I got a telephone call from my aunt, and I made the trip up here to Oshkosh to be with my ailing mother. Her condition worsened, the consumption had set in and quickly took over. I have been here just two days. I last saw my mother alive eleven months ago, in June of last year, for a twenty days, on a three-week shore leave from the Navy. She passed away on Wednesday last ... and we buried her Saturday ... in her family's plot at Saint Joseph right here in town. The services were excellent, properly done and with a respect I cannot recall at any other ... a glorious Mass ... and there were so many people ... but besides my aunt and cousins ... and some old neighbors ... I can honestly say that there was nobody else I knew. Now all that's left is the settling of her estate ... and filing the papers … it's been a tough haul these past few days … but I'm working through it all ... with the help of God … my aunt Marie … her family … and a lawyer of course ... cannot forget the lawyer … it's all going to be all right." His voice trailed off. He spoke in a deliberate and firm tone, with pauses of thought. His hands were fully around the coffee cup, warming his fingers and calming his uneasiness. He wondered if he perhaps had offered too much information, and why he would even mention all this to a woman he met only moments ago.

He quickly found comfort in the alluring eyes of the young woman sitting across from him. He looked down at the table, back up into her eyes, and back to the table again. Her hands were wrapped around his and the cup of hot coffee. Alex could not remember when she did that.

"Ohhh," Annie empathized. She moved her hands warmly on his. She had witnessed this man's personality carry the full spectrum of emotion. The bold, brassy, and confident stranger of a few moments ago became subdued. She watched him blink quickly twice, and wondered: *Could he be forcing back a tear?*

6

The brief silence was broken as the raspy voice of the cook announced from the kitchen window, "Order up, Annie!"

Alex sat back in the chair and pulled himself away from the momentary grasp of melancholy. Her eyes wide, Annie realized she was holding his hands and smoothly lifted hers away. He smiled at her, watching as she got up from the table to bring his dinner from the kitchen.

She took a deep breath and spoke quietly, "Enjoy your meal. Just ask if you would like anything else." In the few moments that just passed, Annie experienced much more insight into this man's life than she could have ever expected. She felt a feather tickle and tease her heart from deep within her chest. It felt strange, uneasy, and dangerously thrilling at the same time. Back behind the counter, Annie was keeping busy, almost overtly, and trying to pass the time until she could walk back to Alex's table. She felt awkward and thought everyone in the diner was watching and knew about the butterflies in her belly.

She was keeping an eye on the stranger as she began the required chores for closing up the restaurant. The next fifteen minutes slowly ticked off the clock. As he finished his meal, Annie brought over the apple pie and set his bill on the table. She smiled as she said, "Here's your dessert, sir. I hope you enjoyed your meal and maybe I'll see you again. Would you like anything else, sir?"

"Now, Annie ... I did tell you that my name is Alex ... it's not 'sir'.

"The meal was excellent, the service superb, and it was extremely comforting to talk with you. Thanks for listening. And you will see me again. Are you working tomorrow?"

"Well, yes, I am, as a matter of fact. I work lunch and dinners all week then Saturday breakfast, yes I do," she answered. Annie was astounded that she just told this man her work schedule for the entire week. Her words flowed. She was incredulous of what she had revealed but held a pleasant anticipation for tomorrow.

Alex got up, straightened his jacket, pulled a few singles out of his wallet, placed them on the table, turned to the young waitress and said, "Tomorrow evening then, Annie."

He could not muster the courage to tell her that her form made him think of a '36 Ford. He knew better, and decided it was most certainly better left unsaid; at least for now.

"Super-duper," Annie nodded, smiled and watched him walk out of the diner. He turned and gave a brief smile back, walking out the door, as he tucked his scarf inside his jacket. Annie picked up the money and looked at it in astonishment. *A three-dollar tip! Golly!*

Maxine was watching all this unfold while leaning on the counter with one hand. She was standing in front of two truckers at the far end of the counter who were making small talk, smoking cigarettes and drinking some 'hundred-mile' coffee for the road. She encouraged them, "Time to hit the asphalt, boys."

One of the drivers answered, "Sure enough, Maxie. Just as soon as the jukebox cranks out my last nickel, okay?" He was talking about the big, solid Seeburg against the wall and loaded with 45-rpm records. There were lighted color wheels spinning green, red, yellow, and blue up and down along the inside of the frosty white plastic corners. Hank Williams and his Drifting Cowboys were pining and twanging out *Your Cheating Heart*.

"Yeah, all right, all right. Let's go, then," Maxine said, trying to hurry the men along.

Maxine's attention moved back to the dining room. The truckers cranked their heads around to catch a fleeting glimpse of a smiling Annie walking back to the kitchen with a full bus pan of dirty dishes. Bert, the surly cook, was in the back of the kitchen rattling a day's worth of pots and pans in and out of the sinks. He always turned it up a notch when it was time to go home. His t-shirt was soaked with sweat, dishwater, and soap. His big, tattooed arms were plunging in and out of the deep sinks like bobbing telephone poles.

Maxine was humming to the Hank Williams song and wiping down the counter. The thought crossed her mind that she could be looking for another waitress soon.

## Shake, Rattle, and Roll

**Wednesday, May 26, College Ave. & Oneida St., Appleton, Wisconsin, 7:10 AM**

Annie drifted in and out of sleep all night. She was restless, in body and mind, like a kid on Christmas Eve. Her thoughts danced back and forth from the stranger named Alex to childhood memories and all the events that unfolded the past year. She held wondrous anticipation of her future and sentimental recollection of the past.

Annie and her sister Beth have continued to share strong bonds since early childhood. As young girls aged ten and eight, they lost their father, Herbert Dahl, in the North Africa campaign of the World War. Their mother, Irene, remarried in 1949 to a paper man, Walter Hendricks: a newsprint-manufacturing foreman she met while working at Atlas Paper during the war. Annie graduated high school in 1950, and with her mother's help, landed a desk job in the payroll department at the paper mill. Annie was always the person to 'jump from the frying pan right into the fire' and was more than happy not to continue school. She felt the need to get on with her life, whatever it may bring, and gladly put academics behind her.

In February 1953, Kimberly Clark Paper transferred Irene's husband from Atlas in Appleton to a newer mill in Vermont. The pending move forced a shift in the dynamics of the Dahl-Hendricks family. Her husband's reassignment to Vermont was a significant force pulling on Irene's life. Her daughters were woven into the fabric of Appleton's small-town world, and not too keen on the idea of moving to the Northeast. Annie had her full-time clerical job at Atlas and Beth was a freshman at Lawrence College.

The move to Vermont became the primary subject of conversation in the living room and at the dinner table of the Dahl house on South Walnut Street. The situation came to a head one Friday evening in March of 1952. Annie Dahl was neither reserved nor quiet, and she certainly was not a timid wallflower. She told her mother and Walter that she and Beth would stay in Appleton.

If something needed said, Annie said it without hesitation. Annie had convinced her mother and stepfather that she and Beth were competent young adults and able to get along fine by themselves.

In late February 1953, Irene and Walter moved to Vermont, leaving Beth and Annie on their own. The Dahl family in Appleton was now Maryanne and Elisabeth. In April, the cape cod home on South Walnut and Sixth Streets was sold to an elderly couple from Fond du Lac and events began to snowball; like the old adage 'everything happens at once'. The sisters needed to secure an apartment quickly and a mere two days after the home sold, Annie became the recipient of bad news. The personnel office of Atlas paper had given Annie and three co-workers a month's notice of pending layoff. The paper mill contracted the payroll functions to an expanding accounting firm in town. Annie and her co-workers were excess, redundant, and being let go. Word gets around fast in small, close-knit communities and within a day, Robert Wilkerson, the deacon at Bethany Lutheran, let the girls know that a large room with a bath and kitchenette was available downtown, above Moore's drugs. The College Avenue apartment was close to all the stores and within walking distance to the college. The rent was affordable at thirty-five dollars a month, and the sisters were able to move right in. The wheel of fate had spun like yet another old adage: 'what goes around comes around.' The same accountants that took over Annie's payroll job at Atlas Paper were the former tenants of the large upstairs room.

10

Annie's stepfather Walter left his old 1936 Ford behind for the girls to get around in and told Annie to 'take care of it and it will take care of you'. She passed her driver's test on the first attempt and was excited to be able to move around freely in Appleton. Annie remembered when she was growing up, her father, Herbert told her more than once that 'everything works out for the best'.

Now, with the car and her driver's license, she was seeing some evidence that her father's words of wisdom were correct. Things have indeed been 'working out for the best' but Annie still needed to find another job. Annie, the optimist, was not one to let grass grow under her feet. Her father's words proved correct yet again: exactly one week after her layoff, Annie had a new job. She hired on as a full-time waitress at *Maxine's Roadside Rest* ... a modest truck-stop and homespun diner a few miles down the road.

Annie was proud of the old jalopy Walter gave her. The old Ford was not much to look at, but it always started with a simple turn of the key and went down the road. She of course didn't know it, but in the not too terribly distant future, there would be a tall handsome stranger admiring all the attributes of that 1936 Ford.

The siblings worked out a successful living arrangement. The College Avenue apartment was sparsely furnished with items from the house on South Walnut Street; twin beds, two dressers, and a small table with three wooden high-back chairs. The old maroon, paisley-print sofa from the Dahl house on South Walnut sat right in the middle of the room, somewhat out of place, like a duck in a hen house. As it was throughout their youth, the sisters got along famously and enjoyed each other's company. Annie, always unreserved, described the austere apartment as *an oversized room with a kitchen sink; a tub and toilet stuck in a closet; an old gas stove, a couple of twin beds, and a beat-up couch jammed in just for laughs.* Beth once told Annie with candor: *'The only thing right about this place is the door.''* Their time together was limited primarily to mornings and late evenings. They shared laughs, played Scrabble, and listened to radio shows like *Amos and Andy, Jack Benny, Dave Garroway,* and *Gunsmoke*. Beth kept her nose right at the grindstone, went to class, studied and practiced her music. Their lives went on, blending the right amount of self-reliance with mutual respect. Beth continued college on a partial scholarship from the Lutheran Brotherhood and worked afternoons on Tuesday, Thursday, Friday and Saturday until noon at McKinney's shoe store just down the street. Annie developed the knack for restaurant work and was making fifty cents an hour plus tips. Life was grand.

The morning sun filtered through the tall windows and filled the apartment with bright light. Annie awoke from her restless sleep, stretched the length of her body on the twin bed, and wiggled her toes; her bare feet sticking out from under the flannel sheets. She smiled and thought again of the tall, handsome stranger she met last night. The street noise found its way upwards and through a slightly open window of the Spartan one-room apartment. Beth was at the table with an open *Classical Music Theory* textbook.

Beth held the same delightfully cheerful disposition as Annie. Not much ever got her upset, and she always was fast to put any worries straight to bed. Except for the color of their hair, the girls shared many features. Beth got the blond hair of her mother and Annie got the muted red of her father. Beth always made the unashamed distinction that she still carried some of her baby fat.

"Been up long, have you?" Annie was looking over to her sister and attempting to wipe the sleep from her eyes.

"A while," Elisabeth replied. "You were half asleep and tossing and turning when I got in at eleven-thirty last night. Yesterday we had that rehearsal at Weber Hall for the graduation concert. I'll tell you; the Music Conservatory was as full as I've ever seen it. This year's ceremony is certainly going to be one full-blown extravaganza. Bells, whistles,

trombones, and tubas!  Maybe even an accordion!  Yes sirree!"
They giggled.

Beth was finishing her sophomore year at Lawrence College
right in town.  Last year she struggled through the two essential
terms of Freshman Studies, and now devotes her efforts toward
a Bachelor of Music degree with a Performance Major.  Beth's
goal was to teach classical music, but she hoped to become an
accompanying pianist someday.  Her dreams put her on stage
with Mario Lanza at Radio City Music Hall in New York City.
Annie's interest in music, on the other hand, went about as far
as doing the Lindy Hop to Big Joe Turner's *Shake, Rattle, and
Roll*.

Beth walked to the sink and half-filled the percolator and a
saucepan with water, and asked, "I got about an hour before
Language Arts.  Want me to fix you some Cream of Wheat or
Ralston and warm buttered toast before I leave for class?"  The
water pipes burped and clanged.  They always did.  She
dropped two scoops of Chock Full O' Nuts coffee into the
basket.

Annie thought a second.  "Yeah.  Sure.  Ralston's fine."

She listened to the coffee pot bubbling and burping for about
five minutes before she slid out of the covers.  The scraping
sound of a butter knife across crisp toast and the clunk of a
steaming bowl of hot cereal onto the table signaled the time to
get up.  Annie sat on the edge of her bed, pulled on her ankle
socks, threw her dressing robe over her shoulders, and walked
across the creaky wood floor to the old green enamel stove.
She poured a cup of coffee for herself, another for her sister,
and sat at the table.  Staring out the window at nothing, she
blew on the hot beverage and took a sip.  She was anxiously
awaiting the opportunity to tell Beth all about a man named
Alex.

Beth closed the textbook and began, "The spring semester
ends on Friday and Bobby Olsen asked me after class yesterday
if we could go out for dinner and dancing at Babe Vanderpol's
on Saturday night, and maybe we could double date with you

13

and that Jimmy Malone, what do you think, Sis?" Her excited words flowed non-stop.

Annie was waiting for an opening like this. She took the opportunity and started, "You know, that sounds like fun. But it could be someone other than Jimmy Malone I go to Babe's with. Somebody new."

With wide eyes, Beth asked, "Oh really? What's this all about, then, eh?" She looked across the table and Annie immediately started in.

"Well, I met someone last night. I met a man and I truly believe this fellow is something special. I can't get him out of my mind. He's tall, good looking, well dressed, well mannered, well-spoken and did I say handsome? Well, I'll tell you, he's all that and more, I bet. And we just met last evening at the diner. He came in, sat down, ordered his meal and I sat down with him. We talked, and he told me so much, and we really got on. I'll tell you, Beth, this guy could be the one. He just got out of the Navy, and he bought a small farm and home in Florida. But he's not a farmer. He works on engines. He said he's coming back tonight. I hope he doesn't forget. But he won't, I know. But I'm not rushing into anything. But he's no Jimmy Malone, I'll tell you. He's made from a different fabric, he is. His name is Alexander. Alex."

"Well good golly, big Sister! Sounds to me like you're sweet on this Alex fellow already, eh!" Beth teased.

"Do you think so? Do I sound that silly?"

"I don't know about the *silly* part, but, like I said, it sure is sounding like you're sweet on this fellow you just met, don't you know."

"Maybe you're right. Maybe I'm being silly and over-reacting about this man. Maybe I'm dreaming and reading too much into this. Maybe it's not chemistry, but some sort of infatuation. But I got this funny feeling. And the way his eyes melt into mine. I'm telling you, Beth, there has to be something going on here. And I think I should find out. If my Alexander comes into Maxine's tonight, I'm going ask him

14

about going dancing with me on Saturday. That's what I'm going to do. I just decided."

Beth reached across the table and took Annie's hand. She held it gently and said, "That does sound like a good idea. You go right ahead and ask this fellow Alex out to Babe's with us on Saturday. And besides, there's always Jimmy Malone, in case your new fellow tells you 'no'." Beth was reassuring, and Annie needed that.

"Beth, I can't even think about Jimmy Malone now! Uff! It's about time I ditch that lout. You don't think that it's too bold of me to ask Alex? No, I suppose not. This is the fifties, for goodness' sake! Us girls have rights, too.

"Thanks for listening, Beth. I didn't sleep too good last night. I was so excited and could hardly wait to tell you all about this fellow. And I don't know a whole lot to tell, but I know his mom just passed away, and was buried in Oshkosh, and that he has a farm somewhere down in Florida. I think. I think I remember that. I feel calmer now. Before I go to work this morning, I think I'm going to Moore's or maybe Zahm's and get some new nail polish and maybe some mascara. Some of that new Max Factor stuff that's supposed to last all day."

Beth smiled and said, "Yes, Annie, that sounds like what you should do. But I don't know if Max Factor can help. I think you got *The Lovebug Itch*, just like that Eddy Arnold sings about!"

Annie shot right back, "You bet! I got it! The lovebug itch. That's what I got ... and it needs scratching!"

The sisters laughed.

*Secret Love*

**Wednesday, May 26, US Route 10, Appleton, Wisconsin, 9:45 AM**

Annie's thoughts were churning all morning. At the cosmetic counter of Zahm Brothers Dry Goods Emporium, she spent several minutes picking out the right shade of red nail lacquer with matching lipstick. There were so many possibilities. The mascara decision was easy; she figured that out back at the apartment: black Max Factor. As an afterthought, she purchased two pair of nylon stockings. She thought about spending this money, but soon justified it as a necessary investment. Furthermore, she thought, *A girl is allowed to pamper herself once in a while.* There was barely enough time to hurry upstairs to the apartment, put her hair in curlers, shower, and paint her nails before she left for work.

Annie parked her old Ford alongside Maxine's Hudson. Her shoes crunched on the little stones of the parking lot and sounded the transition to the boardwalk of the diner with a subtle tap-tap. She could feel her heart thumping oh, so steadily within her; every sound of the world around her was more distinctive. She was keenly aware of her being. Everything: sights and sounds seemed so clear. Life glistened.

It was a slow mid-week morning at the roadside restaurant. A couple of regulars, the occasional trucker, and only a few locals stopped in. Maxine was writing the lunch special on the little blackboard behind the counter and the chalk made that annoying, penetrating, squeaky, scratching sound. Earlier, Annie topped off the sugar shakers, wiped off the catsup bottles, and filled the napkin dispensers. She was working hard at working to pass the time. Fred, the heating-oil driver from Green Bay, was enjoying coffee and a piece of lemon pie at the counter. Annie topped off his cup and slid the pot back into the Sunbeam coffee machine. She reached into her apron, pulled out a dime, and asked, "Hey, Fred, do you want to hear something special? I'm going to spin a couple songs on the jukebox."

"Yeah, alrighty, Annie. See if you can find Rosemary Clooney, you know, that Mambo song she does."

Annie punched in the letter *'A'* and number *'14'* buttons for Fred's *Mambo Italiano*. The big Seeburg jukebox came to life; the record automated out of its slot, flipped sideways, and flopped onto the turntable. Rosemary Clooney's voice filled the diner as Annie looked for the new record by Doris Day. It took a moment. She found it, *Secret Love*, and pressed the buttons for '*B*-16'. Annie went back to her busy work, waiting to hear her song and wishing for the time to fly along. The evening and Alex seemed so far away.

It was a beautiful spring morning with no shortage of sunshine. Maxine moved down near Fred the driver, leaned on the counter, and watched the occasional car or truck pass by on the highway outside. Sally was in the kitchen cutting up cooled boiled potatoes for home fries. When the Seeburg started playing the Doris Day record, Maxine looked over the top of her glasses at Annie. She was swaying her hips, almost dancing across the dining room, setting the little white flower vases with the daffodils on each table.

Maxine shook her head, smiled, and thought, *This girl's got it bad, she does.*

*Till I Waltz Again With You*

**Wednesday, May 26, US Route 10, Appleton, Wisconsin, 6:00 PM**

The day could not be going by any slower. Annie was a bundle of nerves, watching the clock, and wondering if the stranger named Alexander would be returning this afternoon. She was second-guessing her decision to ask him out to Babe's dance club on Saturday. She thought, *I don't even know how old this fellow is, what he does for a living, or even what his last name is, by golly.* It went on all morning and afternoon. Occasionally, Annie would put a dime in the jukebox and play two songs just to fill the diner with sound and hoping to blanket her wandering nervous thoughts. During the lunch crush, she dropped a customer's grilled cheese sandwich and French fries onto the floor. It was the first time she ever dropped an order, but Maxine gave her a stern look and admonished, "Careful!"

Bert knew Annie was a bundle of nerves, and he took the blame, telling Maxine that it was his fault, and that the plate was slippery with cooking oil off the grill.

At one o'clock, Sally, the morning waitress was ready to go home for the day. She took Annie aside and said, "Girl, you better get a grip on yourself and don't go worrying yourself all baldheaded. That would turn your new fellow right away from you, don't you know? A baldheaded woman ain't anything to look at, so calm yourself Annie. This Alex fellow will show up sure enough." Annie realized that Sally was right and made an effort to steady her stubborn nerves.

The dinner crowd gradually drifted in, and time began to pass better for Annie. The meatloaf and gravy, and open-faced turkey sandwiches with potato salad were coming out of the kitchen in good numbers. The place was busy and that was helping Annie avoid watching the clock as well as the front door.

As the evening edged on and darkness set in, the little restaurant emptied out. Customers began to head home, and the truckers hit the road. The headlights of cars and trucks leaving the parking lot threw strange shadows all along the back wall of the diner. Tire noise from the gravel parking lot was filtering in through the screen door as it banged shut. Annie looked up. It was Alex, with his tall frame backlit by a pair of high beams. He walked in and sat down at the same table he was at last night.

Like a kid in a candy store, Annie quickly walked across the dining room and greeted him, "Hello Alex. I've been expecting you." She wore a beaming smile.

"It's nice to see you, Annie. It's nice to see you, indeed," he said. A few seconds passed, their eyes busy, and their thoughts swirling. "You look just wonderful." He paused, nodded the slightest bit, and asked, "What's good tonight, any specials?"

"The meatloaf is pretty darn good. Everyone seemed to enjoy it. And we got an open turkey sandwich with potato

18

salad," she answered. Her heart was racing, and she was sure that she was blushing. There was so much to say, so much to ask about, and so much to find out. She could not think of what words to say, and in what order to say them.

Maxine walked from the coffee station and carried the full pot around the restaurant for refills and warm-ups. She spoke from across the dining room, "Take your break, Annie. You've been here all day. Take your ten minutes."

Annie turned her head and smiled at her boss. "Thanks, Maxie."

Alex heard that exchange and decided quickly. "I'll have the meatloaf, Annie, and a coffee. Thanks, and come and sit down if you can, won't you?"

"Okey dokey. Will do. I want to. Be right back." Writing as she walked, Annie made her way to the kitchen window, announced, "Order in, Bert", and hurried over to the coffee machine. She moved sideways, squeezed passed, and behind Maxine. She whispered, "Thanks, boss," turned, and started back into the dining room with two cups of coffee. As she sat down, she looked directly into Alex's eyes and said, "I've had a long day, believe it or not. I feel like I've been going non-stop. This is the first chance I've had to sit down. And it feels good, don't you know."

He repeated himself, "It's nice to see you, Annie. Very nice to see you. I've been in Oshkosh with my Aunt Marie most all day, in and out of the attorney's office, Probate Court, County Hall, and Tax Office. Even had to go to the newspaper. But that's my merry-go-round ride and not yours. So, what's going on in your life? Anything Earth shattering? Any new life-altering events?"

He was smiling, looking right into her green eyes, giving her all his attention.

Annie piped up, "Well, how about you and I go out dancing with my sister, Elisabeth and her date this Saturday? Saturday evening .... how about that? To a dinner-dance club called Babe Vanderpol's. How's that? How am I doing? I've never asked a man out before in my entire life!" Annie spoke quickly, like an excited little girl asking for another piece of chocolate. She had been waiting all day for this moment to ask him, going over it in her mind. When the chance arose for the words to come out, the dam broke, and they flowed like a tidal wave.

With a hint of a smile, Alex nodded ever so slightly, and leaned back in his chair. He picked up the heavy china cup and took a sip. He looked over the rim and directly into Annie's eyes, and deep into her soul. He spoke slowly, "That sounds like one helluva good idea, Annie girl. Just what I need. A night out dancing with a fantastic-looking woman and enjoying her company. I was going to ask you to a movie, or dinner, or something myself. Good idea, thanks for asking, and it sounds like a date. It's a done deal."

The conversation stopped for a few seconds as Maxine came across the dining room towards them. She brought Alex's order and set the plate quietly on the table. When Annie moved to get up, Maxine placed a hand on her shoulder. "No .... stay seated, Annie. Things are under control. Take a few more minutes, and then we need to get started with closing, okay?"

"Oh, thanks! Thanks, I'll be right there." Annie spoke with sincerity.

"So how long before you're done?"

"Not too long, probably thirty minutes, maybe a little more or a little less. Why?"

"Well, if it's alright, I'll sit right here, finish my coffee, and wait for you. Okay?"

"Okey dokey, but I can't go anywhere, my sister expects me by eight o'clock"

"Sure, that's fine. We can sit and talk some more."

"Super. I'll be right back. I'll get today's Post Crescent for you to look at while you wait, okay?" Annie got up, turned, smiled, and walked quickly to the counter. She reached one hand into the raised glass case and brought out a piece of apple pie. Her other hand went under the counter, grabbed the

20

Appleton newspaper, and brought the pie and paper over to Alex.

"Be back with you in a flash." She was off to the far side of the dining room and started clearing tables. She was excited and apprehensive at the same time. She thought, *something is clicking with this fellow.* Something was indeed clicking, something that would dramatically change her life. She didn't realize what it was, but she was loving every single moment of it.

### *Goodnight, Irene*

**Wednesday, May 26, US Route 10, Appleton, Wisconsin, 6:55 PM**

Maxine's voice filled the restaurant, "That's it! Annie! .. Bert! Let's call it a day. Time to go home!"

Bert bolted from the kitchen, gruffly uttered "Goodnight, Irene," walked past Maxine, and directly out the door. It banged shut behind him. Alex got up and brought the newspaper and his cup over to the counter. He set them down with four dollars and his check. Maxine quickly gave him an automatic smile, grabbed the cup, and put it in a bus bin underneath the counter. She stuck the paper under her arm and shoved the cash and guest check into a glass by the register.

Annie came out of the kitchen carrying a soft pink cardigan over her arm and smiling right at Alex. "Goodnight, Maxie. Thanks. See you tomorrow," she said.

"Okay, kid. See you tomorrow. Goodnight, Mister Alex." Maxine gazed at Alex and Annie over the brim of her eyeglasses with a knowing smile.

Alex offered his arm and led Annie toward the door. She announced, "Goodnight, Maxine," one more time as they stepped out of the diner. Maxine was right behind them, flipping the light switches. She locked the heavy interior wood

21

door and allowed the screen door to shut with a bang behind her. The porch floor and wooden steps moaned and squeaked under Maxine's shoes. Alex and Annie stood under the two yellow bug lights and watched Maxine walk over to her black Hudson. In a moment, she was out of the parking lot.

"Let me help you with your sweater, Annie." She handed it to him and switched her handbag from one hand to the other as he maneuvered the sweater. It was a chilly evening, just getting dark with not a breath of a breeze. He motioned toward the bench and said, "How about we sit here for a while?"

"That sounds good. It's beautiful out here tonight." A handful of night flies buzzed around the bulbs.

"Thanks for asking me to that dinner-dance place on Saturday, Annie. It saved me from trying to figure out what I could ask you to do in a town I know nothing about. I knew last night I wanted very much to get to know you. Very much. I know my way around Oshkosh pretty well, but up here in Appleton, I'm poking around like a blindfolded drunk. I'm an actual stranger in paradise here," he said.

Annie chuckled, "Appleton is nice, but I don't know about the paradise part. And do you often play the role of a blindfolded drunk?"

Alex let out a muffled giggle, "No, no! As soon as I laid eyes on you, I knew I wasn't blindfolded. And didn't want to be. You are seriously easy on the eyes, Annie girl. And from the first time I saw you, last night, in this diner, I knew there was someone truly remarkable wrapped up in that waitress uniform. And now I want to get to know her. Get to know her much, much better."

She felt awkward with all his flattery directed her way. She was not at all accustomed to this line of talk from anyone, let alone a man she just met. She felt herself flush and shifted her weight on the bench as she started, "I'm sorry to hear about your mother's passing, honestly. I lost my Dad in the World War. I was younger, but no matter what age you are, it's tough losing a parent. And it's got to be even harder to travel all the way up here from Florida, like you said, right?" She was hoping to change the direction of the conversation.

"Yeah, it's been a busy week. Tomorrow, I intend to stay in Oshkosh all day. I'm the Executor of my mother's estate and my two cousins are here from Green Bay and Eau Claire. I want to spend some time with them and their mom, my aunt. Then we have a ten o'clock appointment with the attorney. As Executor, there are some requirements needed, such as final signatures, the property transfer, and the closing of the bank account. Then we'll be done, and later things have to get back to normal ... so to speak. There is so much I still don't know about the Old Man, my father, I mean. I hope to find out more tomorrow ... I suppose ... maybe. At least I'll be putting all my ducks in a row."

"Oh, you got a lot of ducks, do you?" Annie giggled.

He looked straight at her. He leaned slightly to his right and Annie willingly moved left. It was the most passionate kiss she ever had. Her toes tingled. She felt a deep charge going up and down her spine. Annie was lost in the moment and his kiss. She felt his arm move around her shoulder, onto her back, and the other around her waist. He held her. They embraced uncomfortably on the wooden bench. Time stood still. The bench creaked. Moments passed. Alex kissed her neck and mussed her hair. Annie started making little noises. Alex slowed things down.

Annie breathed a melodious *whew* and whispered, "There wasn't any ducks that needed any lining up there!" She was twirling her fingers on the back of his neck, gazing into his deep brown eyes, and wholly captivated. She was his.

Alex slowed and dropped it down a gear. He felt it was necessary because his passion could have easily taken over. He did not want to take a chance or allow things to get awkward. This young woman meant something, seemed special, and he decided to proceed slowly. "Like I mentioned, Annie, tomorrow I must be away in Oshkosh, but I will be back here on Friday. I will come to see you on Friday. That's the plan. You're working on Friday, right?"

Annie collected herself, "Yes … yes, I am. I'll be here around ten; that's when I start."

"That works. I can be here on Friday and have lunch. And I can see you again. And what should I wear for this date of ours on Saturday? I didn't pack all that much when I rushed up here," he said.

"Just a tie and jacket. Babe's place isn't all that fancy." She paused a second, set her head slightly back, studying him, "A tie will do just right with what you're wearing right now, as a matter-of-fact. Just right." Annie, too, realized she nearly lost control of her thoughts. She was completely oblivious to the world for a minute or two.

Alex gave her another kiss, gentle this time ... and another ... and one on her cheek.

He spoke as he stood and straightened his jacket, "I'll see you on Friday, then. About noon, thereabouts. But now it's time for me to go." He offered his hand to Annie, and they started down the steps to the gravel lot. They kissed one more time and Annie walked toward her car. Alex closely watched her form sway across the lot. She opened the door, turned, and gave him a finger-wiggle wave.

He had a sudden realization. "Annie! Is that your car? That's your '36 Ford?"

"Yes sirree, it's newer than me, don't you know, but it doesn't look it, does it?" Annie giggled from across the lot.

Alex smiled, "That's a fantastic car, that 1936 Ford. My old man had one just like it."

He paused a second, and said, "Well, ... goodnight, Annie."
"Goodnight, Alex."

He watched as she drove off. He thought about his father and remembered what his father told him about Betty Grable. He smiled to himself, ... and thought about Annie. Again.

## Thursday, May 27, 216 New York Ave, Oshkosh, Wisconsin, 8:15 AM

Alex walked up the steps, onto the porch, and knocked on the door of the white Victorian home. He turned his head and looked around the neighborhood. There was an emptiness knowing his mother would not be coming to the door, but nothing else had changed since he was here last; or since the time before that. The same two robins he remembered from his youth were still hopping across the lawn looking for an earthy meal. He was in a blue mood.

His aunt Marie opened the door, "Good morning, Alex. Come on in and have some coffee. I'm making flap jacks for breakfast."

"Sounds terrific, Aunt Marie. Are Ben and Patty still here?" Alex spoke as he entered the home.

"They sure are. Your cousins are in the kitchen, but I think they'll probably go back to their families tomorrow morning. Ben took a week of vacation for the funeral, don't you know? And I'm sure Pat wants to go home to her husband up in Eau Claire."

"We all have our own lives, don't we, Marie? And we all will go on with them." Alex hated hollow sentiments, and spoke in a subdued tone on his way down the hall, "But, it has been nice seeing you all again despite the circumstances."

Prior to this week, Alex had not seen his aunt or cousins since he left Oshkosh back in 1947 to join the Navy. His uncle David, Marie's husband, was killed in action on Guadalcanal in 1942. Alex only barely remembered him. Time and distance can make total strangers of family members. Family reunions at funerals oftentimes turn out to be nothing more than catching up with everyone else's distressing news and misfortunes.

The morning's coffee, hot buttered pancakes and maple syrup warmed the conversation, despite the pending tedious legal transactions. After breakfast, all four got into Alex's new Packard and went to the attorney's office in town. Once the family got inside and sat down in front of the lawyer's desk, it was all straightforward business. Alex sat directly in front of the lawyer with his aunt on his left and his cousins to his right.

The attorney had a two-day growth of whiskers, unkempt graying dark hair, thick bifocals, a worn brown suit, and a pair of oxfords in dire need of a brush and polish. There were flecks of tobacco ash clinging to his jacket. His voice was raspy and would occasionally break into a higher pitch. He rose up from his chair and stood behind the cluttered desk. A soggy, spent two-inch cigar butt sat in a large green glass ashtray. He started, "Good morning, everyone. My name is Abe Suskind, and I am representing Alexander in these proceedings. Today we will affect the transfer of properties, real and tangible, for the estate of Nora Jolan Throckmorton. Does anyone have any questions? If not, we can begin." It seemed that he didn't intend to wait for any questions, as he started right in with a legal narration that was clearly memorized from repetition.

Alexander's mother had left her entire estate as well as the New York Avenue house to her son. Since he recently had purchased his small farm in Florida, and he had no interest to relocate to Wisconsin, he decided to deed the house to his aunt. He had planned to do that despite his attorney's private and strongly worded recommendations against doing so.

Ten days earlier, on May 15, Marie called him in Florida about his mother's rapid decline in health after a perilous bout with pneumonia. His aunt was with his mother during her brief and sudden illness, and over the years, Marie helped Nora with the care of their aging Hungarian immigrant parents. Marie also lived in Oshkosh, only a few blocks away, and was often there with his mother. Alex assumed that the home would likely become his Cousin Patricia's residence along with her husband Frank and two children. She was returning to teaching

26

next year in Oshkosh, since her husband became disabled. He had lost one hand and two fingers off the other in a sawmill accident the previous year. So, the house on New York Avenue would become the home of a family of four real soon.

The deed and tax roll title transfer took a few minutes. Signatures were required twice here, four times there, and initials on each page. His cousin Pat had tears of gratitude in her eyes when it was final, leaned sideways off her chair, and hugged Alex.

"Patty, live well and keep yourself and your family healthy. Enjoy the home, and there is no need to thank me. Your mother is an angel on Earth. She helped my mother so much. God bless you all," Alex said. Cousin Patty gave him a sincere thank you yet again, as did Ben.

His mother left a bank account with just over three thousand dollars, a tribute to her frugal lifestyle. She never wanted for anything, and always watched her pennies. Living through the Great Depression turned common folks into thrifty savers. The bank account easily covered the funeral and burial charges at the church cemetery, with well over two thousand remaining. Countless signatures were required here, there, and everywhere on the bank papers as well.

His mother owned a 1947 Plymouth that Alex transferred title to his cousin Benjamin. The furniture in the home was a combination of his mother's and his grandparents'. None of that would be going to Florida with him but staying in the home. The lawyer drew up a property transfer for all the furniture, clothing, and any residual items that would be left in the house. More signatures were floated onto the endless flood of paper. Whatever jewelry was in the house Alex signed to his aunt, and she would allow him access to and control of any unique pieces he may want.

It was an hour later that the last items in his mother's will and testament were transferred. The attorney stood up behind his desk, cricked his neck, looked around to those in the room, cleared his throat and spoke, "Well, Alexander, we are finished here. You have transferred several tangible assets to your family members, but please remember, that was your personal decision." He cleared his throat once again. "I want to thank everyone for your attention and presence. Does anyone have any questions?" This time he waited for an answer.

Alex, his cousins, and aunt all replied *"No"*.

The attorney continued, "Well, thank you all again, but I need to have a few words with Alexander here and alone for just a quick moment."

Alex wondered what this could be about. He stood and watched as the others left the office. On her way out the door, his Aunt Marie said, "We'll be in the hall, Alexander."

Alex expected the lawyer to scold him again for his decisions to gift or transfer the estate. He didn't. It was a quick and cordial conversation. Alex ended up with a fist-full of papers, a set of keys, and some cash. Trying to understand everything that happened over the past hour, he knew he would need to sort it all out later.

Out of the stagnant office and into the musty hallway, Alex led the fragments of his family directly to the curb and the parked car, ready for the quick return trip to New York Avenue. He unlocked the trunk and put some of the documents into a leather shoulder bag. The remaining papers he brought with him inside the car and handed them to his aunt. "The lawyer said these are your copies, Marie."

Alex spoke as he pulled away from the curb. "That went well, didn't it? We got everything done and settled in one easy trip. How did you like that lawyer? Huh? Was he strange or what?" He didn't expect an answer. He didn't get any. The ride back to the New York Avenue home was silent.

"I think some tuna salad sandwiches on toast and hot tomato soup sounds good for lunch, doesn't it?" Marie asked.

Everyone agreed.

Alex was relieved that the whole affair was over and the uncertainty of it all was gone. He anticipated the rest of his

28

family was also.  Nevertheless, the lunch table was relatively quiet also.

Alex broke an uneasy silence, "Aunt Marie, I'd like to go through my mother's snapshot album, and keep any photographs that may mean something to me.  Can we do that this afternoon?"

"Sure enough, Alex.  You can have the whole book.  It was your mother's."

"Well, let's go through them.  There may be some of you and Grandma and Grandpa Sterescu that you may want to keep for yourself."

"Okay, Alex.  That sounds good," and Marie finished her soup.

After lunch, Marie went upstairs and retrieved the photograph album.  It was well worn.  The dining room table was where Alexander, his aunt, and the book ended up.  They sat next to each other and paused on every single page.  Alex and his aunt pointed to various photographs and made sentimental comments.  Each one was years old and carried a story of some importance to someone.

An upholstered dark cherry dining room chair became a magical time machine for Alexander.  Memories abounded in pictures from his boyhood home in Mount Clemens, Michigan, family outings, and the occasional trip to his grandparents in Oshkosh; right here in the house he had signed over to his aunt. He saw Christmases, birthdays, and family events from long ago captured on black and white Kodak Verichrome film.  All with little black photograph corners, glued into an album for posterity, and destined to become faded old memories.

The photographs garnering most of his attention were those of his father.  An indefinable numbness inside made Alex realize he was now parentless.  While he looked at the pages of snapshots, his thoughts drifted back to boyhood.  Pictures inside and out of the house off Eleven Mile Road, and trips to Belle Isle Park stirred his memory.  There were some taken on the banks of the Detroit River.  He figured those were from

1932 or 1933, when he was about five years old. He recalled that his father spent a lot of time alone with him while he was young.

He remembered his father holding him on his knee and cheering for a thunderously loud speedboat. The boat was *Miss America*, and its builder was Gar Wood. His father often spoke of Garfield Arthur Wood and what a mechanical genius he was. His father briefly worked at Wood's machine shop in the late 1920's. The race the he and his father witnessed was for The Harmsworth Trophy, the jewel of speedboat racing. His father's stories allowed him to relive that race numerous times. His father always got animated and excited as if the boat race just happened. That day, *Miss England* was driven by Englishwoman Joe Carstairs, her mechanic Kaye Don, and Gar Wood was behind the wheel of *Miss America*. His mechanic, Orlin Johnson, sat right next to him. The large boat was powered by four 12-cylinder Packard aircraft engines, rated at 1800 horsepower each. His father would laugh and tell him the boat became known as the 'madman's dream' with all its noise and power. It was his father's greatest story. Alex left his memories for a moment and looked around the room. He paused and wondered if it was his father's story about the race, the boat, and the powerful engines that drove him to purchase a Packard automobile. On the way to Belle Isle for picnics, they would drive past the vast Packard Motor Car assembly plant on East Grand Boulevard in Detroit. His father would point it out and talk about the advanced engineering that the company used in its automobiles.

Alex pushed the photograph album away from him and gazed out the dining room window at a spreading oak tree. His aunt looked over to him. A black squirrel interrupted his daydream. The furry rascal scampered up the tree trunk and waved his bushy tail wildly in the breeze. *He's either after an acorn or chasing a lady squirrel,* he thought.

Immediately Annie came to mind. He missed her and realized how terribly disappointed he was that he would not be seeing her tonight. He desired her company. He looked at his watch. It was a quarter past four. Annie was twenty miles and just a bit less than an hour down the road. He could not wait until Friday.

"Marie, I'm going to head back to Appleton," he said. He stood up from the table, closed the book, and stuck it under his arm. "I'm done here, Aunt Marie, and I think it would be best if I leave the past to the past for now. I want to move on from here, but I'm going to keep the picture album, okay?"

His statement took his aunt by surprise; she answered, "Of course, keep the photographs. They're yours, Alex.

"And really? You're going back up to Appleton tonight? It's nearly an hour drive, and you've had a long, busy day. I'm keeping a big pot of stew warm on the stove, and it's almost dinnertime. Can't you stay?" His aunt had asked a question she already knew the answer to.

"I'm heading out, Marie. There's a place up in Appleton where I can get a delicious meal. I have a weekly rate at *Bloomer's Motel* up there, and, anyway, well, my clothes are there, and I'm ready for a short drive. It will clear my head and do me good. There has been so much going on here today, I need a break. Thanks for everything, Marie." He continued talking as he turned and walked away, "Where's Pat and Ben? I've got to say *'so long'* to them."

"They're on the porch with a Vernor's, I think," Marie walked with Alex toward the door and out to the porch. He told his cousins good-bye, gave Ben a handshake, and hugged them both.

"Aunt Marie, Ben, and Patty, God Bless you and your families. Thank you for all your support, understanding, and your help. Especially you, Marie. Thank you all sincerely. And I'll drop you a note when I get back to Florida, and let you know my address. And don't forget Christmas cards. And I know how to use long distance."

He hugged his aunt again and walked to the driveway. Alex made his way to the Packard and put the photograph album in

31

the trunk.  He gave a wave as he got in the driver's seat, and with a turn of the key, the engine fired up.  Three people on the porch waved goodbye right back.

Alex looked around at the surrounding homes and neighborhood.  When he put the car in gear and pulled away from the curb, he realized he was leaving Oshkosh, and it would be a while, if ever, he would return.  As he started to drive down New York Avenue, an unfamiliar sensation of relief came over him.

Certainly, he was gratified to have all the estate business finished and done with.  He was also very happy to be driving north to Appleton and toward young woman named Annie.  He wished that Saturday would hurry.


*Let's Go Steady*

**Thursday, May 27, US Route 10, Appleton, Wisconsin, 3:10 PM**

Annie's day was going by well.  She had thoughts full of Alex, wondering how his day with the lawyer, his aunt, and cousins was going.

She was also daydreaming about Friday night and dancing at Babe Vanderpol's with a new, mystifying, charming fella on her arm.

All during lunch hour, the customers were coming in steadily and without any real rushes.  She fed the jukebox with dimes and worked in excellent spirits all morning and early afternoon.  Annie gave *Let's Go Steady* by the Davis Sisters a spin and that was all Maxine needed to start teasing her about Alex.  The good-natured ribbing didn't bother Annie a bit.  She remembered what Alex said last night, about getting his ducks in a row.  That seemed so humorous to her, and she pictured ducks in a row all morning.  Those ducks, his embrace, and his kiss captured all her thoughts.

32

With a little convincing from Beth, Annie decided that she should get a new dress for the dance on Saturday. Her only chance to do any shopping would be Friday, if Sally could work lunch and dinner for her. Annie asked her if she would be able to change shifts tomorrow, Friday, and she agreed. After a little more teasing from Maxine and Sally, Annie's shopping trip was all arranged. Alex had promised he would stop in around noon on Friday, and she was nervously worried he might not be in until after one o'clock, when she would have left. Maxine reassured her that if Alex did stop in, she would let him know what was going on. Maxine had alleviated Annie's nervous apprehension.

It was getting close to four o'clock when a young man came storming through the front door of the diner. It was Jimmy Malone, and he was clearly upset with clenched teeth and a flushed face. He walked straight to the counter, swung his leg around the red plastic upholstered stool, and sat down. Tall, lanky, and with messy black hair, he was the picture of an automobile mechanic. He was wearing a worn white t-shirt under a pair of blue bib coveralls stained with motor oil and axle grease. He reached into his pant pocket, took out a half-crushed pack of Camels, lit one, and banged the pack down onto the counter with a slap.

Annie took a deep breath and looked around the dining room. She was hoping to find an emergency exit, escape hatch, or something. She walked slowly to the counter. Her pulse quickened and her scalp tingled. Fighting her nerves, she asked, "Hi, Jimmy. Coffee?" She knew what was coming. She just knew; somehow the cat got out of the bag. She didn't bother pouring a cup of coffee for Jimmy Malone. Jimmy didn't answer and didn't seem to be in the mood for coffee.

He looked at Annie with a scowl. His heavy black eyebrows were pushed together as one. His voice thundered and bounced off one wall to the other and back to the counter. He growled, "What's this I hear from Bobby Olsen? What's this ya going with another man to Babe's on Saturday, huh? What's going

33

on, Annie? Are ya running around on me like a dog in heat? Are ya dumping me? Well, are ya?"

Maxine was watching it all from the kitchen window. There was only one other customer in the restaurant. A truck driver was sitting at the far end of the counter and looking over with indifferent curiosity.

Annie's voice crackled with nerves. "Shush, Jimmy! Quiet down. Calm down. I'm not dumping you, but yes, I am going to Babe's on Saturday with my Beth and Bobby Olsen. You know Bobby. Of course, you do. He's the blabbermouth who told you, didn't he? Well, I'm telling you now. I'm going with a charming gentleman I just met named Alex. He's fresh out of the Navy and he's from Oshkosh ... no, Florida ... and he's a neat guy."

"Sounds like ya dumping me, Maryanne Dahl. I wanna know why ya dumping me for some guy from Florida. You going somewheres, are ya, girl?" Jimmy's cigarette hung from the side of his mouth and bounced up and down with each burning word that erupted from his throat.

Annie was aggravated, embarrassed, annoyed, and frightened all at once. "Jimmy, hush up! I'm going to Babe's on Saturday with Alex. That's it. That's all. Now you can have a coffee or a soda or not, but you have to quiet down and act grown-up. I work here, this is my job, and you are embarrassing me, Jimmy. This is not right what you're doing to me, Jimmy."

Jimmy shouted, "I'll show ya what's not right, Annie Dahl!" He crashed one hand down onto his pack of cigarettes and made a fist of the other. Maxine's bulky frame was already coming out of the kitchen and around the corner. Behind the counter, she was standing directly in front of Jimmy Malone, leaning over toward him, her belly pushing tight against the counter, and holding an eight-inch cast iron fry pan at her right hip. She and Jimmy were matched up eye-to-eye and they may as well been nose-to-nose.

34

She spoke in a guttural growl, "Calm down right now young fellow, and understand that you're going to leave this place right now." Maxine's eyes were afire. Tiny beads of sweat appeared on her brow. Her glasses fogged up.

Jimmie roared, "Annie is my girl, and I'm getting mad now!" His eyes bulged in their sockets. He became blotched with a deep, beet red.

Maxine slammed the pan onto the counter with a thunderous crash, reached across and squarely grabbed Jimmy by the arms. She spoke clearly and with stern admonishment, "Get the hell out of my restaurant, young man!"

In one motion, Maxine forcefully pulled him toward her, then away with such force he was off the stool and onto the asphalt tile floor. It was then, in anticipation of an imminent fight, the trucker at the far end of the counter stood up, waited and watched with clenched fists.

Jimmy took a deep breath and came to his feet. His eyes and attention went directly to Annie, then back again to the large woman who had admonished, dominated, and embarrassed him. "Okay, okay. I'm leaving. I don't like this one bit, Annie!"

"Jimmy, I do not care! This is it. We are done, Jimmy Malone! Done: D-O-N-E … done! We are done," Annie spoke with all the anger-induced confidence she could muster.

Maxine came out from behind the counter, and stood staring at the ruffian Jimmy Malone. The trucker chuckled quietly and realized that the big woman had the situation under control. She ordered, "Get out of here. Now, young man, out! Now!"

Jimmy Malone spoke with defiance, "OK, OK. I'm leaving now."

He stopped at the door, turned and said, "Goodbye, Annie! You're out of my life for good, Sweetie. Goodbye, so long, bye-bye, you two-timing hussy." The door banged shut.

Bert laughed from the kitchen window, "Give 'em hell, Maxine!"

"I did, Bert. I did." She took a step toward Annie. "You all right, kid? You all right, Annie?" Maxine took another step and gave Annie a hug.

"Yes, I'm fine. Thanks Maxie. I'll tell you; I need to have a soda." Annie returned the hug, exhaled a sigh of relief and walked to the back of the counter.

The trucker sat back down and watched as Annie opened a bottle of Faygo Cola. She stuck a straw in it and stood with an extended arm, bracing herself behind the counter. Annie drew a deep breath and slowly exhaled. "Thanks for looking out for me, Maxine. Really, thanks a lot. I don't know what would have happened if I was here by myself. Boy, I'm glad that's all over. That Jimmy was downright mean, wasn't he? He never was very nice, only when he was sweet-talking me. And he had awfully dirty hands most all the time. The only thing he was good at was telling bad lies. Jimmy told big bad lies and he had dirty hands. I was downright stupid to get all mixed up with him to begin with. I hope he doesn't ever come back. Never ever."

Maxine was back behind the counter and standing next to Annie. She picked up Jimmy's crushed pack of Camels, lit one, and said, "I seriously doubt it, kid. If he does, I'll toss his backside right out the door.

"And don't go blaming yourself. Jimmy's a jerk, an outright jerk. He just proved it. But I think you might be looking at a good one with that Alex fellow. Is he coming in tonight?" Maxine was standing next to Annie. She picked up Jimmy's crushed pack of Camels and lit one.

Annie looked across the dining room toward the door and answered, "No, not tonight. He could still be in Oshkosh and settling his mother's estate. But he'll be here tomorrow afternoon for sure. He told me so. He promised."

## Thursday, May 27, US Route 10, Appleton, Wisconsin, 5:10 PM

The storm door opened with a squeak and closed with a bang, just as it always did. Nobody paid any attention to the noise. It was a busy late afternoon at Maxine's and unusually busy for a Thursday dinner shift. All facets of restaurant work are unpredictable.

Alex stood at the door holding his hat and looked across the room at Annie. She didn't notice him. She was attentively writing down a dinner order for an elderly couple seated at a far table. Alex smiled and nodded to Maxine, who was busy giving re-fills of coffee. He walked to a small table for two near the wall by the counter. He took off his wool jacket, loosened his tie and sat down.

Maxine turned, giggled and teased, "Hey Annie! Look who ain't coming in tonight!" Everyone inside the diner heard the exclamation.

Annie was still busy taking the dinner order. When she heard Maxine's announcement, her heart began to dance. She glanced over her shoulder and was never so happy to see a man. She smiled, sighed and welcomed the sense of relief that came over her. After her upset with Jimmy and the ruckus he had caused, Annie was absolutely beyond joy to see Alex. She finished with her customers and walked over to his table carrying a menu and the Green Bay newspaper.

She felt a flush as she said, "Hey, you came today after all! That is great! Here is today's paper. We do not have the local one. I hope the Green Bay paper will be okay?" Her words ran together like syrup from a soda fountain. She was beside herself. He had that smile from the first time they met. His brown eyes were locked onto her green.

He noticed her glow, and spoke in a teasing tone, "I was reading your green eyes just now, so sure, the Green Bay paper's fine, Annie. I can read it, too."

"I finished the lawyer and drove right here, thinking about you every mile of the way. I was thinking that after my meal, we could talk. Like we did last night. I'll wait for you again, is that all right?" he asked.

"Sure enough. That works for me! Be back in a minute for your order ... we're awful busy tonight," Annie apologized and had started off before he spoke.

She stopped to hear him say, "Wait, wait, Annie. Never mind, the menu. Just the meatloaf special and a glass of water. And don't hurry on my account. I can wait. Bring it out together and I'll be happy. There's no hurry."

Maxine's Roadside Rest was much busier than it was the day before. The place was in the middle of a dinner rush: the typical unforeseen flood of customers that can be experienced in popular eateries. He sat eyeing the customers and paging through the Green Bay *Press & Gazette*.

Understandably, there was a short wait before his order came out of the kitchen but, when it did, Annie brought it over with a beaming smile. Alex leisurely finished his meal, waited for the dust of the dinner hour to settle and for Annie to be able to sit down.

It was past six o'clock when Annie returned to his table and asked if he'd like a piece of pie and perhaps a coffee.

"No, no. No thanks. I'm done. Full to the brim with meatloaf, mashed potatoes, and peas. And no coffee. I've had enough water. My teeth are floating."

She twittered just a bit, and said, "Oh, alrighty then. I'll be over in few minutes. I'm just finishing up. Back in two shakes ... two wags of a doggie tail." She smiled, nodded, and turned toward the counter and kitchen.

Alex was obliged to watch her gentle sway before looking down at the paper's headline: *Chiang Kai-shek becomes president of Nationalist China; President Eisenhower sends message of congratulation.*

He was irritated, and thought again what a waste that entire Korean War was, then quickly unfolded the paper and snapped it open to the sports page. The newspapers were always full of bad news and international crises. Things that he absolutely could not control.

He didn't feel like being annoyed. He had decided to read the baseball box scores instead. He started: *Right-hander Billy Hoeft hurls for the Detroit Tigers to defeat the Baltimore Orioles; left fielder Jim Delsing led the Tigers with four hits and one run batted in.* Alex preferred the sports pages.

Until a couple days ago, when he first met Annie, baseball had been his favorite diversion.

The place had cleared out about half past six. Alex watched Annie buzz through her work like a honeybee flying to an apple blossom. When the last customer left, Maxine took notice and told Annie, "Go home, kid. You got the early start tomorrow. Go home and get some rest."

Annie turned in her steps, looked at Alex, smiled and back to Maxine. "Okey dokey, boss. Thanks. See you tomorrow." She immediately walked to the kitchen, got her sweater and walked back over to Alex's table. He stood, took her by the hand and told Maxine, "I left the money and check on the table, Maxine. Thanks. I'll see you tomorrow afternoon."

"Oh, I'm sure you will!" Maxine said, swinging a dishrag in their direction.

On the way out the door, Alex asked, "You're going to work early tomorrow, Annie? How come?" and offered her his arm. She took it and placed hers through.

"Well, Mister Alex, it's so I can do some shopping before we go to Babe's on Saturday. I want to get a new dress and maybe shoes. I need to look good if I want to impress you, don't I?" She tugged at his arm, playfully pushed her hip sideways into his and walked with him down the steps. "It's chilly tonight, don't you know, how about we sit in your car?"

39

"Good idea, but the truth is that you've already impressed me, Annie. Impressed me in more ways than one." He walked to the passenger side and opened the door for her. There was a chill in the air; it was colder than it had been.

"New car, isn't it?" Annie asked.

Alex got in and Annie slid over to him. Their lips met for a gentle kiss. "I missed you. I had to come and see you again. And, yes, it's a new car. It's a little over a week out of the showroom." Annie pushed up against him and looked up to his eyes. She had one hand on his thigh and held his hand with the other. "Really? You bought it just to drive up here?"

Alex began to tell her about his trip from Pensacola to Oshkosh. He started out a week ago Saturday with his bags and around five hundred dollars cash. His 1947 Chevrolet Fleetmaster made it as far as Cincinnati when the engine seized up after the main bearing seals burst. He sold the crippled car to the service station mechanic for twenty dollars and bought a bus ticket to Milwaukee; a monotonous ten-hour trip on a Greyhound Silverside bus from Cincinnati. In Milwaukee on Monday morning, he carried his suitcases and bag directly to the Packard Motor Car showroom on Grand Avenue. The dealership owner was on the telephone with Alex's bank in Pensacola for around ten minutes, enabling him to write him a check for $3,500. With a handshake and a smile, the dealer handed him the keys to the new pale-yellow Patrician.

"Now you know how I got here and how I got the car, Annie. There's just something about a Packard. Maybe it's the way the name sounds: brisk, solid and strong. I don't know." Alex changed the subject and continued, "I had a compelling and eventful day today. We got all the estate business done and I transferred my mother's house to my aunt Marie, signed her '47 Plymouth over to my Cousin Ben, closed her bank account, paid for the funeral and made a donation to Saint Joseph for the Funeral Mass. Then, when we were leaving, the lawyer let my aunt and cousins go and he calls me to the side. This is the interesting part. This is where it gets good. He told me a story

40

and gave me something. There's something I really need to show you, Annie. This is what's making me crazy curious with nervous wonder."

He reached into his breast pocket and brought out a tight bundle of cash and two chrome keys connected by a knotted piece of rawhide. He held them in the open palm of his hand and said, "This is what that lawyer Suskind, gave me ... look. Five thousand dollars in hundred-dollar bills. And these two keys. He said my father gave these to my mother back in 1946. Back then, my father also left another five thousand in an account for me, for college. I never used any of that until I got out of the Navy. I never went to college. I put some of it toward my place in Florida and had to use just about all the rest on the Packard. My father was Nicholas Throckmorton ... I'm Alex Throckmorton; I don't think I mentioned my last name yet."

"No, not yet. It's an unusual name." Her hands were cold, and she held onto Alex, "Now that I know your full name, Mister Throckmorton, you can't get away with anything! So, watch yourself!" She giggled and watched him put the keys and money back in his coat.

"Seriously, Annie," Alex continued, "Seriously ... the lawyer said my father wanted my mother to have this money, just like he put the other five thousand aside for me. The keys are supposed to fit two bank deposit boxes in Detroit, and he explained that my mother had no idea what was in those boxes and that she refused to spend the money. It's like she completely ignored what my father gave her. The attorney said he only knew what my mother had told him. So, I guess I'll find out when I get to Detroit."

"Are you going to Detroit now?" asked Annie.

"Hell no, not now. I got a dance to go to on Saturday night ... and I'm going with a girl who's much too good looking to be working in a roadside hash house in Wisconsin. Her name is Annie, if anybody should drive up and ask you."

Her green eyes looked up at him. "Hmmm. Alrighty then!"

The windows were beginning to steam up, prompting Alex to start the engine. When he turned the heater on, the fan briefly chattered, then went to a whisper. Maxine and Bert were pulling out of the parking lot. A fog was beginning to settle down and the lights of the diner were a blur through the haze. The dashboard lights showed the sparkle in Annie's eyes each time she looked up at Alex. He was holding her hands in his, warming them, moving his fingers all around hers, up and over and around her red lacquered nails. They kissed again; he released her hands, put his arms around her and pressed her closer. After a brief impassioned embrace, he started to tell her about his father, Nicholas, a young rough-cut mechanic and new pilot working out of Port Huron, Michigan as a crop duster. He signed up for the Army Air Corps in 1938.

Annie listened intently to Alex's history. She realized she was beginning to understand all about this well-dressed man. His story was captivating, his eyes were steady, and his voice was believable. Excited and intrigued, she felt assured he could be trusted. She looked at his hands, again holding hers. They were clean and strong. After today's clash with Jimmy Malone, clean hands were a plus for Annie.

"Sounds like all the answers you're looking for are locked inside those boxes at that bank in Detroit, Alex," Annie said, looking up at him again.

Alex went on, "My mother got these keys back in 1946 when my father came back from the World War. The lawyer said they would open two lock boxes at the Bank of Detroit building on Griswold Street. As I said, the lawyer told me that the Old Man gave them to my mother in the spring of 1946. It was just before he left for Okinawa on his way back to China. The World War was over, but he was staying in the Air Corps and going back overseas. I was young and didn't pay any attention to details. He wasn't home very long, maybe a week at the most. I remember they had some noisy disagreements that time; not real arguments, but disagreements I would call them. They always ended with each of them giving the other

42

the silent treatment. All I can remember is that he left for China again. My old man left for the Orient, and I never saw him again. He came home, turned right around and went back."

Alex paused. He turned the car's heater down, and began again, "My mother got the infamous and dreaded telegram from the Army about a month or so after he left. It was a *Missing Air Crew Report* that stated he was Presumed Dead as a direct result of hostile action. I remember that. You remember bad news. My mother cried for days. Then, suddenly, it appeared that she got completely over it. She even seemed to block me out and ignore me, like she withdrew into a shell. I had a very hard time figuring out what 'hostile action' it could have been that took my father. And I was wondering why the Old Man would go back to the same area of the world that he just left. The World War was over. And nobody even heard of Korea yet. He came home, took off again and never returned. I was a kid of eighteen and it didn't make much sense. The world was racing by and I wasn't paying much attention to it. I was alone in my own little world." Alex lit a cigarette and opened the window an inch or two.

"Right after my mother got that telegram, she became withdrawn. She wanted to move from Royal Oak, relocate to Oshkosh and live with her aging parents. The fact is, my mother and father didn't get along all that well before the war. They had their differences for sure. Funny how these memories come back. When you're young, I think you try to block out things that upset you. I didn't remember, or didn't want to remember, a lot of this stuff. Now I do. Funerals always bring back forgotten memories. I think you try to ignore and forget things that are upsetting and unpleasant. Now that my father was gone, I suppose there wasn't much to keep my mother there in Michigan. I wasn't too happy about that. All my friends were there in Mount Clemens. That's where I grew up, just north of Detroit. I was pretty upset. I was young and pigheaded, I guess. The Old Man wanted me to go to college or something. I didn't want any part of that. I almost ran off and joined the Army right then and there. As it was, I gave in to my family obligations. It was a sense of duty or commitment, I guess. After my grandfather died, I moved to Oshkosh with my mother. She was alone and I knew I had to go. We ended up living upstairs at my grandparent's house right there off New York Avenue. I felt stranded there. I was stuck living in a strange town, with no friends, my withdrawn mother and her Hungarian mother. I lived there for about a year with my mother and grandmother. I worked at a grocery store for a while and then I joined the Navy and signed on for six years. I ended up going to aircraft mechanic school outside of Ypsilanti, Michigan. Eventually, I went to sea aboard the aircraft carrier Valley Forge. I rode the waves in the far Pacific for a few years and spent some time off the coast of Korea during that so-called conflict. While I was in the service, my grandmother passed away and my mother stayed in the house in Oshkosh. Her sister Marie lived nearby, about a half hour away. In June of last year, the Valley Forge left the Korean coast for the San Diego Navy Yard. That's when I came up to Oshkosh on shore leave to spend three weeks with my mother. The Navy then reassigned me off the carrier and gave me my discharge in Pensacola just three months ago. That's it, Annie. That's where I'm today: twenty-six years old and sitting here in Appleton, Wisconsin with a terrific looking gal on my arm and with a lot more questions about my life than I could have ever imagined." As he spoke, he shrugged his shoulders and flicked his cigarette out the window. "I think I've rambled on long enough, Annie."

"Goodness," Annie quickly blinked her eyes a few times and took a deep breath.

Alex looked at the dashboard clock. It was a quarter to eight. He asked Annie, "Hey, you have to get home, right? Early start and all."

There was stillness, calm and a blanket of silence inside the car. All the information Alex had given Annie was spinning around and finding a place in her memory. "Yes, I do start early. I need to be back here at five-thirty tomorrow morning. I better be going home."

"How about you leave your car right here at the diner tonight and I can drive you home, and even pick you up in the morning? I get up early anyway ... I always did. A gift of the Navy."

Annie thought a moment, looked at the man holding her hands and spoke softly. "Sure. Why not. I live right in town. I'll show you the way." She moved her body closer and playfully continued, "Onward, Alex. Take me home. Home to beautiful downtown Appleton."

Alex put the Packard in gear and left the parking lot of Maxine's Roadside Rest with Annie leaning against his shoulder. Neither spoke. The short drive to Annie's upstairs apartment was over before they noticed.

"Here we are," Annie announced as the car approached the corner of Oneida Street. "I live upstairs, right over the drug store here. Right here."

Alex pulled the car to the curb.

"Thanks for the ride, Alex. What time in the morning should I be ready for you?"

"Quarter-past five would be good ... I think, don't you?"

"Yes sirree. That will work. See you then." She leaned over, gave him a kiss on the cheek and exited the car.

"Goodnight, Annie. See you again, right here tomorrow morning. Goodnight."

Annie carefully closed the car door. Alex closely watched as her hips swayed to each step she took down the sidewalk. She rang the bell once, opened the door and entered to go upstairs. She turned, looked at him and gave a little wave before the door closed. The streetlights laid a warm glow all over the world. He sat a minute, looking at the door before he drove off. He knew there was a dynamic new force in his life.

Annie took the stairs two at a time, banged on the door, put the key in the lock and announced, "Hey, Beth! It's me!" She opened the door and locked it behind her. She threw her

45

sweater over a chair at the table, put her purse down and kicked off her shoes. She walked across the room to the over-stuffed sofa in her stocking feet and sat down with a plop.

"I'll tell you, Sis ... my life is changing and I'm loving every single minute of it!"

Her sister Beth watched all this from the table. She closed the textbook in front of her, took off her glasses and walked over to the couch and sat down. She settled in and said, "Tell me all about it, Annie."

## You Belong To Me

### Friday, May 28, College Ave. & Oneida St., Appleton, Wisconsin, 5:05 AM

Sitting at the table in dim light, Annie was pulling up her stockings and snapping them onto the garter snaps. Her crimson red nail polish had dried, and she slid her hands slowly upwards from her ankles to her upper thighs, gently straightening the seam, and smoothing the hosiery on her legs. The smoky grey nylon shimmered in the subdued light. There was only a forty-watt bulb burning in the apartment, and she was trying to be extremely quiet so as not to wake Beth. She walked to the tiny bathroom, shut the door slowly and pulled the chain on the single-bulb ceiling fixture. She carefully drew a brush through her hair, put on her lipstick and rubbed some of the wrinkles out of her waitress uniform. Annie studied herself in the brownish reflection of the old mirror and used the rouge brush on her cheeks just right. Looking left, right and forward, she decided that her hair needed a body treatment. A visit to Margaret's Beauty Parlor down the street was a definite requirement prior to Saturday night's date at Babe's. As she pulled the string on the light and opened the door, her sister sleepily muttered, "Annie? You're up?"

"Beth! I'm sorry, I really was trying to be quiet." Annie was standing on one leg at a time, slipping her feet into her brown pumps.

"Shhh, yourself, Annie! I'm awake. I was thinking last night after we went to bed ... my last class is at noon, so I should be home when you get here. Let's go shopping together, it'll be fun." Beth was putting on her bathrobe and walking to the table.

"Super! I will be done at one o'clock, so expect me right around one thirty at the latest. We can go to Kronenberg's and Piper's and Neuman's! We'll make a day of it. Sound okay?" Annie picked up her purse and started toward the door, throwing her sweater over her shoulders.

Beth was smiling ear-to-ear, "Sounds terrific. See you later."

"Bye! I've got to go; I bet Alex is waiting at the curb." With that, she was out the door. Beth walked over, locked it, leaned her back against the door and smiled again. She knew her sister had fallen in love. She had not seen her this happy in years.

Down the stairs and to the door, Annie was still primping her hair and the wisps at her forehead and temples. Alex was at the curb with the engine idling as he reached across the front seat and opened the door for her.

She sat down, closed the car door, slid across the seat and put her lips to his. "This is the kind of ride every girl should have to work: a warm car with a good-looking man in complete control." It was a quiet, almost sultry, whisper. She was surprised at her words and tone. As Annie so often did, she spoke the words without regard to propriety, and released a little chuckle.

Annie's warm, wistful voice had triggered an urge to reply, and Alex fought to suppress it. "Good morning, Annie," he said, putting the car in gear. "Did you sleep well last night? Get enough sleep?"

"Yes, I did. And Beth and I are going shopping together today, so we should have fun. How was your night?"

"To be perfectly honest with you, I had a wonderful night's sleep." Alex looked down at the woman on his shoulder and continued, "I fell asleep thinking about you." He landed a tender kiss on her lips.

There was silence. Alex put his arm around Annie, and she leaned into him during the short ride to the restaurant. It seemed to be only a few seconds before he pulled the Packard right up to the steps of the diner.

"This evening why don't we do a movie or something?" Annie asked.

"Are there any quiet parks or places by the river where we could have a picnic if the weather holds? We could bring a couple sandwiches, pop, lemonade, beer, or something? It's just that at a movie you honestly can't talk. You know what I mean?" Alex led on. He was making plans already.

"That sounds terrific ... and I'll pack a picnic. I know just the place. Peabody Park; it's right on the river. And it has pavilions and those gazebo things. You can pick me up about six o'clock then? Goodness, I'm sorry. Is six o'clock, okay?"

Alex gave her a kiss on the forehead and said, "That's a plan, Annie, girl. I'll pick you up at six o'clock." Alex gave her another gentle kiss on the lips. He was playing with her fingers again, over, under and around, holding her hand. "I'm falling in love with you, and I don't know your last name, your birthday, or shoe size."

His question took her by surprise. She sat straight up and turned her body toward him. With wide eyes, she blinked and smiled. She took the opportunity to give him a tender kiss back on the lips, and started, "My name is Maryanne Louisa Dahl. I was born on July 10, 1932. I'm 21 years old and my shoe size is seven. I'm five feet, three inches tall and weigh a hundred and ten. I think."

"I guess I better write that down ... so I don't forget your birthday, I mean." Alex chuckled, reached over her, and across the front seat to open the door.

"Are you coming in for breakfast?" She grabbed the door handle.

"I'll come in later, Annie. I need to call my neighbor in Florida. He's been checking on my house and boarding my horse for me. He goes out to the fields early, so I need to call soon."

"Alex ..."

"Yes, Annie?"

There was a second of silence, then, "See you later." Annie got out, blew him a kiss and bounced up the stairs to the diner.


*Heart and Soul*

**Friday, May 28, US Route 10, Appleton, Wisconsin, 10:10 AM**

The noisy storm door on Maxine's restaurant could be an early warning system or a resounding goodbye. The noise telegraphed that someone was coming, or someone was going.

Alex walked straight to the counter and sat down. The late-for-breakfast and early-for-lunch dilemma was at hand. The place was empty, excepting Maxine, Annie and of course, Bert somewhere back there in the kitchen.

Maxine poured the coffee and looked over her glasses at Alex and queried, "So, you're not going to be sitting at a table today then, Mister Alex?"

"Lunch is a little less formal than dinner, isn't it, Maxine?"

He smiled at her, Maxine nodded, and replied, "You're right about that!"

"I'll leave you two alone." Maxine moved to the side and back to the end of the counter. She was refilling catsup bottles and topping off sugar shakers.

"Hey, Alex."

He teased, "Long time, no see. Is your day going all right?" Alex lit a cigarette. "Want one?"

"No. No thanks. The day is going good. This is usually the quiet time. 'Between time,' is what I call it. In between breakfast and lunch, when we catch up on busy work, refill stations, wrap silverware, wipe counters, you know, get ready for the next rush. She paused a second or two, glanced side to side and continued in a sultry tone, "And now's the time I usually flirt with all the good-looking men sitting at the counter." Annie boldly leaned over the Formica top and squarely planted a kiss on his lips.

His felt his pulse quicken. He looked deeply into the green eyes of the chestnut-haired beauty in front of him and slowly stirred the cream into his coffee. "What's good for lunch? Any ideas?"

"Bert's doing a bratwurst and sauerkraut plate with a salted Kaiser roll. Or he does up a respectable Rueben. People like that a lot too."

"Well, I think I'll pass on the bratwurst and sauerkraut. So, I'll go for that Rueben sandwich, with some potato salad on the side. How's that? With a root beer."

She was writing as he talked and almost immediately turned around to the kitchen window. Annie hung the order, and announced, "Order in, Bert." Just as quickly, she put her hands on the counter in front of Alex and asked, "Did you get in touch with your neighbor to check your place, Alex? Were you able to drive back to Oshkosh all right?"

"Yes. I called and he says the place is still standing and he's been checking on it every other day or so since I left. Oh, and by the way, I'm not staying in Oshkosh, Annie. When I came up here on May 17, all the hotel and motel rooms in Oshkosh were booked. There was some sort of private pilot, private plane show, or exhibition thing going on. There wasn't a room in town, so I ended up here. I've been staying over at Bloomer's Motel, over on US 41. They have a pretty decent weekly rate … radio and TV. I've been pleased with them, no complaints. And it's quiet."

Annie was surprised. "You mean that you've been hiding in plain sight, right under my nose, right up the road, for over a week? And I never noticed you until this week Tuesday!?"

Alex leaned toward her from across the counter and began to ramble tenderly, "Annie, I came in here for the first time Tuesday evening. That was what? Two, three days ago? The first time I saw you ... the first time I saw your soft hair, your walk, the way you carried yourself across the floor, the bounce in your step, the sparkle in those unbelievable green eyes, the softness of your glance, your voice, your smile, your giggle ... your form ... your legs ... that wiggle ... the first time I walked in this place ... and the way you listened to my trials, tribulations and everything that I was going through ... I knew."

"What did you know?" Annie was flushed. She was flattered like never before. She asked again, "What did you know, Alex? Tell me!"

The storm door banged shut and all attention went toward the noise. A truck driver walked in and sat down three stools away.

After the brief commotion, Alex smiled, "I knew ... I knew that you were one helluva special waitress. And that I would be back to bother you each and every chance I could."

"Smart aleck!" She took a playful swipe at him with her order book.

As he finished his sandwich, the regular lunch crowd sifted in. The diner became busy. He watched every move she made: up and down the counter, in and out of the dining room and back to the kitchen window. He allowed his thoughts to wander. He enjoyed it. They exchanged several brief glances and smiles as the place filled up. Waiting for what could pass as a private moment, he paid his check and told her quietly, "Pick you up at six, Annie. Have a terrific day shopping, Sweetheart." He smiled and left.

Annie didn't tell him, but she was already having a great day. She could not remember anyone ever calling her *sweetheart*.

51

When quitting time came, Annie could not get out of the restaurant and into her old car fast enough. She was well aware there was plenty for her to do that afternoon. She had a lot on her plate.

## I Still Get a Thrill

**Friday, May 28, College Ave, Appleton, Wisconsin, 1:22 PM**

Beth was expecting Annie at any minute, so when she heard her sister bounding up the stairs, she was ready for her. She hurried over to the door and opened it as Annie reached the landing. She gave a buoyant, cheerful greeting, "Howdy, sis! Now, let's get this show on the road! We'll call it the *get ready for the big night at Babe's* shopping trip!"

Annie was excited, measurably more about the night out than the shopping trip. Just as upbeat she answered, "Yes sirree, Beth! Today is Friday, it's payday, and I'm ready." All day she was anticipating her Saturday date with Alex at the dinner-dance club. At one time around noon, she realized she had not been this excited about a date since her high school prom. She remembered what a disaster that was. Everything that could have gone wrong that night did, from shoes that hurt her feet every way to Sunday to her boyfriend, Arnie Ericson buying her a red rose corsage to wear on her pink dress. Arnie was so fashion blind that he would have worn a plaid cummerbund with his tuxedo if one were available. To finish that total train wreck, he got sick to his stomach on Vernors ginger ale and Oreos.

Quickly, Annie shed her seersucker waitress uniform, garters and stockings. She then wiggled her way into a pair of blue jeans and pulled her Badgers football sweatshirt over her head. With ankle socks on her feet, she slipped into her penny loafers. Together with her sister Beth, who was wearing a button cardigan, poodle skirt and Montgomery Ward red-rubber-soled saddle shoes, the sisters looked more like high school girls than women of twenty and twenty-one. "All right, Beth, I'm ready to go," Annie said, taking a rubber band from between her lips and pulling her hair into a ponytail. "How about we start down the street, right where you work, at McKinney's Shoes?"

Beth raised her eyebrows slowly, "Really? You want to get another pair of shoes?"

"A while ago I saw an ivory T-strap pump with a nice heel in the window. I think I would like to look at them, and then we'll walk back here, jump in the jalopy, and drive over to the big stores on Richmond. Sound okay?" Annie grabbed her pocketbook and was making her way toward the door with Beth close behind. Beth was excited to see her sister on such a mission. She knew it was going to be a fun afternoon.

"That sounds like a plan, Annie." Beth smiled to herself. The girls took to the stairs and out onto the street.

Annie ended up buying that pair of pumps at McKinney's. The brand name sold them; they were *Enna Jetticks* and with a name like that, Annie knew she would be dancing the entire night away, twisting and twirling long past the twilight. She also picked up a pair of black patent leather pumps with two and a half inch Cuban heels. When she shared her thoughts with her sister, they giggled and pushed each other. Beth knew Annie was a real shoe enthusiast and asked, "So when do you plan to wear those shiny black ones?" Annie didn't immediately answer and picked up the pace instead. They walked down the sidewalk to the alley parking lot where her 1936 Ford was parked.

When they got to the car, Annie replied, "Someday I'll wear those black heels, Beth. Someday I know I'll be wearing them ... someday soon."

From the stores on Richmond, down to Wisconsin Boulevard and back to College Avenue, they filled the afternoon with laughter, shopping and gossip. Annie made all the purchases she intended and then some. She even splurged on a small bottle of Lanvin eau de Cologne at Anderson's. The most important item by far was the dress which she got at Isabella's Fashions on the corner of Wisconsin and Richmond Avenue. Neither of them had ever set a foot inside that store before, and they discovered that it was far pricier than what they were accustomed to, but Annie explained to Beth, "Alex is worth it."

At every chance, Beth would prod her sister about the new man in her life, and Annie was more than happy to tell her every little detail and each single tidbit of conversation. They ended up at *Woolworth's* where they bought some dainties and Annie bought another four pair of stockings. That prompted Beth to ask, "Do you wear them out quick, walking like you do when your waitressing?"

"Yeah, I do. I also like the way a fresh pair feels, too. The seam is easier to keep straight when they are new, don't you know? I think those taupe ones will look terrific with my new dress."

Of course, Beth had to tease, "I bet you're even going to shave your legs for this Alex fellow, too!"

Annie shoved her sister playfully. Walking past the soda fountain, Annie insisted on paying for hotdogs and cola. They sat at the counter, ate their hot dogs and shared memories. Beth bought a little bag of Planter's redskin Spanish peanuts. They gossiped, laughed and put peanuts in their colas.

"This has been great fun. You know, Sis, we make a fantastic team, you and I." Annie reached over and put her hand on Beth's.

"It sure has been a super day, Annie. It sure has. We did some serious shopping today, don't you know?"

Annie was wondering aloud, "Just think, in a couple of months that giant shopping center is going to be open. Then we can really go crazy shopping. There's supposed to be over a dozen stores inside when it's all done. I cannot imagine that. All under one roof. Can you picture that? All under one roof?"

Annie, like most of the folks in Appleton, found difficulty in comprehending the concept of an all-indoor shopping experience. The Valley Fair Shopping Center was to open in August of 1954 and would arguably be the first enclosed shopping mall in the United States.

"You know, Annie, I can't get that image in my head. I mean, when you drive past that place and see the construction going on, you still can't picture what it will look like inside, don't you know? I mean, golly, sometimes I can get totally lost right here in Woolworth's looking up and down the aisles at stuff. bangles, beads, *Buster Browns*, bedspreads, *Boraxo*, brassieres and *Bromo Seltzer* all in one place!" exclaimed Beth. Turning to look at Annie, she made cross-eyes and put on a crazy look of confusion.

With that, the sisters laughed once again. They were sipping their Royal Crown cola through straws and looking into the mirrored back wall of the soda fountain. Their shopping adventure was ending, and they went over everything they purchased. They were extremely satisfied and enjoyed their time together. Beth was second-guessing her decision not to get a dress for Saturday, so with some encouragement from Annie, she decided to go out and get one in the morning. Beth also made a hair appointment for herself and Annie, for two o'clock Saturday afternoon at Margaret's Beauty Shop on College Avenue, a little way down the street from their apartment. Everything was under control.

Annie spoke with affirmation, "When we get back to the apartment, I need to call Maxine. I think I'll have Bert put some of his pan-fried chicken and potato salad in bowls, so I can bag it all up and have it ready for tonight. That should work out just great."

"What are you talking about?" Beth asked, looking at her sister cross-eyed again.

Giggling, Annie answered, "Alex is picking me up at six o'clock. We're planning on a picnic at Peabody Park tonight."

55

"Really? A picnic? At least the radio said it's going to be about sixty-five and it's not supposed to rain. It sounds to me like you and this Alex fellow are getting serious, big Sister. No, you're not getting serious; you guys are more than serious. I can see and feel it myself. And fried chicken and potato salad? Golly, that is not a picnic, that's a five-star dinner at the Ritz! It seems to me that you already have turned up the heat on this Alex guy!"

They laughed again. Annie looked far away, deep into the mirror and went on, "Well, I suppose you could say that Alex and I are seriously interested in each other. When we're together, it seems like we know exactly what the other is thinking. We click. I think there's a connection between us. But don't ask me what's going to happen. I just do not know. I just do not know yet. Right now, we're just enjoying being together. But what's going to happen? I just do not know. After all, he has a place in Florida."

Beth was silent for a moment. She leaned an elbow onto the counter, rested her chin in the palm of her hand and asked, "You mean you're not sure if you want to live with alligators?"

Annie reached over and playfully pushed her sister's elbow off the counter. They got up, looked at each other square in the eye and laughed. They hugged one another right there, in front of the whole world, reflected in the long, mirrored wall of the F.W. Woolworth soda fountain counter.

"Hey, it's five o'clock. We've got to get going if you want to call Maxine for the chicken," Beth said, gathering her few items.

Annie grabbed her bags, turned towards the door and looked to Beth. "Let's go, Sister."

Their seats at the counter were now empty. The Royal Crown cola was gone, but each bottle had peanuts inside. It was a good day.

### Friday, May 28, College Ave. & Oneida St, Appleton, Wisconsin, 5:30 PM

Alex rounded the corner onto Oneida Street and spotted Annie's car in the alley behind Moore's drug store. He parked the Packard curbside at the door to the sisters' apartment. Standing on the sidewalk, he rang the bell and opened the door to look up the stairway. A cheerful looking young blonde opened the upper door and asked, "Hello, yes?"

"I'm Alex. I'm here to pick up Annie," Alex spoke each word carefully.

Beth looked sideways into the apartment and asked teasingly, "Hey, Annie, it's Alex. Are you all right, dressed and everything, I mean?"

Annie was standing next to her bed. She hurriedly buttoned the front of her white long-sleeve blouse and tucked it into her new Blue Bell jeans. She called out, "I'm ready," and sprung over to the open door. "Alex! Come on up and meet my sister. Come on up!"

Annie and Beth stood shoulder-to-shoulder inside the landing as Alex came up. With a friendly smile, he extended his hand to Beth.

"Beth, this is Alexander Throckmorton, and Alex, this is my sister Elisabeth … Beth," Annie nodded and moved her hand as a presentation.

Beth smiled devilishly and said, "Pleased to meet you, Alex. My sister has told me all about you."

"Hello, Beth, it's my pleasure. It's my pleasure to know two such beautiful women." He reached out and took Annie's hand in his. "Annie means a lot to me; a whole lot."

Annie looked flabbergasted and was obviously unprepared for him to say anything like that in front of her sister. Beth's eyes opened wide, and her head jerked backwards a little. She took the chance to give Annie the business. Beth started to grin

57

and broke the short silence by teasing her further. "Really, now? Wow! Hey, Sister, that's a new development, don't you know."

Annie quickly shifted her weight to one foot. She put a hand on one hip, pushing out the other. "Well, not exactly, Beth. I think this whole thing has been simmering on the back burner for a few days now. And it's possible that I may turn up the heat!" Annie spoke in the fearless approach her sister knew all too well. She moved next to Alex, stood up on her tiptoes, gave him a quick kiss on the lips and came down close to him. She briefly, boldly rested her hands on his buttocks. "I'm glad you're a little early, Alex. We need to make a quick stop before we run out to the park. Bert made up the picnic and we need to pick it up at Maxine's. I'm pretty sure you know where that is, Alex?" Annie giggled and didn't wait for an answer. She walked over to the table, sat down, quickly rolled up the cuffs of her jeans and picked up her grey wool cardigan and purse. Alex smiled at Beth as they watched Annie move back across the room. It was at that moment Beth realized her sister could very well be in love.

"It was nice meeting you, Beth. I'll be seeing you again tomorrow," Alex gave her a nod, went out the door to the landing and started slowly down the stairs ahead of Annie.

Beth reached out, gave her sister's ponytail a flip, and said, "See you later, big Sister. Have fun." She called down the stairs, "See you tomorrow, Alex. Nice meeting you, too."

Alex gave her a wave and was out the bottom door. Beth asked, "You have your key? Right, Annie?"

"Yes, I do." She gave Beth a peck on the cheek and started down the stairs. She whispered, "Don't wait up." Halfway down, Annie turned and looked up to the landing. Beth was grinning and giving her the thumbs-up.

Alex held the door open on the Packard. Annie got in and slid across the seat. Walking around the car, he looked up to see Beth waving from one of the two large windows of the apartment. He gave a quick wave back and got behind the wheel. "You have a great sister there, Annie. One nice person, she is. Very pleasant I think." He looked at Annie and asked, "I didn't embarrass you up there, did I? Did I go too far, Annie?"

Annie turned and gave Alex her full attention. She calmly started, "Well, it was a surprise, the way it came out. But we both feel what's going on here, don't we? We know what's happening. I mean, Alex, I meant what I said upstairs ... I'm thinking the heat is getting turned up, don't you? And it ain't just urges. It's feelings, Alex. I have real feelings, Alex. Feelings for you ... and quite frankly, I'm loving it. This is something I have never, ever felt before. You got me good, Mister Alex. You got me good."

He reached over and held her. They shared the most meaningful kiss they have had. They embraced for minutes before he straightened up and turned the key in the ignition. "Let's go get our picnic started, Annie girl."

Down the road a few minutes, Alex pulled into Maxine's parking lot. Annie announced, "I'll be back out in a minute," jumped out of the car and up the wooden stairs.

And it was just a minute or two. As Annie came out of the diner, Alex got out of the car, opened the trunk and stood to the side. Tucked away in the back was a six-pack of *Blatz*, a fifth of *Jim Beam* Kentucky bourbon, a small eighteen-inch suitcase and a black leather satchel with *"USN"* embossed on the side.

Annie walked over to the car carrying two paper sacks and set them into the open trunk. She spotted a dark blue blanket with a bottle of champagne resting on it. "What's this? *Great Western* New York State Champagne? The royal treatment?" Annie joked. "And what's up with the leather bag?"

Alex was enjoying all this. "Well, I wouldn't call it the royal treatment. The blanket is not royal blue, just dark blue. I took it from the motel, only borrowing it, for our picnic. You simply have to have a blanket at a picnic, right? I think it's an absolute requirement, as a matter of fact. And the bottle? Well, since I am going to be enjoying the great outdoors with such a great looking woman, I figured we better have something great to drink. The salesclerk told me Great Western was positively the right champagne for occasions like this. And the shoulder bag? Well, that's a souvenir from my hitch with the Navy. I got my checkbook, and the estate transfer papers in there. Last week when I left Florida to come up here, I simply threw it in the trunk of my '47 Chevy along with my other bags."

"It looks as if you have things under control, Alex."

Alex was still standing with his arm extended upward, holding onto the trunk lid. "Well, Annie, to be perfectly honest, the toughest time I had all morning was finding a corkscrew for the champagne."

Annie giggled. Alex continued, "No, really! It was like a three-ring circus! The fellow at Mid-City Liquor sent me to Schlater's hardware store, then, they sent me to Bailey's Dry Goods. I went all over town for a twenty-cent corkscrew and bottle opener. I finally ended up at Woolworth's!"

Annie giggled again and shook her head. "Well, you can find just about anything in a Woolworth store. They say if Woolworth doesn't sell it, you don't need it. Beth and I were there today, too. But ... wait here a minute more. We need something to drink out of, don't we? I'll run back in and get a couple glasses for the bubbly stuff."

Annie came back out of Maxine's with two heavy, white china coffee cups. Again, she giggled, and said, "No clean glasses! Just mugs!", and carefully set them down onto the blanket. Alex closed the trunk, and they left for the river.

They arrived at Peabody Park and found the perfect spot: a covered gazebo sitting at a gentle bend along the Fox River. It seemed intended for special occasions like this. The water was calm despite the spring snowmelt; gently lapping and pushing along the banks. There was barely a breeze.

Alex parked the Packard right up to the shelter and he turned down the radio volume. The evening was unusually warm for late May, and Annie was quite comfortable with her sweater. They sat close on the bench, laughed, kissed and leaned on one another. Bert's fried chicken and potato salad were as delicious as ever. The food, however, was not the real focus for either of them. The world was truly magnificent, with time standing still. It could not have been any better.

He removed the foil top from the champagne bottle and unwound the wires surrounding the cork. With a resounding *pop!* it rocketed away, bounced off the gazebo roof and came to rest somewhere in the shelter. Alex was beyond surprise and looked perplexed at Annie. "I didn't need that corkscrew after all! Why didn't the clerk at the liquor store tell me?!" They laughed. It was Alexander's first champagne opening.

They toasted each other often with good clangs. It was downright fun drinking champagne from the heavy Buffalo China coffee cups. Annie joked that they were closest thing to fine crystal Appleton had to offer.

They kept the bottle lying at the water's edge. The river cooled the glass up and all around, falling down onto the little stones on the grassy bank. The sun was going down behind them, reflecting its fading light onto the water and creating little diamond sparkles on the surface. With the diminishing sun, it gradually became considerably cooler. It seemed as if the world had suddenly decided that the warm day needed to end, and the cool night begin.

A half dozen or so Canadian geese noisily honked their way northwest across the darkening grey sky above. Alex put the blanket around Annie's shoulders, and they sat together inside the gazebo. They could not get any closer. Annie considered herself the most fortunate woman in Appleton and perhaps even the world. It was glorious.

He reached inside his coat, brought out a small box and set in on the table in front of Annie. "Open that up and tell me what you think, Annie girl."

She turned her head and said, "Alex!" Her hands came out from under the blanket, and she popped open the maroon felt-covered box. Inside was a dark green jade in a bezel setting on a narrow, gently curved gold band. She slipped the ring on her

right hand.  With only the slightest twist, it went on
.comfortably and fit perfectly.

She gazed at the ring and the stone ... moved her hand gently
back and forth ... she let the setting sun's waning light create
little green stars on the jade ... and she gave Alex a heartfelt
kiss.

"Like it?  I saw it and I thought of your wonderful green
eyes and how it would complement you."

"Oh, yes.  Yes.  How did you know it would fit?  How did
you know my size?  It's wonderful.  Beautiful.  Thank you.
Thank you, Alex, so very much.  I love it."

It was dark when they were ready to leave.  They put the
two cups and plates in one paper sack, and the empty
champagne bottle in the other.  He put his arm around Annie,
and they walked to the car for the ride back to College Avenue.
Five minutes later, he pulled his car to the curb right at her
apartment door.

The dashboard clock read eleven thirty.  Alex gave Annie
one last kiss, "Goodnight, Annie, girl.  I love you."

Annie kissed him back, "I love you."  They held each other.

"Alex, please tell me, how did you guess the ring size?  Just
luck?"

"Well, you told me your shoe size was 7.  Someone once
told me that was a good way to determine ring size.  And do
you remember the other night, outside Maxine's, when I was
holding your hand?"

"Yeah!  I remember!  You were feeling my fingers up and
down and over and around, weren't you?"

"Yes, I was ... but enough of this chatter.  You have to get
into bed, Annie.  You have another long day tomorrow."  He
gave her another compassionate kiss on the lips.

Annie sighed and gave him a kiss back.  She smiled, touched
his hand and said, "Goodnight, Alex.  See you tomorrow
evening about six o'clock."

"Six o'clock it is.  Tell Beth we three will easily fit into the
Packard."

Alex watched her ring the bell, open the door and go upstairs. The lights were on.

## Hold Me, Thrill Me, Kiss Me

### Saturday, May 29, College Ave. & Oneida St., Appleton, Wisconsin, 5:50 PM

At about seven o'clock the next morning, Alex had breakfast at Maxine's. He thought about going somewhere else, like Karra's, but decided that would be utterly foolish. After he sat down and saw Annie, he knew he did the right thing. He became accustomed to seeing her. Moreover, her smile and the soft touch of her hand was a gift.

After his eggs and bacon, he drove back to Bloomer's Motel and spent the rest of the morning looking through and reading the Green Bay *Press & Gazette* Friday edition. Alex half-listened to the Farm Bureau and weather reports on WOMT, 1240 radio from Manitowoc. And just to pass time, he spent a few afternoon hours watching a matinee of the African epic *Mogambo*, starring Clark Gable, Ava Gardner and Grace Kelly. The Rio Theater was only a stone's throw down Oneida Street from Annie and Beth's apartment.

After the movie, back at the motel, he took his white shirt and grey double-pleated slacks off their hangers. He decided his dark blue sport jacket would look good with the only tie he had, a black one. Alex paused when he picked up his brown wing tips. He wore them only once, to the church last Saturday. The thought of dancing in new shoes came with a touch of a worry, but he chose style over comfort. After his shower, shave and a splash of Old Spice, Alex was ready for anything Babe Vanderpol's could throw his way. He checked the mirror and tapped his white beaver-belly fedora slightly to one side. In a moment, he was out the motel door and into the Packard.

Annie's day started early, at five in the morning. The sisters stayed up about an hour after Annie got home from Peabody Park. There was plenty of dreamy talk all about the *should-a-could-a-would-a* scenarios concerning Alex and the budding relationship. They knew it was impossible to predict what would happen; everything depended solely on the unknown *Alex factor*. The future was anybody's guess, but Annie saw it as simply wonderful. The jade was not an engagement ring in the classic sense, but Annie considered it to be. Her inner energy was fully charged.

Looking forward to the night at Babe's supper club, Annie and Beth were in a state of wondrous abandon. More so Annie, but they both enjoyed the anticipation of the night to come. Beth went out that morning to Andersons and bought a delicate blue floral print dress and a new pair of pumps with two-inch heels. She was elated that the end of the school year was imminent. Considering the date with Bobby Olsen and Annie's new relationship with Alex, it could certainly be cause for celebration. She reasoned if Annie could be all dolled up for Alex, then she could dress fancy for Bobby. When Annie got home from work, the sisters quickly had some Campbell's chicken noodle soup and saltines before they walked straight down the street to the beauty shop. They hurried like kids out of school and chattered like chipmunks. Annie had her mind made up on a basic body perm and a trim. She always liked the way Ingrid Bergman's hair looked. Beth wanted a permanent wave, one that would last all summer and into the start of the fall semester at Lawrence. It would be one thing less to worry about when school started.

When they got back to the apartment, the girls laid out their dresses on the beds, set their shoes nearby on the floor, and imagined how they would look in them. When it came to wondering what Bobby and Alex would be wearing, all bets were off. Neither of them even dared go down that road of improbability. Annie had a reasonable sense of confidence about how Alex would dress, but she also believed in the accepted stereotype that all men are colorblind and have no fashion sense whatsoever.

Bobby called and Beth told him that Alex was more than willing to take everyone in his car. Beth mentioned that it was a brand-new Packard and Bobby needed no further convincing. He began to ask all types of questions about the car that neither Beth nor Annie could ever answer. Elisabeth finally told him the car was pale yellow and if he wanted to know anything more he would have to wait and ask Alex. It was obvious to Beth that it was going to be an informative and fun night for Bobby too. He excitedly told Beth he would be ready and waiting whenever they got there to pick him up in the Patrician.

Looking into the old bathroom mirror, Annie fixed her mascara, lipstick and powder just right. Beth stood at her side, and they took turns bumping each other out of the way. The single hundred-watt bulb on the ceiling cast its harsh light with no mercy. The sharp incandescent light and strong shadows fell in all the most inconvenient places. Earlier, they spent close to an hour painting each other's nails and pushing chatter to the limit. Some frustration was setting in as the clock neared five-thirty.

Annie had enough. It was time for the dress. It was a solid sea green, with a fully flowing skirt, sleeveless top, gathered bodice and a wide belt in the same color. Beth helped her sister lift it up and over her head while managing to be careful with the hairdo. Annie sat on the edge of the bed and fastened her new T-strap ivory pumps. Beth voiced her approval and Annie continued hooking the clasps of her faux pearl bracelet.

Annie then helped Beth into her new dress with half sleeves and a red plastic belt. Beth's red lipstick and blonde hair in the tight, new curls of the perm set her look. She checked her stockings and straightened the seam down the back. Annie tied her red silk neck scarf off to one side. They stood there, primped, turned around and gave each other final approval. A touch of a comb here, and a tuck there finished the job.

Outside, Alex parked at the curb and walked to the street-level entry door of Annie and Beth's apartment. He rang the bell, waited a second, walked in, and started up the stairs.

They looked at one another. They were finished. Annie raised her eyebrows and Beth smiled. Together, they walked to the door, and Annie opened it. Alex had just reached the landing. "Ladies ... you look beautiful."

They smiled at Alex and back at one another. Annie raised her eyebrows, shrugged her shoulders and Beth smiled again. Annie returned Alex's compliment, "And you look very presentable also, Alex."

Beth added, "Yes, indeed."

Annie picked up her white cardigan and pocketbook. Beth grabbed her red purse. "I think we're ready," Annie said. With that, all three went out the door to the parked Packard.

Beth sat in the back, behind Alex, and they drove off. The trip to Bobby's went fast, with the sisters chattering in between the driving directions that they gave Alex. Bobby was ready and waiting outside his parent's home on North Division Street. He was wearing brown wool slacks and a near-matching sport coat. He immediately performed a quick walk-around on the Packard and totally ignored the door that Beth opened for him. With wide eyes, he beamed a huge smile as he walked. He touched the chrome hood ornament and headlamp visors, allowing his fingers to caress the curvaceous body and rear fenders. The car's shining presence and dazzling chrome overwhelmed him. When he sat inside, he looked all around and managed to take a breath. "This is one heck of a neat car, man. This is what I call *far out*! Nice, really nice. My name is Bobby. This car is far out. Crazy, man!"

Alex looked in the rear-view mirror at the young man, turned around and said, "Hi, Bobby. I'm Alex. Glad to meet you and I'm glad you like the Patrician. She's got a powerful 359 cubic inch Straight Eight and Packard's new Ultramatic automatic transmission."

Bobby nodded, smiled, and repeated, "Far out!"

Alex smiled back and paused a moment, "Is everybody ready to go have dinner and do some dancing?"

There was a unanimous and unified "Yes!"

## Sh-Boom (Life Would Be a Dream)

### Saturday, May 29, South Memorial Drive, Appleton, Wisconsin, 6:25 PM

The parking lot at Vanderpol's was already half full. The warm evening was prompting the spring peepers, those little frogs that signal the end of winter, to fill the air with their shrill calls. Alex locked the car and the group of four made their way to the covered entrance. Their shoes crunched and shuffled the small stones of the lot along the way. Once inside the heavy oak doors, the maitre d' asked Alex if his party were dining, dancing, or both. The patrons who dined were not required to pay the two-dollar cover charge. Alex touched his hand to the brim of his hat, nodded, and said, "Both, my good man. Both. Bobby and I are enjoying the company of these two extraordinary women tonight. We will certainly be dining *and* dancing." He had feigned an English accent, prompting a giggle from Annie.

The maitre d' gestured, "Right that way, sir; the coat check is available to the left, and the hostess will seat you. Ladies, gentlemen, enjoy your meal, have a wonderful evening and I hope you enjoy everything that Babe Vanderpol's has to offer."

Alex checked his hat. Annie and Beth kept their sweaters over their shoulders. On the way to the dining room, they passed the long bar and the wood parquet dance floor. The large easel standing in the doorway announced the night's live entertainment was Frank Wachewski and the Dizzie Tunes from Milwaukee. The bar was long, polished dark cherry and gently curved away toward the dining room for about 30 feet. Barstools went the entire length, with men and women standing and seated. The din of conversation and the clinging

67

of bottles and glasses filled the room. Four bartenders were on the job, wearing white long-sleeve shirts and pitch-black garters on their upper arms. A half dozen slowly rotating, large, wicker blade ceiling fans were dispersing the air above the bar, churning the smell of cigars, cigarettes and perfume. The adjoining dining room was large, open and walled on the far side by connecting plate glass picture windows. The view of the Fox River and its grassy banks gave the room a feeling of a subtle transition to the outside world.

They sat at a table close to the dance floor. The band members were bringing in their instruments, moving music stands and two large, round, chrome microphones on the raised stage. A waitress in a black tailored skirt and white blouse came and took their drink orders. A young waiter in a fitted white denim jacket, black slacks and red bow tie, followed her and brought the dinner menus. They were heavy stock, burgundy paper and bordered in gold braided chord piping. Alex made a brief announcement that the dinner would be his treat and there would be no arguments accepted. Bobby did object and Alex ensured the peace by saying he could leave the tip. Babe's claim to fame in the Fox River Valley was aged charcoal grilled steaks. Oddly, only Alex ordered beef, the New York strip. Rather, it was chicken Parmesan for Annie, Rainbow Trout for Beth and a Salisbury steak for Bobby. The place was buzzing, and by the time their meals arrived, the dining room was full. The Dizzy Tunes were warming up. There was a twang, a cymbal clang, a drumbeat, a trombone blat and a clarinet peep. Someone was snapping a finger on one of the large round microphones. The accordion player was pumping up his button box and creating mechanical moans.

All around the table, they shared stories about their lives, past and present. There was plenty of humor and a flashing touch of pathos now and then. Alex learned that Beth was indeed a warm and loving sister. He also discovered that Bobby was a young man interested in fast cars, big engines and Beth. Annie and Alex spent most of the time holding hands under the table and pushing close to one another. At a discreet, private moment, Annie would rub her calves along Alex's legs. Her stockings made a whooshing sound that one time caught her sister's attention. Beth looked across the table and winked at Alex. He smiled back and started to talk to Bobby about engines, transmissions and the Patrician 400.

Wisconsin has a good share of Poles and Norwegians, and understandably, the band started with a sequence of polkas. It seemed half the dining room got up and began jumping. Bobby and Beth joined in after the first number and remained out on the floor. Alex and Annie sat closer. They continued to talk, rub legs and touch thighs.

"I have not ever experienced such a lovely time. I have never been this dressed up before. And I have not enjoyed any evening more than this." Annie spoke in a silken tone.

"And never in my life have I been in the company of such a beautiful woman. I cannot explain it any other way. You are simply remarkable to me Annie, very special." Alex was holding her hand on his lap.

Frank, the band leader, announced in a deep baritone, "Ladieeees, and Gentlemennnn, it's dance time! Here we go with a brand-new number just released by The Chords: *Sh-boom, Life Would Be a Dream.*"

The band started and Alex stood up, beaming a huge smile. "Come on, Annie. Let's show them how it's done!" In one smooth motion, he took her hand out from under the table and led her onto the dance floor. She smiled and hurried right behind him, with her shoes tapping along, tippity-tapping on the wood parquet. Other couples made some room as Alex and Annie began to dance the Lindy. Beth watched them dance and was having almost as much fun. They danced across the floor, mixing together like warm oil paint. Her green dress and auburn hair flowed along like an artist's brush, applied in smooth, wide strokes with Alex's grey slacks and white shirt.

The band ended the five-song set with Fats Waller's hit *I Ain't Got Nobody,* and announced a break. Annie needed a pause. She stood on the dance floor with her arms outstretched on Alex's shoulders, taking deep breaths. She shook her head slightly and ruffled her hair. "Where did you learn to dance like that, Mister Alex?"

He caught his breath and smiled wryly. "It was part of my Navy training, Annie. Call it mandatory dance training at USO clubs in Japan and Guam. And a little at Pearl Harbor, too. When a thousand or so sailors go on shore leave and only thirty girls are at the USO, you darn well better be able to dance or you're going to be sitting on the sidelines for the entire evening."

They walked back to their table and to Bobby and Beth. They gave Alex and Annie a polite short applause, agreeing that they were indeed quite a dance team.

They all shared more stories and personal histories. Alex sipped Kentucky bourbon over ice with dinner, and later switched to Canada Dry. Annie and Beth enjoyed several refills of sloe gin and Squirt. Bobby made it clear early in the evening that he was a Milwaukee Schlitz beer man.

The Dizzie Tunes with Frank Wachewski proved to be an eclectic mix of talent, styles and music. Frank wore a polo shirt and baggy slacks. The accordion player had a beige, red and green plaid topcoat with a broad red tie. The big Negro bass man did most of the vocals and wore a dark blue suit with a skinny red tie. The trumpet and trombone players had matching seersucker summer suits. The drummer, messy hair and goatee, was wearing a blue denim work shirt. Another large Negro, the saxophone player was in a white shirt way too small for him, red vest and dark blue slacks. The group continued animating the dancers and vibrating the floor and walls. The Dizzie Tunes played everything from polkas, rockabilly, country to rock and roll. Beth and Bobby almost stayed on the dance floor. They bopped to songs like *Crazy, Man, Crazy* and *Rocket 88*. The crowd loved the band, and long periods of applause and whistles broke out after every set of songs. Annie and Alex would go out and dance an

70

occasional Swing or Lindy when the band went into their rhythm, blues and jazz sets. At one point in the evening, Annie and Beth joked that it was a possibility the smiles they wore could be freezing on their faces.

The stage became quiet at midnight. It was time for everyone to go home, back to the apartment, bedroom, cabin or motel room. On the way out to the parking lot, Annie walked slowly and pushed close to Alex. She started, virtually repeating some of her words from earlier in the evening, "This is the most fun I've ever had, being this much dressed up, being with a handsome man and being in love, in my entire Wisconsin life." She said the secret word. Alex noticed.

Alex stopped, bent his head down, and kissed her under the arching lights of the parking lot. He held her tight, arms around her shoulders and waist. She pushed into him.

Bobby and Beth were waiting at the Packard.

## Be My Life's Companion

### Sunday, May 30, College Ave. & Oneida St, Appleton, Wisconsin, 12:42 AM

Alex stopped the Packard outside Bobby Olsen's home on North Division. The porch light was on and so were lights inside the home. Beth and Bobby exited the car, walked up the sidewalk to the front door where they stood and kissed.

Annie sat close to Alexander, watching and fully aware that the night was ending. "Do you think his parents are still up?"

"Without a doubt, Annie. Without a doubt. Bobby seems to be a young man who parents would wait up for."

Annie nodded in agreement and watched Beth walk back to the car. Alex put it in drive and went off in the direction of College Avenue. The trip seemed over in an instant. As soon as the car came to a stop, Beth opened the rear door and said, "Thank you, Alex. Bobby and I had a fantastic time. See you

71

upstairs, Sis." She hopped out, stepped across the sidewalk and started upstairs.

Alex parked the Packard directly under a streetlight a little further down on Oneida Street. There was not another car anywhere nearby; the shops were dark and the streets empty. The lights went on upstairs in Annie and Beth's apartment. The bar located half a block down had the only neon lights in sight and two cars were parked at the curb outside the gin mill. Somewhere not too far away, a dog was barking. Moths and night flies were darting and dodging into and out of the fragile grasp of the streetlights.

Annie was resting her head on Alex's shoulder. She sat up and whispered, "Thank you, Alex. It was terrific." Alex looked at her and didn't say a word. She paused and wondered: *How come he's so quiet? What is he thinking about?*

As if he read her mind, Alex started, "For the last four days, Annie, I have only had one thing on my mind: you. You and only you are what I've been thinking of." He paused and thought for a minute. "I have something to say and don't know how. And you have no idea of what I want to say, do you?"

"No, not really. Why are you teasing me and what do you want to say?"

He gently took her hand and placed it inside his coat, against his chest. "I don't have the words that my heart has. My heart is talking to you, Annie. Can you feel my heart talking? Can you feel it beating?"

She whispered, "Yes, I can. I can feel every beat."

"It's saying: *I love you; I love you, I love you.*" He then paused ... and asked, "Will you marry me?"

Annie kept her hand against his chest. She looked straight into his eyes and said, "Yes. Yes, I will."

He held her. Their lips touched. They whispered to one another, twisted their bodies and held each other close. The Packard's leather seat began to moan and stretch.

He reached into the inside right chest pocket of his coat and brought out a little blue box. He opened the lid and handed the box to her. "I bought one for you and one for me." She held the open box in her hand.

"You bought these when you bought the Jade, didn't you?"

"Yes, I did."

"I guess you already knew what I was going to say, didn't you?" Annie teased.

"Yes, I did. I'm guilty as charged." Alex smiled at her.

"Well, it's a good thing I'm so gosh darn predictable," she whispered, and kissed him again.

She needed to ask, "And when is the wedding?"

He teased, "Any day now. Soon."

Her head was swirling with thoughts. Alex was relishing every moment with the woman he loved. They were still dancing the Lindy together, lost in a sexual stupor fueled by dreams, wishes and their deepest, private desires. Their hands and lips moved on one another with a passion neither of them had ever before encountered. Annie was experiencing the most intense feeling of sensual abandon of her twenty-one years. Her warm body surrendered under his firm touch. The supple leather of the Patrician whispered as the weight of their bodies shifted. Annie's legs rubbed her nylons into a steady silken purr under the caress of her new dress and Alex's touch.

About half an hour later, an Outagamie County Sheriff's two-door Mercury coupe drove past ... ever so slowly and parked across from the bar down the street. Annie slipped the little blue box in her purse. The passion quickly cooled.

It was early Sunday morning. Alex suggested he could pick her up at ten o'clock and they could catch brunch at Karin's Kitchen, a cafe downtown. Annie agreed. She practically ran upstairs and exclaimed, "Guess what, Beth!"


*Botch-A-Me*


**Sunday, May 30, Richmond Avenue, Appleton, Wisconsin, 9:15 AM**

Alex stood at the mirror and twirled the wet brush in the cup of Old Spice shaving soap. He turned his head to one side, and began sloshing the frothy stuff onto his chin, neck and cheeks. It was second nature, a habit, to turn the handle of the safety razor and pop out the old blade into the small bathroom trash can. He slid a new Gillette Blue Blade out of its tin dispenser, tightened the handle and pulled the razor across his face. A nick or cut was inevitable. Alex stuck tiny pieces of toilet tissue on the two he just got. The bedside table radio was tuned to the Lutheran Hour from radio 1240, Manitowoc. He checked his watch; it was quarter past. He walked across the room and shook the wrinkles out of his white shirt. As he buttoned it up and tucked it into his slacks, he stepped into his Cordovan loafers. Alex pulled his grey sweater over his head, turned off the radio and was out the motel room door. Annie would be expecting him.

A few miles up the road and about an hour earlier, Beth opened her eyes to stare at the ceiling. She turned to see her sister looking at the ceiling too, lying on her bed with her hands behind her head. "Good morning. Sleep good, did you, Annie?" The sisters didn't get to bed until 2 AM.

"I did. Well, after I managed to get to sleep. My thoughts were boiling and bubbling around with all kinds of stuff last night. Still are. I'll tell you, Beth. I'm lost in love. I'm way past and way far beyond the point of no return."

"I can imagine. It's pretty plain to see how you and Alex both feel about each other. And it's not every day you get a marriage proposal, don't you know."

Annie still had her eyes fixed on the patterned, pressed metal ceiling above her bed. "Alex is picking me up at ten and taking me to Karin's this morning for brunch. So, I think I'll shower, have a quick coffee and get myself put together. I think it's going to be a busy day." She hopped out of bed and into the bathroom.

74

*Young At Heart*

## Sunday, May 30, College Avenue, Appleton, Wisconsin, 10:45 AM

At a booth inside Karin's, Alex looked across the table at Annie. He was marveling at how refreshing she looked and how her presence made him feel so alive. "Sweetheart, you look fantastic," he told her. He meant every word. She was wearing a light brown skirt and had her hair pulled back in a ponytail. The round white collar lying on the outside of her dark green sweater looked as a frame around a portrait. The sunlight coming through the window fell upon the jade ring and it reaffirmed his decision to buy it for her. He leaned across the table and spoke quietly, "Annie girl, I love you."

The waitress came and went several times. The tables around them became empty and occupied again. They talked, laughed, whispered and discussed their immediate future. Annie asked him early on, direct and on-point, "When is this wedding going to be?"

Alex replied, "Well, soon. I have a young colt at the farm in Florida, and my mechanic job in Pensacola. My boss told me to take all the time I need, but I don't have forever. And I've been relying on my neighbor down the road to keep an eye on the house and barn for me. Louis has a small horse ranch, and he has been boarding two-year old Sebastian for me. So, I think 'soon' would be the answer to that question."

"The two-year old is the pony, right?" Annie had her eyes open a little wider than normal.

Alex let out a chuckle, "Sebastian is the colt, Annie. I don't have any children running around back in Florida."

Alex then realized he had not told Annie anything at all about the farm he bought last month. They recognized there were some significant details about each other's lives that would be coming to the forefront quickly. He started telling Annie about his twenty-acre farm near Milton, Santa Rosa

County, about half an hour north of Pensacola. He described the grasslands around the county and the great possibilities for raising beef cattle or horses. The untapped resources of abundant grass, fresh water and the warm weather created an idyllic year-round location. He explained that he developed an affinity for farm life; a notion he embraced while on an aircraft carrier in the Sea of Japan. He admitted it sounded foolish, but that he dreamed of raising quarter horses. He was slowly drawing circles with his finger on the table. He smiled and told Annie that maybe he saw one too many John Wayne movies aboard ship. He joked that the dream of a cowboy lifestyle went to his head. Annie listened to every word. She tried to imagine starting a ranch life like Maureen O'Hara did at the end of that movie, *The Redhead From Wyoming*. She watched Alex intently. Deep inside, Annie longed to be in his daydream. She wanted the opportunity to tell him so and deep within her, she knew the chance would come. She truly believed she would be living her dream.

"Well, then we better get the ball rolling, don't you know? And as far as a big wedding, forget it. I'm not that kind of girl. A Justice Of The Peace will do just fine. I do not need any of the hoopla a big wedding would mean. No, thank you. I'm a small-town Midwest country girl all the way. And I knew we would end up in Florida … Beth and I already went over that, and it's a given fact. So, I think this week would do just right, don't you think?" Annie spoke quickly, hardly stopping for a breath, smiled, reached across the table and took his hands. With an immediate afterthought, she added, "And you got that bank box in Detroit. You need to open that up, too." She bent her head sideways and raised her eyebrows, encouraging him to answer.

"Yeah. There's that too. I forgot about that, didn't I? How could I forget that? Well, I guess we need to get this show on the road … it looks like this wedding is going to be just like all the others you hear about: busy, busy, busy." He sat straight up, took a sip of lukewarm coffee, grimaced and shuddered. "What do we do first?"

"Why don't we aim for Friday? Does that sound okay?"

He pushed away his cold coffee and looked into her green eyes. "That's it then. Let's do it. We'll shoot for Friday. We got some work to do, starting tomorrow."

They got up and walked to the cash register at the counter. As they waited to pay their check, they ran through a few of their plans for the day. Annie said she needed a nap and would have to call her mother to tell her all the news. Alex thought he would go back to Bloomer's and try to get a ball game on the television or radio. He knew the Tigers were in Cleveland playing a weekend stretch with the Indians.

Annie's apartment was only two blocks away. When he dropped Annie off, he asked, "Give me your telephone number, Annie, and I'll call you later." He pulled a pencil and scrap of paper out of the glove box.

"It's Regent ten-twelve, Alex. RE-1012."


*Honeymoon on A Rocket Ship*

**Sunday, May 30, College Ave. & Oneida St, Appleton, Wisconsin, 1:40 PM**

Beth was sitting on the sofa, looking through last week's Saturday Evening Post for the third time. Annie was lying on her bed half-asleep and listening to the radio, the sound barely audible.

Beth set the open magazine down next to her and started, "You know, Sister, this ain't one of those whirlwind romances you hear about all the time when the girl gets swept off her feet. Nope. This isn't a whirlwind romance. It's one of them hurricanes, that's what it is. A Florida hurricane ... No, no ... it's a gosh darn Wisconsin tornado. You and Alex are flying around inside a tornado ... a love tornado. And you are headed for one of those rocket ship honeymoons." Beth paused and

77

became serious, "But hey … are you going to telephone Mama soon?"

"Yeah, I guess I better. But I really don't know how to start the conversation. You got any ideas?"

"Since when don't you have any ideas about how to start talking? You've never had any problems before… just come right out and say it. Say: 'Mama, I'm getting married this week!' That's all. Don't be afraid, Annie. It's Mama. It's just like talking to me for goodness' sake ... well … almost."

Annie got out of bed, walked across the room, grabbed a chair and set it by the counter, next to the sink and the big black telephone. She put the receiver to her ear and dialed *"0"*.

"Operator, I'd like to call long-distance. To Putney, Vermont. The number is Bridgestone five-six-nine. BR- 569."

Annie tried for thirty minutes without any luck. The operator always got a busy signal. Frustrated, Annie gave up and waited for an hour. At three o'clock, she tried again. Two, three, four times. Each time the result was a busy signal. She got annoyed. While Annie had a nervous anticipation about talking to her mother, she was anxious to tell her all the monumental news in her life.

She tried again. "Operator, I have been trying for two hours. This is important; it's not an emergency, but I want to tell my mother that I'm getting married this Friday and I can't get through. I know my mother's on a party line, but gosh darn it, aren't they supposed to hang up after five rings or something?"

The Wisconsin Bell operator broke into the line. She connected Annie to her mother and stepfather's home on US Route 5 in Putney, Vermont. Annie started, "Hey, Mama! Guess what!"

The conversation began in earnest. They hadn't spoken in nearly six months. Irene Hendricks talked at length with Annie and Beth. At the beginning of the telephone call, when Annie told her mother the exciting news, Irene tiptoed around the subject and seemed to avoid the topic of the upcoming wedding. Naturally, she spent most of the telephone time with

Annie. The two sisters and their mother shared laughter and emotion over things past and present. Their mother wondered how they were getting along on their own since she last talked to them at Christmas and told them that Walter received a promotion to Lead Supervisor of Newsprint Production at the paper mill.

After some uncomfortable and lengthy chatter around the small tidbits of life, the topic of the man in Annie's life, Alex, finally became front and center. A lot of time was spent describing the tall stranger who came from Oshkosh by way of Florida, the Navy, and Michigan. How he looked, how he talked and how he asked her to marry him. The romantic details of the proposal were skipped, passed over. As Annie and Beth were accustomed to, their mother continued with her thinly veiled criticisms and well-intentioned but mundane motherly advice. They talked about *Sincerity, Honesty, Certainty* and whether or not anyone can learn enough about a future spouse in five days.

Irene warned Annie that she was taking a big gamble with her life and that she should make her decisions based on purity rather than lust. That comment caused Annie to grit her teeth. She felt she was sitting in the forward pew of Christ The King Lutheran church with *Adulteress* written in giant red letters across the front of her white blouse.

Next, her mother continued talking without regard to graciousness and boldly told Annie that after the wedding night sex, she would know if she had made the right choice. Annie was surprised, shocked, stymied and more than slightly irritated. Her mother had the talent to make well-intentioned statements sound derogatory. Annie even thought of telling her mother she and Alex had already made love. She quickly decided against it, and rightfully so. Annie knew it would not help matters at all and would only further complicate the conversation.

On occasion, her mother could be downright brutal with some of her opinions. It was probably unintentional, but she was talking to her daughter as if she were still a schoolgirl. She was more than straightforward, and Annie wondered if she inherited some of her own boldness from her mother. Irene eventually brought up the subject of children and exactly how to avoid an unwanted pregnancy. She didn't use the words 'condom' or 'diaphragm' but she described them at length. Annie rolled and crossed her eyes more than once.

Annie was wondering if it was perhaps a big mistake to make this call to Vermont. Despite her mother's ranting and raving, however, she knew she did the required thing. She knew she had an obligation to share her good news with her mother. Exactly how her mother dealt with it was beyond Annie's control. She thought, *Even the perfect bowl of oatmeal can have its lumps.*

Her mother asked when the wedding was planned to take place. Annie was perhaps shockingly honest, and said, "Well Mama, I don't know. Alex and I haven't made those plans yet. But I guess it could be anytime now."

Irene then dropped the biggest bombshell: the marriage license. That part of the conversation became the single snowflake that created a blizzard from the few flurries of worry already in the wind. Annie, of course, knew that she and Alex needed a marriage license, however, it's one of those things you need to be reminded of.

"Of course, Mama. I know that," Annie said in her own defense. But the unspoken truth was that it was not even considered, not up until that moment anyway. The license was the single thing that caught Annie by surprise, and it made her nervous. Thoughts were flashing through her head like lightning. She knew she would have to go to the Outagamie County building on Monday and ask the County Clerk or someone who handles the marriage licenses. Annie was getting so much information at once. She was frustrated at her mother's all-seeing, all-knowing demeanor. She needed a break. Without saying a word, she handed the telephone handset to her sister, got up from the chair, and let Beth sit down.

Annie walked to the sink, stared out the window and gazed down College Avenue. She felt unsure of herself, and squeezed her hands into fists. She stood, clenched her jaw and calmed herself with determination.

Beth went on about last night's double date at Babe's, and her mother genuinely wished she could have been there with them. "Well, Beth, you tell Annie for me again what I already told her once and you tell her again that I wish I could be there for her wedding. I love you, girls." Beth pictured her mother wiping away a tear. She could only picture it. She could not tell for sure, not by her tone anyway. Beth stood and passed the receiver back to Annie.

Their stepfather, Walter, also wished the girls well, telling Annie that he too, would have liked to attend her wedding. Annie told him, "Well, you both will be there with me in my thoughts." She briefly talked to her mother again and said a mild good-bye. "I love you, but you know this is a party line, Mama, so we better go," and with that, Annie hung up. One of the most uncomfortable conversations of her life was over.

Annie sat in the chair by the counter for a minute. She took a few deep breaths, stood up and brought the chair back to the table. Beth was watching her sister and knew she was troubled.

"Beth, I've got to go see Alex." Annie went to the bathroom, rinsed the sting out of her eyes and touched up her mascara and lipstick. Looking into the old, brown, mercury-stained mirror, she undid her ponytail and ran a brush through her hair. Annie threw her green cardigan back on, walked over to the table and picked up her purse. "I'll be back before too long. I'm going to see Alex. He's staying just down the road at Bloomer's."

"Take your time … take your time," Beth said. She looked over to the big window by the sink and shook her head. Beth was aware how their mother could tarnish the silver lining of any cloud. She realized that her mother must have said something to get her sister this upset. She picked up the magazine again.

On her way down the stairs, Annie had a thought. She remembered that Deacon Wilkerson performed marriages. She suddenly had a spring in her step. Annie hurriedly walked to the alley and started up her 1936 Ford. She drove to the deacon's home on West Marquette Street, adjacent to the church. It was Sunday after services, and he would be home. She just knew it.

*Wanted*

**Sunday, May 30, Richmond Avenue, US Route 41, Appleton, Wisconsin, 4:10 PM**

Alex had his feet up on the bed, sitting back in the brown Naugahyde chair, and watching the Milwaukee Braves and Saint Louis Cardinals on WBAY, Channel 2 out of Green Bay. The picture on the seventeen-inch black and white RCA console was snowy and rolling, but the sound was loud and clear. The knock on the door came in the middle of the sixth inning.

He walked to the door and opened it. Annie was visibly nervous as she began to speak, "Hi Alex. We need to talk. Now … right now. I saw your car right outside the room, but I went to the motel office to make sure, and made certain which room was yours. I hope you don't mind, and I hope you don't think I'm too bold, but we need to talk."

He noticed her red eyes. He took her hand, led her into the room and clicked the knob of the television to the *off* position. He noticed Annie's demeanor and tried to exert every bit of confidence. He pulled the other chair from the small table by the window, set it across from him and motioned Annie to sit down. She settled down onto the edge of the chair. He made the effort to exhibit a calm and steady bearing. "What's going on?" He leaned forward on his chair, getting closer to her.

She began by telling him first about the difficult time she had experienced making the telephone connection to her mother in Vermont. She continued and described the whole conversation that ensued and detailed how her mother brought up the subjects of the wedding night, family planning, obligation, and even the marriage license. Annie said she felt treated like a teenager and believed that her mother didn't mean to get her upset. Nevertheless, her mother's know-it-all attitude didn't help matters much. She then explained how she ended up at the deacon's home on West Marquette for his advice and guidance. Annie talked non-stop. It seemed she didn't take a breath between words. Finally, it came down to the big question; the real reason she made this trip to his motel room. Annie feared she already knew the answer. She took a deep breath and paused for just a second. "Alex, Deacon Wilkerson told me that you need either your birth certificate or a Wisconsin driver's identification. Do you have either one of those things?"

Alex leaned back in the chair and nodded with confidence. "We'll fix this. Soon everything will be under control. Together, there isn't a problem we can't handle." He got up and picked up his keys. "I'm getting something out of the car. I'll be back in a flash." Annie felt relief but she didn't expect that Alex went to the car to bring in his birth certificate. She just knew it and she was right. He went outside to the Packard, opened the trunk and brought in the unopened bottle of Jim Beam. He came back in, set the Beam down on the dresser, went to the bathroom and rinsed out the glass standing by the sink. He poured two fingers of Kentucky bourbon into the glass, handed it to Annie and set the bottle on the floor.

She drank about half of it, squeezed her eyes shut and made a sour face. She shuddered. It was a moment before she opened her eyes.

"You all right? Bourbon can be a little harsh."

When Annie began talking, she rambled and her words came out as a flood, "Alex, we are not going to solve this by drinking.

Drinking is not going to get us what we need. You don't have your birth certificate, do you? Of course not! Who carries their birth certificate around? And you don't have a Wisconsin driver's card, do you? Of course not! Without a doubt, you have one from Florida!" Annie shook her head in desperation, "What can we do about this?"

"Simple, Annie," he took the glass from her, finished it and set it down on the table. "Simple. I was born in Detroit. I need to go to there anyway, and check out those safe deposit boxes. So, we drive to Michigan, get a copy of my birth certificate, file for our marriage license, get married and then drive south to Florida on our honeymoon. That's all. Plain and simple. We will be on our honeymoon driving south to my place in Florida, Annie. We'll get married in Michigan instead of Wisconsin, that's all." He poured another two fingers into the glass and handed it back to Annie.

She drank half of it again. This time she didn't shut her eyes or make that sour face. Annie looked into Alex's eyes. His eyes gave her confidence and his words had calmed her. She spoke slowly and with relief, "Super-duper."

She reconsidered their situation. Alex was watching her expressions. Annie nodded her head and smiled. Alex's logic had soothed Annie's anxiety. After a short pause, she continued, "That's it, Alex. Just like you said: *plain and simple.*"

They stood and held each other. Alex held her close. Annie held onto him. He was her strength in this whirlwind of emotion. She held her elbows at his waist, her arms up his back and her hands on his shoulders. "Let's go tomorrow," she said, backing away. She locked her eyes onto his. "We'll go tomorrow. I'll pack my stuff and we'll go. We can be on our way tomorrow."

"Are you sure? Tomorrow? So soon?"

"Why not? I'll pack my stuff and we can leave for Detroit tomorrow." Her voice trailed off. Alex watched Annie work her magic. An idea filled her head, a realization. A big smile appeared.

"Alex! *The Badger*! The ferryboat to Michigan! The Badger, it's a ferryboat, and it sails every morning. Every morning at eight o'clock. It takes four hours from Manitowoc to ... to ... Ludington ... Ludington, Michigan, I think. It takes four hours to cross the lake to Michigan. They fill the boat up with rail cars and tourists and automobiles. We'll go tomorrow. Tomorrow morning. How's that?"

They sat back down in the chairs. Alex once again finished off a glass of bourbon. "Are you sure? Tomorrow?" He realized what the ferry ride could do for them. That ferry across Lake Michigan would cut out Milwaukee, Chicago and part of Indiana. He figured it could shave off about ten hours of driving around the lake. He asked again, "Tomorrow? You want to leave tomorrow? Are you sure?"

Annie reached across the small table and took his hand. "Yes, tomorrow. We can get all our stuff together and leave tomorrow morning. Why not? There's nothing holding you here in Appleton, is there Alex?"

"No, not really. The only thing holding me to Appleton is you, Annie. My obligations in Oshkosh are finished. All I have are two suitcases, one full and one empty, a picture album, a satchel full of papers, and me. That's it." Alex poured another two-finger shot. "You're absolutely sure?"

"I've never been so sure of anything in my life as I am right now. I'm ready, Alex. I'm ready to begin my life with you. I'm ready to be your wife."

Alex finished the glass of whiskey and set it back on the dresser with the bottle. "If the ferry steams at eight o'clock, we don't have much time to waste. It's about five now, so how about we grab something to eat somewhere and get our ducks in a row. You have some things to pack, I'm sure."

Annie straightened her hair and said, "I'll get the ducks, Alex. It's your job to line them up." She giggled and stood up. "Karin's is open until six. We can grab a quick burger or something and I can go pack. Come on, I'll follow you. Let's go." They were out the motel room door in mere seconds.

Alex checked his rear-view mirror all the way into town, watching Annie and her '36 Ford following behind him. He thought how fast things have happened these past few days. He felt a tickle inside his chest and remembered how he felt the first time he laid eyes on the woman in the coupe behind him. He looked in the mirror again and was satisfied that he made the right decisions over the past week. He was sure of it.

They walked into Karin's Kitchen together. Their waitress from earlier in the day smiled wryly when she saw them again. She walked over to their booth and quipped, "You guys are back again, I see. Did you get everything talked over?"

Annie took Alex's hand and answered, "Yes we did. We're getting married and we're moving to Florida. We're getting married!"

The waitress handed them the menus and scoffed, "That's nice. Real nice, but you won't be able to spend as much time talking as you did earlier today. We close in forty minutes." She turned and was gone.

Annie gave Alex an incredulous glance. "That was rude. There is no excuse for that snippy attitude. Do not leave her a tip, Alex. Don't you dare."

After a cheeseburger, French fries and a milk shake apiece, they put the exact change on the table and left Karin's Kitchen. Annie knew she would not be back. It was a minute or so past six o'clock.

Annie and Alex drove their cars the short distance back to Oneida and College Avenue. Outside the apartment, Alex gave Annie the empty suitcase from his trunk. When he left Florida on May 15, he anticipated that he would use it for items from his mother's home in Oshkosh. He recalled something he learned while in the Navy: *while foresight can be wrong, it can still be useful.*

Annie knew there was an entire evening of packing ahead of her. They shared a quick embrace and decided that Alex would pick her up at six o'clock the next morning.

*Among My Souvenirs*

### Monday, May 31, College Ave. & Oneida St., Appleton, Wisconsin, 5:50 AM

Alex glanced up and noticed that the lights were on. He rang the doorbell, walked up the stairs to the landing and knocked. Beth opened the door, her eyes heavy from lack of sleep and red with dried tears. She reached out and hugged Alex. "God Bless you, Alex," she said, "I know you'll take good care of my sister. Come on in."

Annie was at the table finishing her packing. She had paper shopping bags, Alex's small suitcase and a worn blue denim-covered overnight bag on the tabletop, stuffed full with her belongings. Empty coffee cups and a few soda bottles were crowded onto the table. She placed a few toiletries into her personal tote and announced, "Done ... all done, Beth." She turned and saw Alex. "Good morning, I didn't hear you come in!"

"Just got here, Annie. I'll start taking some of this down to the car." He moved to the table, grabbed the suitcases and two of the packed paper bags.

Beth walked to the table and hugged Annie. Annie's weary eyes matched those of her sister; she was tired and frazzled but working through it. She was driven by the power of love and excitement of a new life. She stood tall and realized her future was unfolding. The girls were up packing and talking past midnight and when they finally went to bed, Annie just lay there, anxious and only dozed off now and again.

The past evening, as soon as she got back to the apartment from Karin's, she grabbed a paper box from the top dresser drawer. Years ago, their mother had covered an old shoebox with wallpaper scraps. There were small rose buds all over the sides and lid. Her mother would squirrel away small keepsakes, photographs and documents during the years they were growing up on South Walnut Street. When their mother moved to Vermont, her daughters took possession of the treasure chest that they called the 'paper box'.

Annie dumped the contents onto the table and shuffled the pictures, baubles and papers around. She found what she was searching for: her birth certificate from Saint Elizabeth hospital. She folded it carefully and placed it inside her zipper wallet. She patted it as you would touch a puppy and returned the pocketbook to her purse. She decided at Karin's cafe that she would make certain the document was safe and accounted for. The women were busy finding, sorting and packing Annie's things well up to nearly one o'clock in the morning. Annie filled Alex's small suitcase and the larger suitcase of her own. Her five pair of shoes, waitress uniform, old sweatshirts and some odd items were relegated to paper sacks. They stuffed the bed linen, pillow and blankets off Annie's bed into an old laundry bag. At one point, Annie sat and looked at all the things on the table, the suitcases, the paper bags and she laughed. She pointed at the items and said, "There sits my whole life, Beth. All that stuff, packed into paper bags and suitcases, is everything I own. My life is sitting here in front of me. It doesn't look like much, does it?"

Beth stopped that line of conversation right there and let it go no further. "Annie, your entire life is ahead of you, not sitting here scattered on the table or stuffed into those suitcases and sacks. Wonderful times are coming, Annie. Your future will unfold as soon as you're out the door and driving south with Alex."

Late last night, Annie had expressed her concern about leaving Beth behind in Appleton. Beth was adamant she would get along just fine. She told Annie that Laura Wilkerson, the deacon's daughter, said only a week or so ago that she was hoping to move in as a roommate with someone. If worse came to worse, she could post a notice for a roommate in the Student Hall at the college. She clearly explained that Annie had nothing to worry about.

Alex came back up the stairway, knocked just once again and entered the apartment. The sisters were holding each other. Annie backed up and placed the car keys to her '36 Ford into Beth's hand and said, "Walter told me *'take care of it and it will take care of you'* when he passed me these keys a year ago March. The old jalopy keeps on going down the road, Beth. Bobby will help you keep it running." They briefly embraced again before Annie backed gently away.

There was a logjam of emotion. Alex uncomfortably broke the moment and interrupted, "Are we about done here?"

"Yes, I think so, Alex. There's just this laundry bag and two more paper bags." Annie walked toward the door with her overnight bag, purse and a paper sack. She looked over the room again. Alex walked up to Beth, told her goodbye and gave her a hug. He took two steps to the table and picked up the remaining bags and laundry sack. He gingerly made his way around the sisters, turned halfway around and announced, "I'll be in the car, Annie. Bye, Beth. God Bless," and went down the stairs.

The big trunk of the Packard was nearly packed full with one large suitcase of his own, the small one he gave Annie and Annie's denim overnighter. Alex set the laundry bag with Annie's bed linens on the floor behind the front seat. He stood at the passenger door and watched Annie scurry down the stairs with Beth right behind her. There were more goodbyes and clumsy hugs on the sidewalk. Alex held the door open for Annie. She got in, smiled, gave a little wave and blew a kiss to Beth.

The early light of a summer dawn was casting a pink glow onto Oneida Street. Alex spun the steering wheel hard left and made a large U-turn on Oneida Street. Annie looked straight ahead, as Alex drove the Packard south toward US Route 10. A country music station from Iowa was on the radio. He turned the volume down low and said, "Last night the desk jockey at Bloomer's told me that Highway 10 will take us straight to Manitowoc, almost to the dockside, Annie. So, we're about forty miles away, about an hour down the road."

"First, make a right onto Highway 10, please Alex. I need to make a quick stop at Maxine's. I really do. I'm going to quit my job."

*Moonlight Bay*

**Monday, May 31, SS Badger, Dockside at South Lakeview Drive, Manitowoc, Wisconsin, 7:15 AM**

Dry pavement and light overcast skies helped ensure an easy trip from Appleton. Alex's right foot pressed the Packard to the speed limit along the way. They arrived dockside at seven o'clock. When the dockhands at Manitowoc and the below-deck crew of the SS Badger finally directed him exactly where to drive, position and park the car onboard, Alex felt an enormous sense of relief. He locked the car and realized if they had missed this ferry, their trip would have suffered a setback. While it would not have been the end of the modern world, it would have meant either driving all the way around Lake Michigan or waiting another twenty-four hours for the next sailing.

The dockside ticket office gave Alex a foldout brochure when he paid for their passage. The ship was over 400 feet long, 60 feet wide, 7 stories tall and had capacity for 500 automobiles. He estimated that it was about half-full for this trip. Annie looked with child-like wonder at the huge ship. The Badger was not nearly as large as the USS Valley Forge, but Alex was impressed that a vessel of such displacement could navigate Lake Michigan.

With a gentle breeze from the west, the sun on their faces, and standing aboard at the deck railing, Annie put her head on

Alex's shoulder, relaxed her body, and spoke softly, "We are on our way, Alex. We are on the way to our future together."

The bright early morning sun warmed their faces. His arm around her, he said, "I've got a little engagement gift for you, Annie. Let's go find somewhere where we can put our feet up." Holding her hand, he led the way across the deck. She shadowed him, unsure of the destination. Alex was looking for and following the posted directions to the Wolverine Deck. Back at the dock, the man behind the ticket counter had informed him that a few small staterooms were still available for two dollars more per passenger. The ticket agent said the rooms had two beds, a view of the lake and seating for two. The purser wore a sailor hat with three red ribbons coming down the back. Standing there behind the counter, wearing his snappy hat and dark blue uniform, he had Alex convinced. Alex rightfully thought Annie would appreciate a restful, quiet passage.

Without a word, he led Annie secretively, hand-in-hand to their destination and stopped outside cabin number six. Alex reached into his pocket for the key and the oversized fob. He unlocked, and then opened the narrow door.

Annie whispered, "Alexander Throckmorton, you rascal, you!", and they walked inside.

While the room was tiny by any standard, Alex was accustomed to much smaller sleeping quarters aboard the Valley Forge. Crunched into the room were two beds, with a single eighteen-inch porthole on the portside wall in between. Without a doubt, the little window was the *'view of the lake'* the ticket agent talked about. The beds consisted of plastic upholstered pads over plywood frames. Each one came complete with a blanket and small pillow. They were closer to being wide benches than beds. Two short stools were at a fold-down table on the walkway wall.

"Alex, this is perfect. This is wonderful."

"Lie down and rest, Annie. Close your eyes."

"But we can't miss that mandatory lifeboat instruction on deck, can we? They said we are supposed to attend."

"Here's your safety talk, Annie girl: If the ship is sinking, go directly to the lifeboat. That is your official lifeboat instruction, okay. You lie down, relax and let me worry about the lifeboat."

Annie didn't need further persuasion. She set her purse down on the floor, spread out a blanket, fluffed the pillow, kicked off her penny loafers and lay down. Alex took the other blanket and covered her, just as she closed her eyes. Her eyes didn't remain closed very long.

There was an immense blast of The Badger's air horn. The deafening burst swallowed all other sounds. The ship jerked forward, then backward and forward again. Hearing the loud blast of the horn, a startled Annie opened her eyes, looked to Alex for a moment and closed them again. There was yet another colossal blast followed by a sensation of movement. Annie took a deep breath and relaxed in contentment.

Outside, the ship's large funnel spewed a heavy cloud of thick, black smoke from the coal-fired engines. It disappeared upward, into the morning skies.

With Annie so peacefully at rest, Alex was pleased with his decision to pay a four dollar surcharge for the room. Carefully, he was able to maneuver his way between the beds and sit down. The little porthole window fogged over. He kicked off his shoes and stretched out on the other bed. The air squeezed out of the covered mattress as an impolite blat and the plastic made an annoying stretching, squeaking sound. He squashed his pillow under his head, looked over at Annie and recalled the night he first saw her. He folded his arms across his chest and fell asleep as he lay there watching her.

# 2. MICHIGAN

*Thanks For The Boogie Ride*

**Monday, May 31, 11:05 AM**
**On the waters of Lake Michigan**

Alex awoke with a start. He heard the loud, protesting squawks of Great Black-backed Gulls over the monotonous drone of the ship's massive coal-fired steam engines. He immediately looked to Annie and found her awake and watching him. She smiled.

"Did you have a good nap, Alex?"

He smiled back and nodded. "Yes, I did. It was nice. And you?"

"Yeah, I did. I slept for a little while. I needed it, don't you know."

They sat up on the edge of the small beds, and uncomfortably crushed and pushed at one another's knees. They moved forward slowly and shared a kiss. The loud birds, the drone of the engines and gentle undulation of the ship surrounded them like an enormous creaking, moaning metal cocoon.

Annie got up, shivered and wrapped her sweater around her shoulders. They ventured topside, following the signage to the Upper Deck Cafe and found a large dining room enclosed with plate glass windows. They could see Lake Michigan all around them, with a layer of fog lying close to the water, defying the sun above. The gulls were winging all around the ship. The lake was calm, with small, curling whitecaps. Whether it was the chill of the water, or the low-lying fog that chilled Annie, she was pleased with her decision to wear jeans, a sweatshirt and carry her cardigan when she left Appleton.

Yesterday's hoopla was over. Annie was relaxed and happy to be alive. She wondered what it would be like to live in Florida and anticipated a future that would be nothing less than *Heaven on Earth* with the man she loved. She sat in a canvas sling-back chair and looked toward what she guessed was the East.   Annie believed that Michigan must certainly be somewhere just beyond that layer of low fog.

Alex returned from the buffet tables carrying a loaded tray with two Kaiser rolls, sliced cheddar, coffee, orange juice, butter and two strawberry Danish.   Wisconsin was behind them, but the influence was still there.  He set the tray on the small folding table between them. "How's this, Annie?"

"Just right.   This is just right."   She meant it.   "How soon until we dock in Michigan?"

Alex looked at his watch.  "Let's see.  About an hour.  We will be in Ludington, Michigan, right around one o'clock."  He started to wind his *Bulova* and re-set the time.

"It's only four hours to cross the lake, right?"

"Michigan is on Eastern Time, Annie.  It'll be an hour later when we dock," he said, "So it will be about one o'clock Michigan time."

Annie thought a minute and looked out to the East again. The shoreline was barely visible.  "There's Michigan, Alex ... Michigan ... this is the first time I've been out of Wisconsin, and I needed to cross a lake to get here!"

Alex sipped some coffee and set the cup down.  He was reflective.  "You are going to be in a lot of places you have never been before, Annie."

For the rest of the trip, they sat inside the dining deck, looking toward their destination.  The skies remained bright, with high clouds.  The gulls continued their noisy flight all around The Badger.

The booming air horns let loose another blast as the Michigan shoreline and the Ludington docks came into view. Annie joined in when a good number of passengers started clapping their approval.  The cross-lake trip was ending, and the engines moaned defiantly as the ship slowed its approach.

The Badger gently eased into the ferry slip with a slight jerk. After two thumping bumps, the horns gave another loud, short blast.  Most of the folks stood up and started making their way away from the cafe. Alex took his tray back to the buffet and came back with another two cups of coffee. They sat along with a few other passengers undisturbed for a quarter of an hour or so.

It was another half hour before the Packard left the third level of the ship's belly and drove down the apron roll-off onto Michigan. Just outside port, Alex pulled into a *Texaco* station and waited behind two other cars for his turn at the fuel island. The roof of the service station extended boldly out and over the pumps. The attendant could not have been more than seventeen and wore his Dura-Bill baseball hat pushed all the way back on his head, exposing his blonde crew cut. The Texaco star on his cap was straight up into the air. His tongue forced out a wad of bright pink Bazooka bubble gum between his lips. He formed it and proudly popped a big one. He looked very satisfied with himself as he placed the pump's nozzle into the Packard with a clunk.

Alex got out, went inside the station and retrieved the key for the rest room. Annie was in the front seat looking through the brochures about the Badger. The attendant was cleaning the windshield and closely studying Annie. "Have a good crossing this morning, Miss? Did you?"

She looked up and answered, "Yes, we did." The attendant looked Annie up and down and nervously moved his eyes sideways when she caught him. He continued chewing his gum. The advertising poster in the station's window read: *'You can trust your car to the man who wears the star'*.

Alex came out of the station with a Michigan road map, paid the gas jockey and pulled the Packard to the side of the station. He put the transmission in park and announced, "The rest room is clean if you need it, Annie." He then methodically unfolded and popped the road map open.

She sensed Alex was on a mission: a map mission. "I think I'll go and freshen up a bit. It's been a long morning after a tiring night."

Alex didn't respond but pressed the map over the steering wheel and ran his eyes over it. Annie got out of the car, walked around a pile of used tires and into the building. Alex was quickly finished plotting his course and attempted to refold the map. After he realized that map folding was an exercise in futility, he simply opened the glove box and shoved it inside. He looked around the service station lot, across the two-lane blacktop and toward the surrounding countryside. There was a heavy smell of motor oil, gasoline, exhaust, and fresh asphalt. They were in Michigan.

He watched as the young man filled another car and checked the oil. The young station attendant spotted Annie walking back to the car. He cautiously turned and tried to watch her without anyone noticing his leering eyes. Annie had brushed her hair and redid her ponytail. A splash of water, some fresh lipstick and a touch of eye shadow and rouge helped her appear as fresh as a McCall's cover girl. Alex spotted the kid watching Annie walk from the building. Her Blue Bell jeans and grey sweatshirt moved rhythmically with her form. Alex grinned, reached over the front seat and opened the passenger door. Annie slid in and over to him. Alex smiled at the gas jockey and started the Patrician. He checked around him, drove carefully onto the blacktop of US Route 10 and headed east. The busy dock and its surroundings eventually gave way to the open, level Michigan countryside. Freshly plowed fields and grassland were on both sides of the two-lane highway.

"We stay on this road, Annie, US 10, and it will take us right into US Route 23 outside of Saginaw. We'll get a room somewhere around Saginaw tonight. If we can boogie down the road, I figure we should be there in about three hours or so. Are you hungry?"

"A little. I could go for a hotdog or burger and maybe a milkshake. That sounds good, right?"

"Yes, it does." He put his arm around her and gave a gentle hug. A neat, hand-painted sign promised *good food at Ma Harper's Roadside Cafe*, fifteen miles away in Scottville.

"Onward, Alex.  Onward to *Ma Harper's*."

*Let Me Be The One*

## Monday, May 31, US Route 10 & US Route 31, Scottville, Michigan, 2:55 PM

Annie Dahl and Alex Throckmorton cautiously walked across the unpaved parking lot of Ma Harper's Cafe.  The lot was full of trucks and with yesterday's rain; it was a hodgepodge of puddles, stones and mud.  Inside the diner, there was a hearty stew of talk, rattling dishes and coffee cups.  It all was on a scale much larger than Maxine's.  A jukebox was spewing country music and foot traffic swarmed between the fuel counter and dining room.

Alex's order was beef tips and noodles with biscuits: Ma Haper's interpretation of Beef Stroganoff.   The waitress brought the hotdog, French fries and the strawberry milkshake Annie had decided on back in Ludington.  It felt great to get out of the car, walk a little, stretch and take a break from the miles already traveled over land and lake.  Alex opened up the new but crinkled map and put it on the table after their meals.  They looked it over, studied it closer and decided that Bay City, north of Saginaw, would be a good place to overnight.  Bay City was about three hours away and it was within comfortable driving distance for the planned trip to greater Detroit the following day.  After two cups of coffee and some rough measurements with pencil marks made on a table napkin, Alex had a plan of action.

He explained to Annie that Mount Clemens was about two hours south of Bay City.  It was also the county seat for Macomb County, his birthplace.  That was where he would be able to get a copy of his much-needed birth certificate.  Downtown Detroit was no more than thirty miles from Mount Clemens and The Bank of Detroit office on Griswold Street, where a pair of chrome-plated keys should disclose the unknown contents of two deposit boxes.

Annie reached into her purse and brought out a pack of *Chesterfields*. Alex lit one for her and one of his *Lucky Strikes*. Another cup of coffee and they would be ready for the road to Bay City.

Outside, the afternoon sun was warming the world. Alex opened the passenger door for Annie and crossed to the other side.

With a click of the key, and a gentle roar, the Packard fired on all eight cylinders. Alex reached over the front seat, put the Texaco map back into the glove box, and with a turn of the wheel, the Packard was back on US Route 10 and heading east.

The open countryside quickly passed along on both sides of the highway. An isolated farmhouse would appear, stuck in the middle of a field and then, just as lonesome, a weatherworn barn would stand in the landscape all by itself.

"Annie, do you remember when I told you back in Appleton that you were much too good looking to be working at a diner in Wisconsin?"

"Yes."

"Well, how do you feel about living on a horse farm in Florida? I have enough cash now to shop around for a brood mare suitable for Sebastian. And maybe I can set up my own engine shop right on the ranch."

While thumbing the radio knob, she teased Alex, "I think I know what I'm getting into, cowboy."

Annie tuned the radio and found a popular music station without too much static. She leaned into Alex and rested on his shoulder. The wipers were keeping time with Hank Locklin singing *Let Me Be The One*.

Annie was content, happy, and looking down the road. A brief springtime shower began, and tiny droplets of water raced along the windshield as the Packard pushed through the dampness onward to Bay City.

## Monday, May 31, US Route 10 & US Route 23, Bay City, Michigan, 7:05 PM

The rain became steadier and heavier along the way. As they neared Bay City, through the blur of the wet windshield, a motel was visible ahead, off to the left side of the road. It was pouring. A blanket of darkness and a deluge of rain from the heavens above covered the world around them. A large blue neon sign over the roofline flashed the words '*SLEEP INN*'. Right underneath was '*Vacancy*' in red. The words appeared blurry and out of focus in the heavy rain. Thunderstorms give motel neon signs an eerie, special welcoming glow. The windshield wipers diligently attempted the impossible. A crack of lightning and a boom of thunder welcomed them as he parked the car. Alex opened his door and ran through the torrents of rain toward the motel office. There was standing water directly outside the door and all across the parking lot. Rainwater spilled over and into his shoes as he ran. Another crack of lightning and an even louder boom of thunder shook the car.

Annie shuddered and pulled her sweater tight across her shoulders. She was watching closely for Alex. A few minutes later, he came running out of the office. Annie quickly reached over and opened his door. Soaked, he let out a brief sigh of relief. He started the car, drove the short distance to Cabin Six and parked outside.

"Let's sit here a minute, Annie, wait a bit, and see if this lets up."

They turned and looked directly at each other. Alex laughed, "I'm soaked, ain't I?" Annie laughed too. The car windows were fogging up.

They sat inside the car for about ten minutes until the downpour gradually eased. Alex got out, forced his hand into his wet slacks and got the key. He opened the cabin door, flipped the wall switch, and a single, small table lamp came on by the dresser. Annie went inside and dropped her purse and overnight case on the bed. She immediately came out and hurried to the trunk with Alex.

"Do you want the small suitcase or the denim one, Annie?"

"The small one will work."

Alex grabbed the bag and handed it to Annie. He picked up his suitcase and the bottle of Jim Beam from the back of the trunk, stuck it under his arm, and carried the bounty inside.

Alex opened his case on the bed and took out a change of clothes. Dry socks, slacks, a shirt and Fruit Of The Loom briefs came out and over his arm. Annie looked away toward the door as Alex walked to the bathroom. She could feel herself blush and wondered how this arrangement would work in the darkness of night. She looked around. There was only the small table lamp on the dresser to light the room, one full bed, and one overstuffed chair stuck into a corner alongside one small, side table. There was no telephone, no radio and no television set. It was clear to Annie that the room Alex had back in Appleton was much nicer compared to the bare-bones accommodation here. This was her first night in a motel. She was a bit apprehensive, but only slightly nervous.

Alex came out of the bathroom with wet hair and a dry change of clothes. "I hung my wet stuff over the shower curtain, Annie. I hope that's all right. I don't want you to think I'm a slob." His meek apology was halfhearted.

Annie understood. "Nope. That's okay with me, I understand. You were sopping, wringing wet."

Alex looked around for a glass and found two Dixie cups sitting on the bathroom vanity. He brought them out and with a motion of his hand offered one to Annie. "Would you like a bourbon, Annie?"

"Sure …pour me one … a short one. How much did this place cost?"

"Four dollars. There sure isn't anything high-class about this place, Annie." He poured two fingers of Beam into each paper cup and put the bottle on the dresser. He handed one to Annie and walked over to the old fat chair in the corner. He studied it and pulled on the seat cushion before he sat down.

Alex took a deep breath and exhaled, "What a day, Annie. Driving in the pouring rain makes for a long, tiresome trip." He briefly looked around the room. He took a sip, set the glass on the wobbly table, and said, "We're on our way, Annie girl. We're on the road to tomorrow."

Annie was sitting on the edge of the bed and holding her cup of bourbon on her thigh. She smiled at Alex and toasted, "Just like Dale Evans says to Roy Rogers, Alex. *Happy Trails!*" Alex raised his drink and returned Annie's makeshift toast. It felt good to be out of the rain.

"I'll be sleeping on the floor, Annie. I'll take these chair cushions and flop out over there ... against the wall by the bathroom."

Annie looked at the proposed spot and back to the chair again. She studied the cushions and looked up to Alex. "Are you sure? We could sleep back-to-back, right here on the bed. After all, we are getting married," she suggested.

"No. I'll sleep on the floor. If everything goes all right, we will be married tomorrow, Annie. Maybe tomorrow night we can share a bed."

There was a small slice of quiet. Annie mused aloud, "Hmmm. Okey dokey, then." She nodded and lifted her bourbon to take another sip. Her anticipation waned like melting ice cream.

Alex took a drink too, looked over the Dixie cup rim at Annie, chuckled a little and repeated her colloquialism, "Okey dokey it is, then."

She laughed when he said those words. It sounded strange to hear his voice repeat something she used so often.

A good deal of back-and-forth small talk and banter ensued. They talked about the night before, the trip today and what was down the road for tomorrow. They started going over the recent events in their lives since they met a week ago. So many

101

things happened so fast. They were trying to sort it all out and put events in correct order. Several little details of their shared experience were out of place. Annie wondered why, if Alex was staying at Bloomer's Motel, just up the road from Maxine's, why was it Tuesday before he finally came into Maxine's Roadside Rest? He explained that he was eating his meals right across the street from Bloomer's at the *Bright Spot*. He had a bad experience with one of their chicken salad sandwiches and explained, "That sandwich ended my relationship with the Bright Spot. I was driving past Maxine's every day and it took a lousy sandwich to force me into that diner and discover not only the best-looking waitress in Wisconsin, but the love of my life." Annie sprang off the bed and gave him a kiss. She ended up on his lap. They snuggled together for a moment.

"We're going to have a busy day tomorrow, Annie."

"Yes, I guess we will. We better call it a day, Alex, and hit the hay. We've had a busy day, today, too."

She gave Him a peck on the cheek and stood up. He peeled the cushions off the chair and tossed them to the floor by the wall. Annie argued they were not long enough for his height. She walked over to the bed, took off the two pillows and placed them on the floor too. She was fixing Alex's bed with enthusiasm. "We'll get my pillow out of the car," she said. "You can use all the bed linens I brought from Appleton to cover up with. We will fix up a spot for you, Alex. Aww, listen to me. It's like I'm fixing up a bed for a puppy! That's cute! Now go lie down and be a good doggie!" She giggled.

It started to rain heavily once again as Alex brought in the laundry bag from the back seat of the Packard. They arranged the pillows, spread a sheet over the cushions, and folded Annie's bedspread for a pillow. Alex hung his shirt over the chair, removed his socks and crawled onto the makeshift bed. He was able to maneuver enough under the blanket to take off his trousers and toss them to the chair. He closed his eyes and could smell Annie on her Appleton bed linens. Exhausted, in a mere matter of minutes, he was asleep.

Annie crept across the room quietly to the bath. She brushed her teeth and changed into her slip. She walked on tiptoes and folded her clothes onto the dresser. Annie looked down at Alex, turned off the light, slid under the covers and got herself settled into bed.

Annie was lying there, content and smiling. She was enjoying this adventure. She had a peaceful sense of security. Alex was barely snoring.

## Rags To Riches

### Tuesday, June 1, US Route 10 & US Route 23, Bay City, Michigan, 7:00 AM

Annie awoke to the noise of banging pipes and a running shower. While she slept, Alex quietly picked up his bed of chair cushions and linens. Bright sun was barely pushing through the thick drapes. She slept well, right through the night, perhaps because she had her pillow from Appleton. She turned and looked around the room. Daylight exposed the truth: 'Old and run down' was a fitting description. She lifted her blankets and sheets enough to look under them and quickly slid out of bed. Annie picked up her blue jeans and stepped into them just as the shower turned off. She hurried and pulled on her Badger sweatshirt.

Alex came out of the bathroom wearing his slacks and rubbing a towel over his wet hair. He started talking to Annie as he slid bare feet into his wet loafers, threw the towel over the chair and put on his shirt. "I'm going to the office, Annie, there was only one towel in there and I used it for my shave and shower, so I'm going to the office and get at least one more for you." He was out the door.

Annie lifted the blankets and sheets of the bed again. She looked under them, grimaced and put them back down. The sheets were worn and threadbare, with small holes all over. Annie shuddered and muttered, "Uff. What a dump."

She found her toothbrush and the tube of Ipana and walked to the bathroom. As she squeezed out the paste and began to brush, she looked at her mirrored reflection. She started to sway her hips side-to-side, thinking of the toothpaste company's *Bucky Beaver* cartoon character, singing "brusha, brusha, brusha" on the TV commercial. Annie rinsed, smiled, and checked her teeth in the mirror. She heard Alex returning from the office, shutting the door behind him with a clunk. She walked out of the bathroom holding her toothbrush and Bucky Beaver's favorite oral hygiene product.

"I got three clean towels for you, Annie. The clerk, or owner, or whatever he is, was not very helpful, a real jerk. It was like pulling teeth on a chicken, but I got them."

"Hey, Alex … could you bring in the denim suitcase? I want to dress up. A little bird just told me that I'm getting married today." Alex smiled and handed the towels to Annie. He turned and was out the door again.

While Annie showered and dressed, Alex selected the standby combination of a white shirt and grey gabardine slacks. Without a second thought, he rubbed off his wing tips using the badly worn, wet motel towel. He placed Annie's bed linens and pillow back inside the laundry bag and carried it, along with his suitcase, back out to the trunk.

Alex was in the old, overstuffed chair, studying the Michigan road map when Annie came out of the bathroom. She had let her ponytail down and was wearing her green dress, new shoes and white cardigan. She felt much better. After she washed her hair and showered, she was ready to take on the day. It felt good putting on the new clothes she had bought in Appleton. Stockings fresh out of the package and a new pair of delicates made her feel clean, especially after seeing the motel room in the daylight. Her skin crawled that morning when she first looked at those sheets.

Alex looked up from the map and studied her. He felt he was falling even deeper in love. "You look fantastic, Annie." She stood there, tied the little red scarf around her neck and moved the knot to the side.

"Thank you, Alex. And you look pretty darn yummy too … so how about you wear that white silk scarf you wore the first time you walked into the diner? Wear it around your neck and tuck it in into your shirt like Errol Flynn. Okey dokey?"

"Okay, will do." Alex smiled, felt flattered and happy with the thought of being in the company of the beautiful red head from Appleton.

As an afterthought he asked, "Hey, when I took my case out to the car, I noticed your waitress dress jammed into a bag. What on Earth did you bring that for?"

"I can use it for housework, or whatever, Mister Alex. Or I can tear it up for rags. And you told me that I looked good in it, remember? So maybe I'll wear it when I want to get you all jazzed-up and frisky!"

Alex chuckled. They sorted their clothes, put them back in the suitcases and repacked what they needed to. Annie took her smaller suitcase and overnight bag out to the car. Alex found his white silk scarf and tossed it around his neck. He threw the room key on the bed and went out to the car carrying his half-dry clothes and wet loafers. He spread them out over the bags and cases in the trunk.

Alex walked back inside and asked, "Ready, Annie girl?" She was standing in front of the tiny mirror at the dresser, putting on her lipstick and making the final adjustments to her hair.

"Be out in a second."

He started the car and hung his elbow out the window. It was going to be a beautiful day. Evidence of last night's storm was clearly visible in the bright sunshine of a new morning. Bits of broken leaves, piles of dead pine needles and small twigs littered the hood, roof and trunk of the Packard. The parking lot of the Sleep Inn was mud pit with chuckholes.

Annie came out of the motel cabin with her purse and the bottle of Jim Beam. "We almost forgot the jug of whiskey. Oh ... and I didn't lock the door, Alex."

"That's fine, Annie. There isn't anything in there worth locking up. Down the road and away from this hole in the wall, we'll stop and get something to eat."

Annie put the bottle in the glove compartment with the wrinkled road map. Alex put the Packard in gear, and they were on the road again. Annie looked over her shoulder and muttered, "What a dump."


## Little Things Mean A Lot

### Tuesday, June 1, Macomb County Offices, Corner of Cass & Gratiot Ave, Mount Clemens, Mich. 11:05 AM

Just south of Flint, off Dixie Highway, Alex and Annie stopped and took the time to have brunch. Their hearts sang and their souls pulsed with the anticipation of what the day could bring their way. Once they were back on the highway, the miles and minutes went by quickly. They were fast approaching Detroit, and Alex began to recognize more and more of the landscape as familiar territory. When the Packard crossed 24 Mile Road, he felt as if he never left home. It seemed like the last six years of his life had never happened, as memories of his boyhood home in Detroit came drifting back.

Annie closely watched everything around her and marveled at all the bustling traffic. She was impressed by how well it moved, despite the large volume of vehicles. It was obvious that this part of Michigan was a whole lot busier than anything she had ever experienced in Appleton. The vast number of small family or ethnically oriented diners, delicatessens and food stores that dotted every other block fascinated her.

Alex turned off 19 Mile Road and started down Cass Avenue. He nodded in affirmation and observed to Annie and himself, "We're getting close, Annie girl. Real close."

Annie looked around with curiosity, "What are we looking for?"

"Gratiot. When we see Gratiot Avenue, we'll be there."

Soon enough, they reached their destination. Alex spotted a small parking lot half a block away from the Macomb County offices. He reached around and got his fedora off the back seat, ducked his head sideways and put it on. It ended up at a slight angle to the left, just the way he liked it. Annie's heart started to beat faster. She looked inside her purse to verify that the little blue box with the two wedding rings was still there. She looked at the finger where the gold band would go and felt a renewed sense of security. Alex got out of the Packard, opened the trunk and took out the leather bag.

"This is for all the important, life-changing papers we will be getting, Annie girl," he grinned and chuckled. Annie reached up and brushed a wrinkle out of his jacket. She adjusted his scarf, tucking it in here and pulling it out there. Alex stood patiently still as Annie made those important adjustments.

They stepped down off the curb and crossed the busy street to the large brick building. Inside, light grey and pink-flecked granite floors covered the large foyer and halls. There was a nondescript fellow in a blue uniform with messy, unkempt hair sitting behind an elevated desk in the absolute center of the lobby. Alex took off his Ray-Ban aviators and stuck them in his shirt pocket. "We are here to get a certified copy of a birth certificate."

A monotone, mechanical answer came from behind the desk, "Second floor, room 204, to the left. The elevators are to the right and the stairs are straight ahead." A wide, imposing marble stairway was in front of them. Large dark, wooden handrails were on each side and another ran up the middle.

Alex and Annie walked straight to the stairs. Their steps echoed in the large hall. They arrived at the second floor and turned left for Room 204. The room number was in gold lettering on frosted, dimpled and shatterproof glass with embedded chicken wire. Alex held the heavy wooden door open for Annie. Once inside the room, they stood at a long counter. After explaining what he wanted to one clerk and presenting his Florida driver's license to another, they were directed to yet another counter further down in the same room. There were some more questions and even more research by the Macomb County administrative staff. Eventually, someone sat down at a huge black Underwood typewriter and created a certified copy of Alex's birth certificate. After it was notarized and given the raised seal of authenticity, a small woman with pure white hair and wire rim glasses handed the little, blue piece of paper to Alex.

"Thank you. Thank you for your help. Now ... now, we would like to know where we need to go for a Marriage License." Annie reached out and took Alex's hand.

"Right across the hall, sir. Room 201."

"Thank you." Annie and Alex answered together and were out the door. Across the hall, they took a seat on one of the long, polished wood benches in the room. A half hour later, they again stood at another counter. A smiling young man with an extremely wrinkled shirt and a soup-stained tie was more than eager to help. He would occasionally reach under the counter, break off a piece of a Lorna Doone shortbread cookie and munch away. Of course, some crumbs fell on the paperwork. Annie was holding her birth certificate tightly in her hand since they had left Room 204 and finally got the chance to show it to someone here. It was a little anticlimactic when the clerk handed it back to her. She put her birth certificate back in her purse and brought out the little blue box with the two gold rings that Alex gave her in Appleton. She carefully, securely held onto those.

Alex spent two dollars as a 'document preparation charge' and another two dollars for a 'filing charge'. The young clerk took a round rubber stamp and banged purple ink onto the papers in different locations and on all copies.

Again, Alex politely spoke, "Thank you. Thanks. Now ... can you tell us where we can use this license and have someone perform a wedding ceremony right here in this building?"

Annie felt her heart thumping with rapturous expectation. The clerk stuck out his arm and looked at his watch. "Humm, let's see. It's twenty to twelve; twenty minutes to lunch. That should be enough time. Go to the County Justice and Clerk of the Court, on the first floor, Room 105."

They turned on their heels and were out the door, down the stairs and in a flash, they were standing inside Room 105. At the counter was yet another small white-haired woman.

Annie started this time. "We want to get married."

The clerk answered in an antiseptic tone, "Have a seat, and Marion will be right with you."

"Uff. Another bench," Annie scoffed. She felt her hands sweating. She reached out to Alex. His were too.

It seemed like hours, but in another thirty minutes, they were married. When the Macomb County Justice announced they were husband and wife, Annie opened the little box. She rapidly handed Alex the larger gold band and hurriedly slipped hers on. She then helped Alex with his. He stood and smiled as he watched her take charge of the wedding bands. She stood directly in front of him, holding both his hands. Annie looked up at him and stood on her tiptoes. They shared their first kiss as Mister and Missus Throckmorton. A rush went through her body.

A few more papers joined the document collection inside the leather satchel. After they had finished and left each office, Alex tucked all the papers they received neatly into his leather bag. When he placed the marriage certificate inside, he secured the brass clasp and gave the bag a pat. They just crossed a significant milestone, and nobody was more aware of it than Annie was.

Arm-in-arm, they walked out of the Macomb County offices and crossed the street to the car. Once inside the Packard, they looked at each other as if to ask: *What just happened?*

109

They sat and grinned at one another like stray cats in a sardine cannery.

Alex started the car, looked over to Annie and said, "Let's go and find the Bank of Detroit on Griswold Street, Missus Throckmorton."

She slid across the seat and pressed against him. "Yes. Yes indeed. Let's go." Annie was aware of the words Alex used. "After the bank, we will start our honeymoon, Mister Throckmorton." They shared a kiss. She ran her thumb over the bottom of the new gold band on her finger.

Alex steered the Patrician out to the corner and turned south on Gratiot Avenue. In less than an hour, they should discover the contents of two safe deposit boxes. Annie sat close to her husband, watching the world going by. The busy sidewalks and streets of Detroit blended their energy with all the excitement, anticipation and newlywed zeal swirling around inside the Packard.

*That's Amoré*

**Tuesday, June 1, Corner of Griswold and Fort Streets, Detroit, Mich. 1:36 PM**

Fifteen minutes earlier Alex had parked the Patrician at the curb, directly in front of the Penobscot Building's Bank of Detroit. He said he expected to finish his business quickly and would be out shortly.

An extremely anxious Annie sat waiting as patiently as possible for her new husband. The smooth, seductive voice of Dean Martin was bubbling *That's Amoré* from the Galvin vacuum tube radio. Under the long hood, a Packard Straight Eight powerhouse pulsed at idle, ready to flex its muscle. A gentle easterly breeze brought a warm wisp of summer air from across Lake St Clair. Annie sighed, crossed her legs and relaxed back on the tan leather seat. She looked at the gold band on her finger: *Good golly. I'm a married woman.*

Her mind drifted back in time to last Friday night and Peabody Park in Appleton by the river. There was moonlight, champagne and a blue flannel blanket. Her memories quickly sprang forward to Saturday's dinner, dancing and Alex popping the question. He asked her to marry him in a way she would never forget, right there on the front seat of the Packard, under a streetlight on Oneida Street. Annie closed her eyes for a second or two. She recalled how fast things have happened and how much her life has changed in the past week. She ran her thumb over the wedding band on the underside of her ring finger once again and glanced down at the jade on her other hand. She smiled.

She sighed, brought her mind back to the present and reassuringly thought, *This is going to turn out just fine. I trust this man. My instincts were right back there in Appleton. I made the right decision. I just know it.*

The ferryboat ride across Lake Michigan was a day and three hundred miles ago. She felt safe and secure in the company of her new husband. Any minor uncertainties she had were subdued by the excitement of the moment, the street sounds of Detroit and the endless black ribbon of asphalt highways already traveled and yet to come. She was confident that smooth roads were ahead.

The sidewalk was busy with men dressed in suits and some in shirtsleeves; women in light jackets and skirts; shoppers with woven market baskets and paper sacks with handles. Automobile traffic, delivery trucks, taxis and all the rubber on the road affirmed that she was in Detroit: the Motor City. Excitement, expectation and enthusiasm filled the Packard.

Annie's new nylons whooshed as she moved and shifted a restless thigh on the soft leather front seat of the big car, pushing the hemline of her green dress up above her knee. Attempting to calm herself, she reached into her handbag, took out her pack of Chesterfield Kings and lit one with her *Ronson*. As the first puff left her pursed carmine lips and swirled around her hair, the smoke bit at her eyes. She blinked, squinted and gently brushed away an annoying smoker's tear. She reached forward, opened the glove compartment and brought out the Jim Beam. With her cigarette between her fingers, she unscrewed the top and took a drink. Annie swallowed, grimaced and shuddered. It was a harsh tickle all the way down. She got those goose bumps again on the nape of her neck like she did back in Appleton. Bourbon does that to some people.

Four minutes into the cigarette, Annie took a final draw and tossed the spent butt to the curb. She spotted Alex, with his white fedora pushed to one side, quickly coming down the seven steps from the bank. His hat and white silk scarf made him a standout among all the others around him. The warm breeze pressed the white shirt against the form of his chest. He had an almost illegal smile and displayed a strong confidence with his gait. He passed the leather shoulder bag inside the car to Annie and got behind the wheel of the large automobile. She wondered what could be in the bag to make it so heavy. He brought his pack of Lucky Strike out from his shirt pocket and in one continuous movement put a match to one. He slid his sunglasses on, looked around, placed the Packard into drive and pulled away from the curb onto Griswold Street. "Let's get this honeymoon of ours started, Annie girl," he said.

Annie opened the leather flap and looked inside the satchel. She spotted the polished wood grip of a handgun holstered in khaki cloth and secured to a heavy woven belt. The pistol was snuggled between two bulging canvas bank bags, each about six inches wide and long. Her hands trembled slightly as her fingertips gently crossed over the contents inside the black leather bag. There was a large, worn, folded, and stained manila envelope stuck against one side. She gazed over at Alex. He turned his head slightly and gave her a quick, but reassuring, nod. He still had that illegal smile. Her eyes were questioning, and her expression was one of surprise.

"I have no idea what that Smith and Wesson 38 is doing in there, Annie. It was all by itself with a box of bullets in one of the two bank boxes. But that service weapon isn't the most fascinating thing I found inside. The second deposit box had the mysterious and interesting stuff in it … go ahead and take a look inside those two cloth bags," Alex spoke in a sober, serious tone, nodding his head, but still slightly grinning.

Annie looked back into the satchel and gingerly began to loosen the drawstrings, open, and peek inside the canvas bags. Packed inside each of the bank sacks were several tightly bundled rolls of hundred-dollar bills. Annie took a deep breath, pushed the rolls of money around inside the canvas bags and looked for any hidden contents. She found a single roll of brightly colored Chinese Yuan and again she gasped. She caught her breath and grabbed the bottle of Jim Beam from the glove box one more time. She put the bottle to her lips, took another drink, shut her eyes tight, and swallowed. This time she didn't shudder. She held the leather bag tight against her thighs, looked over to Alex and offered him the bottle of Beam. He took two swallows and continued to look straight down the road as he handed it back to Annie. She took one more swallow before she slid it back into the glove box on top of the roadmap. She gazed out the windshield to the road ahead. Her thoughts were racing at full throttle.

Alex turned the Patrician left on Ecorse and right onto Telegraph Road. They were leaving Detroit and heading south. Countless thoughts rushed into and swirled all around inside his head. He was particularly excited about beginning a brand-new life with the chestnut-haired beauty beside him. With two bank bags full of money, a good-looking woman as his new bride, and a fast car, he didn't know exactly why, but he seemed in a hurry. Driving down the road ten miles above the posted limit, he had the big engine throbbing and knew the Packard could easily muscle away from any Michigan State Police black and white Ford. Alex reached across the seat, put a hand on Annie's leg, just above the knee, and gave her nylon covered lower thigh a gentle touch. His fingers caressed her leg and played with the garter snap. He kept his gaze straight ahead and his left hand on the wheel. Alex then moved his right arm up and around his bride's shoulders. The sobering thought of a police cruiser chasing him down the road persuaded him to lighten up on the accelerator pedal. He remembered there was a 38-caliber pistol packed inside the satchel.

Annie smiled through her nerves, looked over to Alex, and thought, *this road can go on forever and the party won't ever end*, unknowing what a jewel of understated truth she just discovered. The warmth of an early June afternoon pushed into the open windows and rushed around inside the Packard. Annie brushed her hair away, blinked and watched the countryside fly by. There were miles and miles of power poles, telephone lines, a lot of open grassland, an occasional newly-planted field, and of course, the lone service station, diner, and grocery at some of the bigger intersecting highways. There was not much else to look at. She decided to wait for Alex to explain the contents of the leather bag and not to ask any questions for the risk of being a nosy bride. It was not just the excitement of the unknown, or anticipation of her future life with Alex that gave her those goose bumps. She recalled something that her mother told her on the phone two days ago in Appleton. Her mother's exact words were *"Annie, after your wedding night you will know for sure if you have the right man. In more ways than one."* The coming night was indeed her wedding night. There was so much happening.

South of Monroe, Michigan, the Packard was rolling down the smooth black asphalt. Annie read aloud the small roadside billboards: *"The Wolf ... Is Shaved ... So Neat And Trim ... Red Riding Hood ... Is Chasing Him ... Burma Shave"*. Annie wondered if life was as painless and simple as the little red and white Burma Shave signs promised.

She grinned and mused, *Probably not: that would be too gosh darn convenient.*

She quickly thought of her own little rhyme and shared it aloud with Alex: *"A Face Of Stubble ... Can Burst Your Bubble ... Smooth Is Good ... Just Ask Red Riding Hood."*

Alex laughed, "Good one, Annie girl." He was beginning to understand her sharp wit.

She smiled, turned to Alex again and laid her left hand softly on his leg. She leaned inward toward his shoulder and gave him a gentle kiss on the cheek. "Smooth", she whispered.

The Patrician purred.

# 3. OHIO

*Baby We're Really In Love*

## Tuesday, June 1, US Route 23, Toledo, Ohio 5:32PM

Alex and Annie did not utter a word about the satchel or its mystifying contents as they traveled the road south through Michigan. Crossing the state line into Ohio, Alex said, "I'm thinking we could stop pretty soon, gas up and grab something to eat. And we need to find a place to stay before everything locks up for the night. Sound okay?" His bride was leaning up against him with her head on his shoulder and eyes closed. She sat up, looked around and awoke from her daydream.

Annie sleepily answered, "Okey dokey. Sounds good to me." Alex noticed her Wisconsin patter. He teased her once or twice on that, and she loved having the opportunity to say it again. He knew it. Moreover, she knew that he knew. He also noticed her tone was not quite as chipper or upbeat as usual. She had something on her mind and Alex sensed it. He too, was considering the contents of the satchel.

On the south side of Toledo, Alex pulled into a Sinclair station, rolled down his window and told the young man to fill it up with HC. The service station attendant was smiling ear to ear as he walked to the rear of the Packard, looking for, and finding the gas cap. He removed the cap and placed the nozzle inside, taking the opportunity to steal a look at the delectable red head in the front seat. He raised his eyebrows in self-gratification and shifted his attention back to the car. He marveled at all the chrome, the wide whitewalls, shiny new paint and all the cream-colored bigness of it as he squeegeed the windshield. The pump stopped at a little over fourteen gallons. The young gas jockey finished wiping the glass, walked past the front door of the Packard, looked inside at Annie again and spoke to Alex, "That'll be three dollars and ninety-four cents, sir. Looks to me like this yellow bolt of

116

lightning will get up and go right down the road!" He then lifted the hood of the Packard and stared in appreciation at the big engine. Annie shifted her weight on the front seat and crossed her legs. Again, the hem of her green dress slid up above her knee and exposed the contrast of her charcoal grey stockings against the supple, pale, off-white leather seat of the Patrician.

"That she does," replied Alex. "How's the food across the street, Bud?" He bobbed his head out the window and toward the restaurant.

"It'll do all right. Not bad at all. The food's good and they have a bar." He paused for a second, and continued to talk, "Your oil is right up there, sir. You're good to go," replied the young man, wiping the dipstick on the faded red rag sticking out of his pant pocket. With a softened clunk, he carefully closed the hood on the big car and walked back to the driver's window. He was sneaking another look at Annie out of the corner of his eye. Annie subtly moved her eyes upwards in his direction. Like a schoolboy, he immediately turned his glance away. Annie smiled to herself, well aware of his embarrassment. Alex got out of the Packard and took a brief moment to stretch his frame. He reached into his back pocket, brought out his wallet and pulled out five dollars. Alex stuck the money into the left shirt pocket of the young man, right underneath the Sinclair 'Dino' dinosaur patch. The young man nodded his head and said, "Thank you, sir, thanks a lot. Yes, sir!"

"Do you got a map inside the station there that will get me to Florida, Bud?" asked Alex.

"Yes, sir!" The attendant sprung inside the station and quickly returned with one of those neatly folded maps, *Roadways Of The Eastern United States*, with the big Sinclair circle and dinosaur on the outside. "Here you are, sir. And our maps are always available with no charge to you, sir."

"Thanks … thanks a lot, Bud," said Alex, "Good job." Alex reached into the front seat, handed the map to Annie and unhooked the flap of the leather satchel. He brought out the brown envelope and handed that to Annie as well. Alex carefully closed the satchel again, snapped the clasp shut, walked to the back of the car and opened the trunk. Alex carefully nested the bag and its weighty contents between the three pieces of luggage. He locked the trunk and gave the gas jockey a nod as he got back into the driver's seat. With a single turn of the key, the powerful engine fired, and the car came to life again. Alex put the Packard in gear and crossed the street to the paved parking lot of the *Maumee Bay Restaurant and Lounge*. He said, "Check this, Honey. This is all fresh blacktop. Business must be good," he spoke as he parked, "Bring in the map and that envelope inside with you, okay?"

Annie looked over at him pleasantly surprised. It was the first time he called her 'honey' and she immediately decided it sounded good. She opened the door, swung her legs around and got out. Annie hung firmly onto the envelope and the map. Alex walked to the back of the Packard and checked to be sure that he had locked the trunk. Annie was hoping some of the mystery inside the satchel could be resolved over their meal.

The restaurant was about half-full of customers. Alex walked toward a booth at the opposite side and away from the bar. Annie sat down and slid into the seat leaving room for Alex. She sat with her hands folded on the envelope and road map. "Let's order, then we'll find out what's in there, Annie. And we'll take a good long look at the map, too," he said.

"Okey dokey," she answered as the waitress came over. They were in an anxious hurry to order and asked if there was a dinner special. Chock full of suspense, they didn't look at the menu, but quickly decided on two $1.75 specials: Salisbury steak, gravy, mashed potatoes and peas. Alex ordered a Carling Red Cap Ale for himself, and Annie requested a cream soda. As the waitress brought the drinks and left, Alex tore open the manila envelope along the top flap and dumped the meager contents onto the table. Annie watched with wide eyes.

Three photographs fell onto the table; edge-tattered, fold damaged, faded and worn. Examining the snapshots, Alex revealed that one was of his father in an Army Air Corps uniform and flight jacket, with another younger pilot standing next to a fighter plane. On the back, written in blue ink: *NJT with pal Robert McElvoy, Eastern Air Command, 1943.* There were two more photographs; a wallet-worn picture of Alex at about ten years old standing by a bicycle, and another of Alex's parents, Nicholas and Nora, probably on their wedding day. There was no writing on the back of those two pictures.

A pair of dog tags on a chain was there, with the following stamped into the metal: *Throckmorton, Nicholas J., O-32487530, T39, A, P.*

Finally, two worn and stained *Stroh's Beer* bar coasters. There was hand printing in the same blue ink on the back. The first: *537 Corinth St, Jacksonville, Fla.* It appeared to have been written in haste. The other was much neater and bore a name of sorts along with the address: *Mac, 14 E. Chestnut St, Asheville, N. Carolina.*

Alex looked inside the envelope again and made sure it was empty. It was. They looked at one another closely. Alex poured the Carling into his glass, let the foam settle and took a drink. Annie tasted the soda.

A chasm of silence opened between them before Alex started to ramble. "What do you suppose these things meant to my old man? And why would it be these things, just these few things? These items ... the sealed envelope ... a pair of Stroh's bar coasters, of all things ... the service weapon ... the revolver in the khaki holster ... the photographs ... the dog tags ... and the cash ... the money ... and the Chinese currency ... who knows how much ... all of it jammed into two safe-deposit boxes in Detroit, untouched for God knows how long ... since 1946 probably. And why? What for? What do you think all this is, Annie?" He was truly puzzled. His words came out carrying a trunk-load of nervous uncertainty. He repeated himself, "What do you think all this is, Annie?"

119

"I have no idea. But I think if we find those addresses in Jacksonville and North Carolina ... if there are such addresses ... if they exist ... then we will find out. Then we will know. Don't you think so?"

Alex took out his pack of Lucky Strikes and lit one. He drew in the smoke and gently bit is lower lip. "You're right, Annie. It seems like we should go to Carolina first. It's the closest. And look at this one with the word *"Mac"* and the address in Asheville. That could be that Robert what's-his-name on the photograph with my father. Yeah, that has to be it; it just has to be ... Robert McElvoy. If we go there, to Carolina and maybe if we find out anything, then maybe Florida ... Jacksonville. Who knows? Then home to my place in Santa Rosa County. We would be taking the long way home, but maybe we should be able to get some answers. What do you think, Annie?"

"Sure, that sounds like a good plan." Annie spoke in an upbeat mood. "We have all the time in the world. After all, this is our honeymoon, right? What else is there to do?" She sighed, leaned sideways into him and put her lips on his. Alex put his hand on her right thigh. They felt the tingle between them. For now, their inner passionate urges smothered the anxiety of the unknown.

Just as their food arrived at the table, he said, "Again, you're right, Annie. We have all the time in the world."

They didn't talk much through the meal. They spent some time fingering the beer coasters, dog tags and looking at the photographs. They didn't bother to take the time to open and fold the road map. The envelope's mysterious, meager contents had all their attention.

When they finished their meals, Annie's thoughts drifted away from the food, and she wondered where they would be staying that night. She decided that from now on, she would check out any motel room before Alex paid for it. That motel outside Bay City had see-through sheets, smelled of stale beer and stunk like a wet dog. They showered before they left, but

120

Annie could smell that place all the way to Detroit. New dress and under-things or not, that motel bothered her, and she expressed it clearly to Alex that there would be *no more Hellholes*. He said he understood and sincerely promised that it would not happen again. Their waitress recommended the *Murphy Hotel* on Findlay Street, a few miles down the road in Perrysburg. She affirmed it had a good reputation and was a decent place. Alex paid the tab and left a dollar on the table. After a short drive, they would be able to put an extremely eventful day to rest.

As they were pulling out of the parking lot and onto the street, Annie teased her husband, "You know, I feel we got the short end of the stick when we got married back there in Detroit. I mean, nobody tied any tin cans to the bumper at all. Now, I suppose it's up to you and me to make all the noise."

*Make Love To Me*

### Tuesday, June 1, Findlay Street, Perrysburg, Ohio, 7:15 PM

Annie had an guarded grin when they arrived at the Murphy Hotel. The building was fresh looking with neatly kept grounds; however, it was actually a motel, not a hotel, as the large wooden sign at the driveway announced. Below it, there were two neon signs that read: *Clean Rooms* and *Vacancy*. He parked the car in front of the office. They went inside, stood at the counter and Alex rang the little chrome bell sitting there. A moment later an unimposing woman with steel grey hair entered from the back. She wore glasses with thin frames and small, round half-lenses. She was smiling and pleasantly greeted them, "Good evening, folks. And a very nice evening it is. I assume you would like a room. Why else would you be here?"

121

"Yes, indeed we do," said Annie. "But I need to see it first. We had a terrible experience at one place in Michigan, don't you know."

The innkeeper said, "All of our units have hot water, plenty of hot water, a shower, and a nice window that opens to the back of the property, and they're clean. The rate is six dollars for a single, ten for a double," she said. "Here's the key to Number Five, Miss, a double for your comfort. And it's two doors down on the right. You are welcome to check it out."

Annie took the key saying, "Thank you, thank you, very much," walked out and down to Unit Number Five. Her pumps were tap-tapping along the boardwalk.

Alex smiled and told the woman, "I can go ahead and sign in right now, Ma'am."

"I think it would be an excellent idea if you wait for the okay from your wife, sir. It's always best to give the woman who is making the inspection the opportunity to voice her opinion, one way or the other, before her husband makes the choice: one way or the other. You see, a woman needs to know that her opinion does indeed mean something to her husband; one way or the other. When given the chance to make a decision, or give an opinion, the husband needs to respect the whole process. The whole process; either one way or the other. That's sound advice, sir. It's an essential part of a marriage to allow that to happen, one way or the other, as I said. The young lady is indeed your wife, sir?" The woman went on and on, speaking rapidly and almost without taking a single breath. Without the slightest pause, one word was followed by another.

"Yes, Ma'am," Alex interrupted, "we are indeed Mister and Missus Throckmorton. Married just this morning. In a pleasant little town called Mount Clemens, Michigan." The smile still on his face, Annie walked into the office as Alex finished speaking. She wondered what could have put that grin on Alex.

"The room is fine, Alex," she said, looking at her husband, the clerk and back to her husband again.

The woman behind the counter began again, "Well, glad to hear it. That's the way we are here at the Murphy. Everything is above-board, clean, and honest. My husband Fred and I keep it that way. Fred is my husband. My name is Alice. Yes indeed, folks. Sometimes our son comes down from Sandusky if we need any big maintenance like the furnace or the water tank or anything crucial, like I said. You folks are going to spend the night here in unit Number One. It's the nicest one we have and just re-done, so it's awful nice. I know you looked at Number Five, Missus, I'm sorry, but Number One is a double, just like Number Five. Of course it's nice too, only better. Better nice. Being newlyweds and everything, that's what counts: *nice*. Isn't it? You know it's important to enjoy yourselves especially on your honeymoon, if that's what you're on. I imagine it is, seeing that you just got married this morning. It's June the first and you're in Unit One. That's pretty exciting, right? Okay, so we'll get you signed in and all, and then you can settle in, and get some rest after coming all the way from Michigan. You can fill out this guest registry card, sir. And don't forget to list your license plate number on there. And oh yes, Unit One has a telephone also. Just dial the number one, and my husband or I will connect you if you need to make a call." It seemed she could ramble on forever.

Alex interrupted again, "Well, let's sign in, Honey, and we can let Alice here get back to whatever she was doing."

"Okey dokey! Sounds good!" Annie understood her husband's grin now. It did seem like another half-hour went by before Alice stopped talking. Eventually, they were able to leave the office with the key to the Murphy Hotel's Unit Number One.

Alex unlocked the door to Unit One and turned on the light. Alice was right. The room was excellent. And it passed Annie's test as well.

"I'll get the bags and be right back," he said, rattling and shaking his keys. Annie put her overnight tote by the sink in the bath, checked the mirror and fluffed her hair. She walked back to the other room and let herself lie down backwards onto the second bed, closing her eyes. It felt fantastic. She kicked off her shoes, spread her toes, took a deep breath and slowly exhaled through pursed lips. It had been an eventful day, and it was not over yet. She enjoyed the quiet for a moment or two, stretched her frame and sat back up. She thought, *Alex will be coming, with the bags.* She ran her thumb along the underside of her wedding ring. It was still there.

There was a noise at the door and then a short knock. "It's me, Annie, the door locked behind me." Annie shot up and let her husband in. He had a suitcase in each hand and the leather bag under his arm. The suitcases went on the bed nearest the door and the small two-drawer dresser. He took two steps back to the door and clicked the dead bolt. Then, he tenderly set the satchel onto the table by the window, as if it were a carton of eggs. He had placed two bottles of Blatz beer from the Packard's trunk inside. *Milwaukee's Best Beer* clanged as he set the bag down. The corkscrew and opener he bought at the Appleton Woolworth rattled against the bottles.

Alex pulled one chair away from the small table, closed the venetian blinds, and drew the plaid window drapes shut. "Let's see what we got inside here, Annie," he said as he pulled out the other chair and sat down. Annie sat down almost before he finished the sentence. They wanted to get the count started: the money count. He grabbed the opener and popped the cap off one of the bottles. The warm beer foamed over and down the sides of the brown bottle as Alex brought it to his lips. He sucked at the suds and took a small sip, handing the bottle to Annie. She took a drink, looking down along the bottle at her husband. "Nothing like a bottle of warm Blatz, is there Alex? Helps take the edge off, don't you know!"

They each took a canvas bank bag, pulled the draw strings open and neatly stood the rolls of bills on the little table. Alex set the pistol, holster and belt on the floor. There was a tattered brown box for twelve 38-caliber cartridges with the *Genuine Smith & Wesson* wording all but worn off. He opened the end.

There were six left.  They sat there, looking at the rolls of hundred-dollar bills, the varied colors of the roll of Chinese Yuan, and back and forth to each other.

"Where do you think all this money came from?"

"Annie girl, I have no idea."

They began unwrapping and thumbing through each bundle of bills.  Alex took to the single roll of Chinese bills first.  There were all sorts of bright colors in varied sizes: pink, turquoise, carmine and blue.  Every bill had the specific denomination written in English and Chinese, and they were all showing signs of excessive wear and tear.  Alex didn't spend very much time with them.  He made a rough estimate of perhaps ten thousand Yuan, in all different denominations.

He joined in what Annie had already started; the labor of opening and counting the rolls of dollars.  The serial numbers were not in sequence, and the bills were in different stages of wear.  Only a few were crisp; the remainder were well-worn from circulation, and some were downright filthy.  Annie counted one bundle, and it contained fifty bills.  There were ten full bundles, each rolled and wrapped tightly with rubber bands, one in either direction.  Some of the rubber bands were so badly cracked and dried out with age, some rolls broke open and the rubber bands flew across the room when handled.  The rolls all wanted to retain their round shape and were difficult to handle.  The one small bundle contained some twenty-dollar and a few fifty-dollar bills.  It counted out to be two thousand dollars.  The money smelled like a potpourri of stale perfume, wet ashtrays, stale beer, and cheap whiskey.

Annie grabbed the bottle of Blatz and took another drink of the warm beer.  She held back a burp and giggled.  She pushed her chair back, walked over to the dresser and pulled a pack of cigarettes from her purse.  Annie put one between her lips; Alex lit it and one of his.  "There's more than fifty grand here.  We counted fifty-two thousand dollars and right around ten thousand Chinese Yuan.  Not bad for a day's work."  He sat back in the chair, inhaled the smoke and let it out with a sigh. "But the question is: what is this about?"

"I'm thinking this is an inheritance, Alex. It has to be. It must be an inheritance. No other explanation. From your father to your mother … and now to you," Annie stopped, took a pull on the cigarette and exhaled. "But I think we should keep this to ourselves. At least for now. We should not tell anyone or let on that we got all this money or anything. We do not want or need to advertise for trouble." Annie flicked the ashes off her Chesterfield and paused. In a minute, she continued, "And we should keep that gun somewhere safe, right in the trunk of the Packard. It's not loaded, is it?"

Alex reached down to the floor and picked up the weapon. He unsnapped the cover of the canvas holster. The revolver was in superior condition and coated with an oily film. Alex turned the cylinder slowly, one click at a time, and discovered that it was not loaded. Annie was watching his every move. He reassured his wife, "No ... it's not loaded ... but Mrs. Murphy would be happy ... it's clean." Annie let out a little sigh and it felt terrific. Her relief broke the tension.

Alexander studied the Smith & Wesson. A number was stamped on the bottom of the handle. He walked over to the dresser, brought the envelope over to the table and dumped out the contents. The pictures, dog tags and coasters fell out of the envelope, onto and on top of the money. Acting on a hunch, Alex compared the dog tags to the number on the pistol grip. It was the same. The number was also engraved on the barrel and across the cylinder. "This was my father's weapon, Annie," he said. "The Old Man's service number is all over the weapon. And here, look at the picture of the other pilot and my father. My father is wearing this belt, this holster, and this pistol. It has to be," he said. "And on the back of this picture here. Look, it has his initials, my old man's initials: *NJT*. Nicholas James Throckmorton. It's certainly him. That's my father with this exact Smith & Wesson. And here, Annie, look at the handwriting on the beer coasters. It's the same as the writing on the back of the photograph of the pilots. The same person wrote on all three things. That could be my father's writing. Must be ... probably is." Alex sounded puzzled and anxious. Annie sat at the table and watched her husband walk back over to the dresser. He picked up the remaining bottle of Blatz and carefully, slowly opened it. This time it didn't foam all over and around the bottle. He took a deep breath, exhaled and took a drink of the beer, shuddering at the lukewarm taste. He sat down and took his wife by the hand, "I'm glad you're here with me. I really am. I love you."

"Right back at you, Mister Alex." She smiled coyly and crushed her cigarette into the ashtray. It was nearly ten o'clock. She got up and turned the light switch off by the door. The only light was from the table lamp. "Let's put this stuff back in the satchel and go to bed. What do you say?"

Alex nodded, smiled and set down the bottle of beer. He started picking up the items off the table and put them back into the bag. Annie walked to the bathroom and announced, "Be right back." The door clicked behind her.

Standing at the mirror, she ran her fingers up and through her hair. She gave it a quick brush and touched up her lipstick. She was experiencing an emotional boldness and nervous anticipation that was new to her. About eight hours ago, Maryanne Dahl became Maryanne Throckmorton. She was bubbling, simmering in a sweet sensuality that was about to boil over. She was acutely aware of the tender tickle in her loins.

In the other room, Alex kicked off his shoes, took off his shirt, let his pants fall to the floor and pulled off his socks. He drew down the bedspread, stacked the two pillows, sat on the far bed and stretched out. Annie walked from the bathroom. Alex could smell the intrigue and sweetness of the Lanvin she had bought in Appleton. Annie stepped smoothly, slowly toward him. Dressed in only her brassiere, panties and silver-grey stockings, she dropped her white panties down around her ankles and kicked them off. She climbed up and straddled Alex

127

with her knees at each side of his hips. With their eyes locked, she reached behind, unhooked her brassiere and gave it a playful toss toward the table, pushing her youthful breasts forward.

"Your troops are giving me quite the salute there, Annie girl."

She put her hands onto his shoulders, let her upper body slowly down upon his chest, shifted her hips upwards just the slightest bit and whispered, "And I expect you to have your soldier standing at full attention, Mister Alex."

With loving humility, Alex grinned and answered, "Yes, Ma'am."

Annie moved her legs back and forth slowly like a cricket on a hot night in August. Her stockings whispered as they brushed the bed sheets. She rubbed her nylon-covered thighs, calves and toes against her husband's legs, and purposely put her lips to his.

"Please promise me that you won't make the seam down the back of my hose all crooked," she whispered.

"I don't believe that will be possible," Alex replied and kissed her back. "Not on our wedding night. Not tonight." He moved his hands slowly down to her buttocks and pressed her closer. Annie let out a sigh of gratification and with a brief quiver, she pushed her body even harder, and tighter, onto him.

About an hour later, Annie thought, *Mama, I got the right man.* That was around ten o'clock.

It was after midnight when they fell asleep.


*Ricochet*

**Wednesday, June 2, Findlay Street, Perrysburg, Ohio, 8:20 AM**

Morning poked through the venetian blinds and left bright lines of sunlight across the wrinkled bedspread. Annie lay resting on her husband's arm. She snuggled even closer, lifted

128

her leg over his and pressed her warm, musky dampness onto him. She opened her eyes enough to catch Alex smiling at her. Annie gently and slowly rolled her libidinous body onto her husband again. They awoke an hour ago, but that was an hour ago. The next thirty minutes brought another round of highly aroused lovemaking, just as intense and gave way to another deeply sensuous fulfillment. Annie's body relaxed and came to rest on the mattress. Her thoughts began to wander, and she wondered aloud, "You know, it seems we are driving south with no idea where we're going. We haven't even looked at the map." She paused and continued, "Where do we go from here? Just keep driving south?"

"We haven't actually needed a map yet, have we?" Alex teased. He rolled over, braced himself on top of her and gave her a gentle kiss. "I love you. But, it's time to get up, Honey. We'll check the map after breakfast." It was one more soft kiss before he got out of bed and into the bathroom.

Annie stretched her form, held up her hands and looked at her two rings. With a smile of contentment, she wiggled her fingers and sat up on the edge of the bed. She heard the shower and walked over to the table at the window. She moved the drapes just far enough apart to see the sun squeezing through the blinds, and filling the day with light. The subdued morning light placed a dusky glow over her naked form.

She picked up the telephone and dialed *"1"*. There was a ring, and Mrs. Murphy chimed a cheerful greeting, "Good Morning Unit One!"

"I want to make a long-distance telephone call to Vermont, Mrs. Murphy," Annie started, "and you will charge us when we check-out, is that correct?" She closed her eyes and sighed. She was worried Mrs. Murphy would start talking non-stop again and that this call could take forever. As it turned out, Mrs. Murphy was more than accommodating, taking the number and information from Annie quickly and efficiently. Annie was surprised and put the handset back on the receiver. She walked back to the dresser, picked up her slip and let it drift smoothly over her head and onto her body. The silky-smooth rayon tickled her nipples and tenderly brushed against her hips. Annie looked into the mirror and pushed at her hair. She was experiencing a wondrous fulfillment she could not explain.

In about two minutes the phone rang back, and Mrs. Murphy said, "Go ahead, Unit One. Your party is on the line." Annie was again surprised. The last time she called her mother it took well over an hour to get through. Now she was hoping the conversation would go as smoothly as the connection did.

Annie exclaimed, excited, "Mama, hello?"

"Yes, it's me, Annie. I'm here. How are you doing, Annie? Where are you? Is everything okay, and are you still going ahead with your wedding plans?"

"Mama, I'm already married! We got married yesterday in Detroit. We got Alex's birth certificate and got married right there."

Annie's happiness caused her eyes to dampen. She began to tell her mother about their ferry ride across Lake Michigan, how Alex slept on the floor of that motel outside of Saginaw, and their marriage at the town clerk's office in Mount Clemens. Annie didn't mention the terrible motel in Bay City, and she didn't talk about the keys, deposit boxes, or the contents. She knew exactly where her mother would take that discussion.

She did, however, say, "You were right about the wedding night, Mama. You were right. I know for sure. Thanks, Mama. And don't you worry about me, Mama. Alex inherited a considerable sum from his mother and father. He has a farm in Florida, and we're going to be just fine. So far, we're having a terrific time driving down south. It rained our first night in Michigan but now the weather is simply beautiful. And Mama, I love this man. And he loves me." Annie spoke clearly and with full confidence. It felt good talking with conviction and telling her mother what she just did. She felt justified and vindicated.

Annie expected her mother to break in but was able to continue without interruption. When Irene did speak, Annie didn't pay full attention to her mother's words. Alex opened the bathroom door with his hair a mess, bits of shaving cream still on his face and a towel around his waist. Annie smiled when she saw her husband and pointed to the phone as she said, "Yes, Mama. We are."

"Say hello from me," Alex said. Annie quickly sensed the opportunity to end the conversation.

"And Alex sends his love, Mama. Say hello to Walter for me. Love you, Mama. I'll call again and I'll write. Bye, bye, Mama," and she put the receiver down. She vowed she would not be upset and decided that the telephone call was best if she kept it short and sweet. She was right. She looked at her husband, got up and walked over to him. They held each other. Annie placed her arms up along her husband's back with her hands onto his shoulders. Alex held his arms around her waist.

Annie felt she did the right thing by making the conversation brief. The quick telephone call didn't give Irene much of an opportunity to criticize, chastise or compare. Annie was relieved that the discussion went smoothly and without any sharp barbs or veiled, well-intentioned but poorly worded advice from her mother.

"Your mother is doing fine then?" asked Alex.

"Yes, yes. Everything is fine. She wished us all the best and told me to say hello to you especially. She's happy we found each other and that we are married." Annie realized she was telling Alex an innocent fib and was only embellishing her mother's condensed dialogue. It made her marginally uncomfortable knowing she was giving Alex a false impression, but she also knew that she was in fact, also fibbing to herself as well. It didn't matter. Now she was holding onto her husband, her head against his chest.

Alex relished the cool and sensuous feel of Annie's slip. His hands moved slowly down to her silky soft, and supple backside and steadily pressed her to him. He whispered, "You feel marvelous, Annie."

She pressed close, and looked up at him. "Is there still hot water for me to shower, you think?" She felt his arousal against her.

"Yes, there is, Annie. You remember that Mrs. Murphy all but guaranteed it and she was right. And there are plenty of fresh, clean towels in there too." He moved away just enough to let the towel around his waist drop to the floor.

With a grin, he stood looking down at his wife. She blushed and quickly walked around him toward the bathroom. She turned her head a bit and peeked to see if he was still there and still naked. He was. He was combing his thick hair with his fingers.

As she closed the bathroom door, she gave Alex instructions from inside, "Don't you dare go anywhere, Mister Throckmorton. Stay just as you are. Right there, just like that. I'll be out in a flash."

*Good Lovin'*

### Wednesday, June 2, Findlay Street, Perrysburg, Ohio, 10:05 AM

Clear skies, a fresh breeze, and a cool morning promised a wonderful early summer day with plenty of sunshine. Alex took the car keys out of his trousers pocket, unlocked the trunk and walked to the driver's door. He reached his arm inside, through the steering wheel and started the Patrician. He listened as the engine went from a rough rumble to a smooth purr. All was well with the world. He returned to the room for the last of the bags.

Alex walked across the room, looked for any forgotten stray items and stood next to his wife. She was dressed in a blue pleated skirt, a white over-blouse, and standing at the dresser mirror with her overnight case open in front of her. They stood

132

close and studied each other's reflection in the glass as she finished her powder, eyes, and lipstick. Annie pushed her fingers at her curls and thought, *that was a good permanent I got back in Appleton.* She pursed and rubbed her lips on the fresh lipstick and clipped on her earrings. She gave Alex a coy wink in the mirror, closed her bag and looked around the room one more time.

"I'm ready. Looks like we got everything. Let's go see Mrs. Murphy," she teased. They walked out the door; Annie closed and locked it behind her. Together, they strolled over to the car. With suitcase and bags placed in the trunk and the door to Cabin Number One closed, their wedding night became a passionate memory.

"You better wait here in the car, Honey. I'll walk over and pay the bill. Perhaps that way I can avoid any detailed long or uncomfortable conversation with her. You know what I mean?"

Annie teased him again, "Oh, yeah, I know what you mean. Tell her that I think this was a nice place, okay?" She watched from inside the Packard as Alex walked to the office. She studied his gait and watched his movements crossing the lot. She crossed her legs and began to bounce a foot up and down. Annie nodded in affirmation.

She adjusted the rear-view mirror, ruffled her hair again and turned her head side to side. She again confirmed to herself that she was very happy with the hair-do she got in Wisconsin. She turned on the car radio, waited for it to warm up and adjusted the dial looking for some music. She found a clear station between the pops, static, whistles and farm reports. She stopped at a clear broadcast playing *Good Lovin'* by the Clovers and looked toward the motel office. There was no sign of Alex. She began to move her foot to the music. "Good loving indeed," she whispered. Her lips curled into a wry smile. She was feeling a tingle deep within and an electric tickle along the inside of her thighs. Annie felt she was the happiest and most loved woman on the entire planet. Life was perfect at that moment, and she considered herself in Heaven.

She looked toward the office again, just as her husband came out of the door with that grin of his and putting his wallet away. He moved his six-foot, two-inch frame quickly toward the car. The brisk breeze pushed the white shirt against his chest and his slacks pressed against his legs. Annie closed her eyes and let out a breath. She thought, *Mama, you didn't tell me everything,* and she smiled again.

"Well, Annie, that's done. Mrs. Murphy told me to say hello." Alex settled in behind the wheel, put the transmission in drive and started off. "She told me the best place for breakfast around here is the *Brown Derby*, a family style restaurant about a mile down the road. Does that sound good?"

"Yes, sounds good. Super." Annie was still lost in her lustful memories of their wedding night.

Three minutes away, they parked at the Brown Derby. Alex took the road map inside and they found a table against a wall, set away from the kitchen and counter, hoping to find a separate slice of quiet. As it turned out, it didn't matter much; the place was crowded. It was considerably busier than Maxine's ever was, and Annie felt relieved that she never needed to endure this level of busy.

After breakfast, Alex opened his map of the Eastern United States. He unfolded, pushed and bent it until Ohio, Kentucky, and part of Tennessee were exposed. Annie got up, moved her chair next to her husband and sat down. They shifted their coffee cups out and from under the map. "It looks like we stay right on US Route 23, Annie. Route 23 all the way. Route 23 is this road right here," he said, following the crooked red line with his finger.

Annie answered, "Alrighty then. I don't know too much about reading maps. I think that's your department." She had briefly studied all the red, green and black lines on the map and dismissed them all as unintelligible gibberish put down on a ridiculously complicated, folded piece of paper. She got up and moved her chair back to the other side of the table. When the waitress returned and refilled their coffee, Annie asked for a piece of apple pie and added, "Can you put a slice of cheddar on top?" The waitress didn't seem to understand, but she obliged. Alex looked up from the map, with a questioning expression. Annie offered a simple explanation: "Pie is perfectly acceptable as a dessert with a late breakfast. And the cheese on top, well, hey, it's a Wisconsin thing, okay?" Alex looked back down at the map and made a half-hearted effort to fold it back up again.

He grabbed his coffee cup, took a sip and said, "We should be able to drive south of Columbus today. We'll see where we end up by around six o'clock or so, Annie. Then we can call it a day and get a motel wherever we are. How does that sound?"

"You're the one doing all the driving, Alex. I'm just along for the ride. If I get really tired and can't make it anymore, I'll tell you."

When the waitress brought Annie's sharp cheddar-covered pie, Alex asked, "That does indeed look good ... Miss, could you please bring me a piece? But, instead of the cheese, a scoop of vanilla ice cream on top, okay?" She answered, "Certainly, sir," and wrote it down, walking away.

It was Annie's turn to give Alex an intentional puzzled look. He expected it and he was ready, "Hey, it's a Florida thing, okay?"

Annie put her head down and continued to enjoy her pie. She looked under her eyebrows at her husband, grinned and decided to needle him right back. "Okey dokey, Alex."


*Walkin' My Baby Back Home*

**Wednesday, June 2, US Route 23, Grove City, Ohio, 2:15 PM**

135

Driving south of Columbus and Grove City, they approached Shadeville, Ohio. The homes were a mixture of traditional Victorian style, newer Cape Cods, and bungalow-type post-war construction. The storefronts were the kind Annie was familiar with back in Appleton: older, small, family-run brick-and-mortar shops were scattered among the larger brand-affiliated retail such as Ace Hardware and A&P.

The landscape and composition of the town suited the name, Shadeville. Large maples arched lazily over the sidewalks and curbs. Annie noticed groups of girls playing hopscotch and others skipping side by side down the sidewalk. Children and dogs ran free. They drove past a mixed group of boys, in worn and patched clothes, playing stickball in a vacant lot. The parking lot of a Kroger market, bordered by the long brick wall of a vacant building, was home court for a street basketball game. The ball players knew that summer was at hand, school was out and times were good.

At the corner of Cottage Street, a long line of customers wrapped halfway around the local Dairy Queen, waiting for their favorite frozen confection. The road leading out of town soon became a rough stretch of concrete slabs. It was pitted with chuckholes, split by cracks and uneven from years of freeze and thaw cycles.

"It's a rotten shame that numbered national highways are deteriorating like this," Alex complained. "If all those big trucks are doing this damage, they should regulate them to secondary roads or something. The motoring public should not be subjected to these poor conditions." His complaints fell on deaf ears. Annie was busy watching the houses, shops, people and lives go by. She ignored his derisive diatribe as best she could. Alex was essentially talking to himself. Eventually, she became compelled to offer assistance, and teased, "Would you want me to drive for a while? You could sit on the passenger side and take a break, and let me complain for a while."

He looked to her, grinned, shook his head, and replied, "No thanks, I'm okay. Just aggravated, that's all. There's no reason for this road to be in such bad shape."

After another twenty miles on the odometer and half an hour on the clock, the pavement changed to newer asphalt. As the highway improved, so did Alexander's demeanor. Alex, Annie and the Packard began running down the road in a much smoother manner.

In Circleville, Ohio, he parked the Patrician outside a bar and grill, where a sign in the window advertised *The Best Darn Chili Con Carne In Town*. That bold promise and a red Carling Black Label neon sign sealed the deal. They sat at a table next to a worn pool table and a colorful, round-top Rockola jukebox. Across the room, three men drinking bottled beer and young lad of perhaps ten or twelve were the only customers. The boy had both hands wrapped around a glass of orange soda. He was slowly swinging his legs from atop the bar stool, looking extremely bored. Empty peanut shells littered the floor. The barmaid's hair was thick, black, and fell straight to the middle of her back. Heavy red lipstick, large red earrings and a red velvet headband consummated her look. When she came over to the table, Annie noticed her red sling-back pumps and gave a nod in approval. "Hey, folks. What can I get for you?"

"Well, I think I'll try your chili ... and one of those Carlings. How about you, Annie girl?"

"Same here, thank you."

"Quiet this time of the day, is it?" asked Alex.

She stood next to their table with one hand on her waist and the other fussing with her hair. "It's slow now but, not for long. In about an hour, the refinery crew will come storming in. Then the whole place will be swarming with men. Then all hell breaks loose. The shift changes then and in they come, hungry and thirsty. Mostly thirsty."

As she was walking away, Alex looked to Annie and affirmed, "I guess we got here at the right time then, Annie. I would not want to be around to see Hell break loose."

She leaned toward Alex and whispered, "She sure looks like a Gypsy to me. Do you think Gypsies make chili?"

"I suppose they could. But I would guess that they make a lot more Goulash, like my grandmother used to." Their mood was in high gear.

After the beans and beer, they were driving south again.

*I Won't Be Home No More*

**Wednesday, June 2, US Route 23, Lucasville, Ohio 4:10 PM**

Annie was looking at the world through a windshield; watching it fly by on the left and on the right. A stiff breeze pushed from the northwest and a few large, white clouds hung in the blue sky above. The back windows of the car were about halfway open, allowing the warm afternoon air to swirl forward against the back of their heads.

Outside of Lucasville, Alex spotted a car with its trunk open, barely sitting off the road on the edge of the pavement. He backed off the accelerator and gently touched the brakes as he came closer. He approached and passed by slowly, noticing a woman and two young children sitting on the side of the ditch in the tall green grass. He was watching them in the rear-view mirror when Annie said, "Stop, Alex." He slowed to a complete stop, backed the Packard beyond the disabled car and parked off the pavement. Alex and Annie stepped out; Alex walked to the disabled vehicle and Annie started toward the woman and children.

Annie called out, "Hello, do you need help?" She held her skirt down, clutching the loose fabric in her fists and started into the ditch, up the other side and approached them. Two girls, about eight or ten, and a young woman stood as Annie came closer.

Red eyes and dried tears exposed her dire plight. The young mother was carrying the weight of the world on her shoulders. Her voice wavered, "I got a flat and I don't got a spare. I don't know what to do." The girls looked up at Annie with eyes wide with worry. Back on the shoulder, Alex was still looking over the car.

Annie asked her, "Are you alone?"

"Yes. It's just me and the kids. We're headed to Kentucky and I'm taking my two daughters with me back to my Mama and Daddy's place in Lynch, down on past Prestonsburg and south of Cumberland. Just off the paved road, this here *Hillbilly Highway*, route twenty-three."

"We'll help you, don't worry. We will help you. Come with me." Annie turned and started back down through the tall grass. The young woman and her children followed Annie through the weeds and across the ditch toward their derelict automobile.

Annie walked up to her husband and whispered for his ears only, "We've got to help them, Alex. Really."

"Yeah. I know." Alex walked around the car again. It was a black 1940 Ford coupe in bad condition, inside and out. He pointed to the car and spoke to his wife quietly, "Look, Annie, she has a flat on the right rear. Two of the other tires are down to the chords. This car won't make it five more miles without another blowout. One tire is shot and the other three are worthless. The inner tubes are obviously junk, too."

Alex spoke to the woman, "Where are you going, Ma'am?"

Annie quickly answered for her, "Kentucky." The young woman immediately echoed Annie's answer.

Alex motioned to them, "Come on over, we can give you a lift to the next service station and help you get on your way again."

"I've got maybe five dollars, that's all, sir." She was speaking nervously and held a child on each hand.

Alex encouraged her, "Five dollars or fifty, you cannot stay here on the side of the road. Come on, we'll get you started

139

and on your way. Come on." They all walked along the shoulder and toward the Packard.

Alex took a paper sack and the laundry bag out of the back seat and stuffed them into the trunk with the other bags and suitcases. Annie invited them into the Patrician. Once inside, the three new passengers seemed immensely relieved, but remained very apprehensive and withdrawn. The young woman introduced herself as Crystal Yoder and her two daughters, Laura and Lynn. She was wearing a threadbare cotton housedress, with worn and dirty canvas shoes. She had a homespun cut with unkempt, stringy and frazzled hair. Annie noticed she had numerous old bruises on her arms and calves. With a whisper, she quietly pointed them out to Alex. Crystal also had a small cut over her right eye with swelling and redness on her forehead. The big round eyes of Lynn and Laura watched Alex and Annie with anguish.

Annie spoke right up, "You're running away, aren't you? You're taking your girls and running away from your man. Am I right?"

Alex didn't wait for a response. He turned around to face the woman and spoke slowly and clearly to Crystal, hoping to deflect any embarrassment. He made it clear to her that he and Annie were going to help them and stated that she was not to argue. Annie strongly repeated her husband's sentiments. Fighting through her teary eyes and trembling hands, the young woman who called herself Crystal Yoder thanked them. The two girls sat wide-eyed and close to their mother.

A *Mobilgas* station was a few minutes down the highway with an adjacent little grocery. Directly across the road sat a small run-down home with a decrepit front porch. Ragged curtains were blowing in the breeze through open windows. Back across the asphalt, a crooked piece of old barn board hung over the station door. It was weatherworn, whitewashed paint with *Mike and Millie's Gas and Food* scrawled in black lettering. Alex pulled up to the pump, got out and stood at the rear of the Patrician. An elderly, disgruntled and unshaven

140

man with a heavy limp made his way outside. His round, beefy belly stretched his denim bib-coveralls to the limit. A woman almost as big, wearing a full apron over a cotton dress, stood in the doorway looking out at Alex and the Packard. Her long grey locks danced all around her head and face in the wind. She pushed her stringy hair aside with a big hand.

Alex started, "Fill it, would you? And do you have any used tires around?"

The big man spit a brown mass of spent tobacco onto the ground next to the pump. With a half-liquid *splat*, it pushed up a little cloud of dust as it landed in the gravel and dirt. He nodded and noisily slid the gas nozzle into the Packard. "You don't need no tires for this here car, buddy."

"No, you're absolutely right, I don't. But I'm looking for four good *seven-fifty-fourteens*; half-way decent ones that will last a couple hundred miles. They're for a 1940 Ford back there; sitting down the road about three miles," Alex pointed down the highway.

"Hummph. Yeah, I guess. I got piles of tires around the back. But they'd be two bucks apiece, if I got any. Used tubes a dollar each. And another buck apiece to mount them. If I got any. I can mix and match some if we need to."

"Do you have a chain? I can tow the Ford up here," Alex said.

"Do you better than that. I got me a big old Autocar hook. A big old tow truck. It can yank that Ford right up here for five bucks. My big old *A-car* will yank that Ford bucket of bolts right up here lickety-split."

Alex took out his wallet and grabbed a twenty-dollar bill. He handed it to the old fellow and explained, "That's for the tires, the mounts and the tow. And I want you to fill up that Ford with gas, too." Alex looked over to his wife, Crystal and the girls. "Is there anything inside that we can use to make up some sandwiches or something?"

The seasoned fellow had one hand resting on the top of the gas pump and the other wrapped around the fuel nozzle. He gave Alex a sheepish grin. "I run this place. I'm Mike. And just like the sign says, we got gas and we got groceries. My wife Millie there can help with them samwitches."

Alex leaned his head into the Packard and asked Annie to shop for some highway food. Crystal looked relieved; the girls remained silent.

Mike topped off the Packard and led Alex around to the back of the station and the Autocar tow truck. The women went into the food store and bought a loaf of Wonder Bread, grape jelly, a can of Peter Pan crunchy peanut butter and quart bottle of milk. Annie put a Baby Ruth, a couple Tootsie Rolls and a Donald Duck comic on the counter. Millie made five peanut butter and jelly sandwiches, wiped off an old, worn butter knife on her apron and wrapped the sandwiches together in waxed paper. She packed it all, along with the butter knife, into a used paper sack and said, "That'll be two dollars and forty cents."

After Annie paid the woman, she, Crystal, and her daughters found a spot in the partial shade of a diseased American elm with small, shriveled and dying leaves. Annie and Crystal began to talk quietly between themselves, and the two girls passed their time with the Tootsie Rolls and comic book.

When Alex and Mike returned with Crystal's old Ford in tow, Alex walked over to the tree and approached the women. Annie and Crystal stood up. "Stay there, girls," their mother instructed. She slowly started away with Annie and Alex.

Annie started, "You're running away, aren't you, like I said?"

There was silence. Crystal looked back toward her children and walked a few more steps away from the tree. She admitted that the day before, she had left her husband back in Sharon, Pennsylvania. He was working the night shift at Bald Knob Mine when she realized her opportunity had come. She took the car and her daughters and headed for home and her parents in Kentucky. She was fifteen when she married and left a Kentucky coal-mining town for another in Pennsylvania. Her husband had repeatedly promised he would change, but his

142

abuse, drinking, and money problems only worsened in the wooded hills outside of Sharon.

At the far side of the service station, Mike had the Ford's front end dangling, suspended up in the air and hooked to the tow chains of the old Autocar. Mike started to pull the wheels off to replace the tubes and tires.

Crystal asked for their address, so she could send repayment when she got back to her Daddy in Lynch. Alex and Annie would not have any of that. Alex gave her twenty dollars and advised her to keep her children safe. She vowed she would and would never have anything to do with her husband again. She added that her father would not allow it either.

Somehow, Annie sincerely believed her. Alex was not so sure, but kept his doubts to himself.

The two girls followed Millie into the store and listened to her stories of other strangers she met over the years. Alex bought three cold Coca Colas and handed them around. Alex, Annie and Crystal drank them under the dying Elm tree. In half an hour, Mike was working on the rear tires of the Ford.

"Time to hit the two-lane again, Annie."

They said goodbye to Crystal, and Annie remembered what her stepfather said about the old car he gave her. She repeated that same advice to Crystal in slightly different words: "Take care of yourself. That way you can take care of your girls."

Alex drove off the dirt and gravel lot of the Mobilgas service station. The Packard kicked up a plume of dust that blew quickly away with the northwest wind. Annie turned halfway around in the front seat and watched Crystal walk over to her daughters. She waved to Crystal, the girls and Millie as the car entered the highway. Johnny Ray was crooning *Cry* on the dashboard radio.

### Wednesday, June 2, Portsmouth, Ohio, US Route 23, 6:55 PM

They stopped in Portsmouth at the Bridge Motel and settled in for the evening. Kentucky was right across the Ohio River. Annie was lying on the bed with two pillows propped behind her head and wiggling her toes in stocking feet like she always did when her shoes came off. She turned her head and watched Alex bring in her denim suitcase along with his leather satchel. He did not want to keep that in the car.

"I have a question, Alex. "Back there when we helped Crystal and her girls ... remember she said her parents lived off the paved road, off the Hillbilly Highway. What is that? What's that mean?"

"I'm pretty sure it refers to US Route 23; this road that we've been following. We've been on this road since Bay City, and we will stay on this road all the way to Jacksonville. Route 23 runs right through the poorest parts of coal country, right through company-owned coal towns and on up north to industrial cities like Columbus, Toledo, Detroit, and all the automobile factories. We're on the road that a great number of men and their families traveled. And the truth is, because they were poor folk coming from the South and looking for work up North, some people started calling it the Hillbilly Highway. We're going to be driving on 23 all day, Annie. There is a difference, though. We are going south. Those folks were going north."

Annie thought for a minute. "Do you think Crystal, do you think she will get off the paved road, off the Hillbilly Highway, and stay with her parents, Alex?"

"I hope so, Annie. We gave her a push. That is all we could do, short of holding her hand and taking her all the way back home ourselves."

"Thanks for helping. You're a decent man, Alexander Throckmorton."

He turned, and suggested, "Well, maybe a decent man would take his wife out and see if they could get a decent meal on the Ohio side of the river."

She agreed and sat on the edge of the bed. "Gosh darn it," she complained. "I got a couple snags in my nylons back there climbing through all that tall grass in the ditch."

"Well, maybe a decent woman should not be out and messing around in the weeds."

She jumped up and chased him to the bathroom door. He stopped right there, and they embraced. "Smart aleck," she said.

Alex washed his hands and rinsed the road dust off his face; Annie stepped out of her skirt and stockings and into a pair of jeans. Their last meal was two hundred miles ago.

When they checked in, the motel clerk suggested Sal's Place, a little Italian restaurant, about a half-mile down the road. They ordered the lasagna special, which ended up being much more than they could finish. During dinner, they could not help but wonder about Crystal and the girls.

Back at the motel, Alex tuned the television set to the only station available, and they watched the *Ray Milland Show* and *Shower of Stars* with Jack Benny and the Harry James orchestra. With an ironic twist of fate, Betty Grable was a guest on the show that night and sang *Put Your Arms Around Me Honey*. Alex refrained once again from saying anything about Betty's figure or the 1936 Ford that Annie left behind in Appleton. He decided once again that he would keep his father's story to himself; at least for now.

Alex checked the road map during commercials and estimated driving distances. He figured they could make it to Kingsport, Tennessee the next day. Appleton was five hundred and fifty miles behind them.

# 4. KENTUCKY

*Sixteen Tons*

**Thursday, June 3, US Route 23, South Shore, Kentucky, 9:00 AM**

Alex walked over to the window in his Jockey shorts, opened the venetian blinds a crack and peeked outside. He was unaware that Annie was awake and watching. The parking lot held half dozen or so more cars than when they had checked in. Through the heavy fog, he could barely distinguish a parked tractor-trailer out toward the road. The window blinds clattered shut with a quick pull of the chord. Annie closed her eyes and Alex walked back to bed. He slowly, gently lifted the blanket and sheet. He covertly, smoothly slid under the covers close to Annie. She whispered and snuggled up next to her husband, "Good morning, Mister Alex."

"Morning, Annie girl."

She slowly shifted, wriggled and slid her legs, hips and her entire self onto him. She gracefully lifted her hips and cajoled him inside. She murmured and propped her body upwards, her arms straight down on the bed above his shoulders. Even slower, she lowered herself back down onto his chest and whispered, "I don't want to get up yet." Alex surrendered with a soft kiss.

An hour passed and the morning fog lifted from the water and the surrounding valley of the Ohio River. The sun was burning through the low cloud cover, with the promise of a glorious day. Annie and Alex checked out of the Bridge Motel and drove onto Route 23 and the Ulysses S. Grant Bridge into Kentucky.

Annie was surprised and taken aback to see the cars and trucks lined up at the bridge. A large overhead sign read *'Stop and pay toll'*. After the uniformed toll collector bluntly, deftly took the quarter from Alex, Annie was incredulous. She

146

admitted that it was the first time she ever saw or even heard of paying a toll on a road. Alex had some fun with the moment.

"Have you ever heard of highway robbery?"

"Is that what this is?" she was genuinely astonished.

"That's what it is, Annie girl. Pure, blatant, highway robbery."

The toll was soon forgotten when Annie looked down at the wide river from the big bridge. It was a thousand times deeper and wider than the Fox River back in Appleton. They soon found a roadside diner and truck stop on the Kentucky side of the Ohio. It was there that Annie would experience yet another first in her life.

Alex ordered a ham and cheese omelet with coffee and Annie requested two eggs over easy, with bacon. When the waitress asked if she would like grits or home fries, Annie was at a loss. Alex explained that grits were a little like cream of wheat, and you could put butter, gravy, or syrup over them. With that kind of variety, Annie chose the grits. After breakfast, she vowed to Alex that she would never again order grits in any way or any form. She tried slathering them with butter and syrup to no avail. Alex chuckled and told her that south of the Mason Dixon, grits were enjoyed like bratwurst, cheese and Kaiser Rolls were in Wisconsin. "No, it's not, Alex," Annie argued. "Bratwurst is meat, cheese is cheese, and Kaisers are bread. There's just no way to tell what grits is." Alex smiled. He didn't dare laugh.

The truck stop was busy and full of noise. When they left, they felt refreshed and ready for the road. They walked to the Packard hand-in-hand, with Annie playfully bouncing off Alex's hips. He got some looks with his white fedora and Ray-Bans, but not as many as Annie. She was wearing her little red scarf with a nicely fitting, white cardigan and blue jeans. Annie filled out her clothes well and Alex stated the obvious: "You're getting some looks."

"I know. I suppose it's because I don't like grits."

"Good one, Annie." He unlocked her door and walked to the driver side. The Packard left another cloud of parking lot dust behind. He enjoyed giving the accelerator pedal a little goose on gravel lots.

Annie spent a considerable part of the morning tuning the radio, looking for a station that didn't have coalmine hiring notices, coalmine closing notices, or United Mine Workers coal safety programs. She didn't have much luck; they were in the middle of coal country. They passed through many little coal-mining towns like Fleming. Some were built entirely by the same mining company that owned the mineral rights to the coal underneath. Rows and rows of cookie-cutter homes filled the countryside, packed like Lincoln Logs on a kitchen table. Mining "company stores" were sitting directly at the roadside. Those company-owned stores sold everything folks needed for survival in the structured coal patch town they lived in. Along the shoulders of the road, men covered in black coal and graphite dust were walking home with their small tin lunch boxes. The only clean part of their bodies was right around their eyes, like a raccoon, only opposite. Many cleaner-looking men were walking in the other direction, toward the mines. The sides of the highway looked as if they were intentionally sprinkled in coal dust. The heavy smell of carbon soot, coal dust and creosote filled the interior of the Packard.

Low clouds and fog shrouded the mountaintops. It felt like the whole world was under a blanket of dark grey dampness. Annie put her head on Alex's lap and ended up dozing off. Climbing and descending the steep grades of the mountains, Alex had the Packard rolling along. The big engine responded smoothly and with power. He passed scores of fully loaded, slow-moving, coal trucks headed to either river barges or railroad yards. The fog on the mountaintops gradually dissipated as noon came and went. The carbon smell waned, and Annie became free of her environmentally induced stupor. About three o'clock she began to stretch and sat up.

Every twenty miles or so, a large barn, usually in a state of poor repair, would be visible from the roadway. *Chew Mail Pouch* appeared brightly painted on one or two sides of some of them. The advertising was clearly visible from the highway, boldly painted in black, red, green and emblazoned with *Treat yourself to the best.*

Annie started playing with the radio again. She finally pulled in a station out of Knoxville, Tennessee, which boomed country music loud and clear. For one reason or another, hearing Hank Williams lament *I'll Never Get Out Of This World Alive* sounded upbeat. As if dictated by fate, the Packard traveled past another set of Burma Shave signs, which broke the dark graphite mood of coal country for good.

Annie read it aloud: *He Asked ... His Kitten ... To Pet And Purr ... She Eyed His Puss ... And Screamed ... What Fur.* They laughed and the radio started playing The Ames Brothers crooning out *You You You.* Alex put his arm around her shoulders and squeezed her softly. She gave him a kiss on the cheek.

"Do you use Burma Shave, Alex?"

"No. I'm an Old Spice cup-soap-and-brush fellow."

"Hmmm. You're living a little dangerously, aren't you? What if I start looking around for a Burma Shave man?"

"That's easy. All I would do is take my big car and drive over all his poetry. That would fix him."

Alex shifted his weight a little and changed his grip on the steering wheel. Annie sighed and leaned against him.

A mile or so further down the road, they pulled into another Mobilgas service station. They looked at one another and silently wondered how Crystal Yoder was doing.

Alex got out and stretched. Annie did too. A young Negro came out wearing a smile as wide as the Ohio River and nodding his head in the affirmative.

"Fill it up, buddy." Alex and Annie walked inside and put two dimes in the Coca Cola machine. One at a time, the bottles clunked, fell loudly and without mercy into the cradle. A noisy chicken suddenly sprang from out behind the counter, clucking and flapping its wings in a frenzy, running across the floor and out the front door. Annie was startled and looked around in total surprise. A rooster immediately appeared from behind the counter and ran off after the chicken. Annie was incredulous and shook her head as she found the opener on the front of the big red vending machine. She pried the cap off her bottle and told her husband, "I'm going to go sit in the car, Alex and watch this comedy from out there." Alex opened his bottle and followed his wife out of the station. They both got into the car.

Alex asked out the window, "How far are we from Kingsport, bud?"

"Just about thirty miles, boss."

"Thank you, young man."

The young fellow made quick work of the windshield. He wiped the headlamps and the outside mirrors. He then stood and looked wide-eyed at the Packard as he slowly lifted the hood to check the oil. "You got one fine automobile, mister, sir. Yessir."

Alex thanked him, paid him and left a dollar tip. The attendant nodded his head vigorously and shooed the chickens back inside and shut the door.

In a little less than an hour, about five o'clock, Alex and Annie were in Kingsport. They checked into the Lee Hotel on Stone Drive. Annie looked around the lobby and decided she didn't need to check the room first. This was another first for Annie. It was a hotel, not a big-city hotel, but a hotel. They carried their own bags inside and took the noisy elevator with folding wood accordion doors to the second floor. Alex had the satchel under his arm, with the strap over his shoulder.

When they got to Room 204, they decided they would clean up before dinner. Annie told Alex to go ahead and shower first, because she had decided on a long hot bath for herself. Annie took full advantage of the little box of Calgon Bubble Bath Beads that she found in the bathroom. She felt fully pampered and that she was indeed on her honeymoon. She got out of the tub and got dressed feeling like a new woman.

After they refreshed themselves, they took the noisy, squeaking, rattling elevator back down to the lobby and walked to the dining room. The ceilings of the Lee Hotel were tall, twelve feet. The long drapes in the dining room were thick brocade in a dark maroon paisley pattern. Heavy multi-light chandeliers hung from the ceiling with their crystals sparkling. Each table had heavy white linen tablecloths and maroon napkins. The richer days of time past were visibly evident with the wear and age of the hotel and its furnishings. The lacquered finish on the doors and woodwork bore the tiny crackling of time. The red and black oriental carpeting covering the floors displayed wear from years of foot traffic. The brass fixtures on the doors and railings had the tiny scratches of endless polishing.

They welcomed a relaxing dinner and experienced their best food so far, on the road. Their meals of fried chicken, sweet potatoes and black-eyed peas were terrific. After dinner, they enjoyed pecan pie and sweet tea with a sprig of mint. They reveled in a sense of calm and tranquility that lasted all night.


## Kiss Of Fire

### Friday, June 4, US Route 23, Kingsport, Tennessee, 7:10 AM

Breakfast at the Lee Hotel began with coffee and a long conversation. Their waitress was wearing a crisp, white, frilly apron and a shiny black rayon dress that whooshed as she walked. She wore her hair twisted up on top of her head, with a mother-of-pearl hairpin on one side. When she brought the menus, Alex ordered his omelet with hot biscuits and Annie asked for the continental breakfast. When the meals came, she learned that *continental* did not mean anything French, or have

151

anything to do with soft-boiled eggs, toast, or fancy sauce. She recognized her faux pas, kept quiet about it and enjoyed her warm cinnamon bun with cream cheese icing. Leisurely picking at it and cutting off neat little pieces with the side of her fork, Annie knew Alex knew.

Alex thought he would tease his wife a little. "How is your continental breakfast?"

She thoughtfully placed her fork down and looked across the table at her husband. "You knew, didn't you? You knew! And you didn't say anything! How come you know all this stuff, Alex? This continental breakfast thing, and the Hillbilly Highway, the grits, you found out my ring size, and you made me fall head over heels for you. How do you know all that stuff? How come you're so smart? Smart aleck. That's what you are. Smart aleck Alexander."

With a little smile, Alex put his biscuit down, reached gently across the table and took Annie by the hand.

"Annie, I know some of this oddball stuff not because I'm smart. I know it by chance. I only went to high school, just like you. For the six years I spent in the Navy, I was aboard ship most of the time. When I was floating around in the Pacific and the Sea of Japan, I did a lot of reading when I wasn't working on airplane engines. All that incidental stuff you mentioned, I picked up through reading or conversation with other sailors. That's the simple truth. I have never spent any time anywhere else in the world. I grew up in Detroit, lived in Oshkosh for a year, spent six years in the Navy, and got honorably discharged from service in Pensacola. Then I met the most beautiful woman in the world working in a hash house in Appleton. I fell in love with her, and I was lucky enough for her to fall in love with me. You know the rest."

She sat motionless and looked at him. He was not quite finished. "And to tell the truth, Annie, you have a helluva lot more going for you than you realize. Don't let anybody, anywhere, tell you different. Don't take a backseat to anyone."

She cocked her head, stood up and walked over to him. Alex stood and they kissed. There were two other tables in the dining room with customers. They pretended not to notice.

Annie ended up having one of Alex's biscuits with jelly. After one last cup of coffee, they took the elevator upstairs. Alex explained that he hoped to make it to Asheville and find that address on the beer coaster. Asheville was about one hundred and forty miles and nearly four hours away. Once they were back in their room, Annie changed out of her cotton dress, stepped into a dark green pencil skirt and slipped on a flowing beige silk blouse. She snapped on her faux pearl necklace and clipped on the earrings. He wore his double pleated grey slacks with the standby white shirt. They had no idea who or what to expect in Asheville. Alex took the old worn manila envelope out of the satchel and checked the address on the coaster. He slid the coaster and the photograph of the two pilots into his shirt pocket. He had butterflies. It was devilishly enticing to be delving into uncertainty: his father's unknown past, the mystifying and murky decade of 1940. Their destination that day was an address on East Chestnut Street, Asheville, North Carolina.

At the lobby check-in desk, they waited patiently for the clerk to finish with the customers ahead of them. When their turn came, they moved up to the counter. Annie leaned into her husband and breathed a deep and sultry *"Thank you"* in Alex's ear that was certainly heard behind the counter. She gave Alex one of her hip-bumps and giggled. The desk clerk gave them a quick look over the top of his glasses and back down again.

Alex picked up his change and pushed the receipt over to Annie. He leaned in toward her and said, "Wait until tonight, Honey." The hotel clerk's eyes bulged, and he gave his dark green jacket a pull on the sleeve. Annie giggled again as they walked out through the lobby. She was certain the clerk heard that. She meant him to hear it, and she exaggerated the shimmy of her hips as they exited the hotel.

153

They loaded their bags in the trunk, took their spots on the front seat and Alex fired up the car. "That was good back there. Super sense of humor. Good job. All day long that fellow will be thinking about what you and I are going to do tonight."

Annie said, "So will I, Alex. So will I."

"That's exactly what I was talking about this morning at breakfast. See what I mean, Annie? You're good. Real good," and he put the Patrician into drive. Annie leaned into him.

There were some family farms down that stretch of the road south of Kingsport; large white homes with porches that went all across the front and sometimes down along one or two sides; small run-down places, some with no window glass or screening. Great distances were in between, with rugged timberlands, logging areas and open grassland. They were on the lower end of the Appalachians, right in the middle of the Great Smoky Mountains. The misty morning fog that shrouds the mountains and gives them their name, was fading. Two hours after they left Kingsport, they were motoring down a long and gradual grade that brought them into the showpiece city. The buildings of downtown Asheville, North Carolina looked like they were plucked out of the 1920's and stuck into a living Art Deco museum.

Alex pulled into a Texaco service station and asked the attendant for directions to East Chestnut Street. It was close; two blocks down and to the right.

Annie got out and went inside the station. She brought out two Coca Colas and the restroom key. Alex was outside the car, stretching his legs when Annie handed him a Coke. As the gas jockey checked his oil, Alex asked where he could have the Packard washed.

"Why, Felix is right inside. He'll do it for ya'll. Yeah, buddy. Felix, he'll wash your automobile up for two dollars, he will. He'll make it all shiny and nice for ya'll."

Alex agreed and parked the car on the side of the building next to the air pump. Felix sprang out of the station, carrying a bucket, a rag and a box of Ivory Flakes. He was a big man, with tufts of grey hair, a red pockmarked face and hands as wide as a catcher's mitt. His huge feet were trying their best to push themselves sideways out of his canvas shoes. Felix started waving a red rubber hose with no nozzle, in all directions over, under and around the Packard. Annie stood next to Alex, watching the soap suds fly in and out of the galvanized bucket, onto and off the car. They backed away toward the station. Annie was wondering what prompted this sudden interest in a clean car and asked, "What brought this on, Alex?"

"The car got dirty back there in Kentucky. It had coal dust, grit and graphite all over it. I just think we should be driving around in a clean car. It feels better."

After the car was all soaped up and bubbling with Ivory, Felix put his large thumb over the open end of the hose. He forced the water into a strong stream and rinsed the suds off and onto the gravel lot. The wide white walls, the chrome and the whole car brightly gleamed. Annie indeed knew that things look better after the dirt is washed off.

Alex stretched, arched his back and glanced around. He looked across the street and spotted Cotton States National Bank. He spoke with quiet enthusiasm, "Annie, that's my bank. I think it's the same one I use back in Florida, Cotton States. It has to be the same."

"And what exactly does that mean?"

He leaned toward Annie and suggested, "I hope it means we are going to get rid of the cash in the trunk. If indeed it is the same bank, we will not have to carry all that money around with us. Let's take the car and find out."

Annie walked to the Packard and got in. Alex gave Felix three dollars and started the car. He drove across the street, pulled to the curb and parked. Annie stood on the sidewalk waiting for her husband. She held her arms crossed in front, holding onto her purse straps with both hands. Alex grabbed the leather satchel out of the trunk. The car was still dripping water as they walked up the two steps and entered the bank.

155

Across the street, Felix and the service station attendant watched with bewildered curiosity.

Inside, the bank's tall imposing ceilings and dark wooden wainscot ended in stucco-surfaced walls. Frosted, dimpled glass and polished brass adorned the teller stations. They walked over to the raised platform floor where busy individuals sat working at their desks. Small lamps with green glass shades sat at the front of each one, casting a muted emerald glow. A balding man with wire glasses, wearing a pinstriped vest and bow tie, gave them his attention.

"We would like to make a deposit," Alex said.

"You can do that over at the teller windows, sir."

"This is a substantial deposit. It's all in cash, to be credited to my account in Pensacola, Florida."

He invited Alex and Annie to take a seat at his desk. After stating his desired deposit amount, they were directed to an office off the lobby floor and behind the teller line. Once inside, an impeccably dressed, tall, thin woman cordially greeted them. She styled her hair twisted up, retained by turquoise pins and was wearing a dark, navy-blue dress with tiny white polka dots. She introduced herself as the Assistant to the Manager and Head Teller, Miss Virginia Lee Shrewsbury. "Call me Ginny Lee," she said.

They were graced with a touch of luck, with all the pieces falling into place. The papers he needed: identification and marriage certificate were all in his satchel. The bank officer studied all the documents closely. She dialed directly, without operator assistance, and telephoned the bank branch office in Pensacola. The direct-dialed call was in itself, a surprise to Alex and Annie. After she slowly and accurately described Alex's physical appearance to the individual at the Florida bank, Ginny Lee was satisfied that it was, in fact, Alexander Throckmorton sitting across from her and she could continue with the transaction. Alex brought out the two bank bags and sat the rolled bundles on the polished desk. The two bank clerks whom Miss Shrewsbury summoned to the office spent a good deal of time with the rolled money. They were at least fifteen minutes counting the cash and straightening all the curled bills on another table in the room. Finally, the bank employees had painstakingly separated, sorted and counted the Chinese currency.

The Assistant Manager again surprised Alex and Annie with another direct-dialed telephone call to the home office of Cotton States Bank in Charlotte, North Carolina. From only hearing one end of the conversation, Alex knew some bad news was coming concerning the Chinese money. After Miss Shrewsbury hung up the heavy black telephone, she told Alex that the Yuan were worthless, and it would not be possible to exchange them to United States Dollars. She explained that as of January 1950, Chinese currency that was not issued and printed by the People's Republic of China was indeed worthless and had "zero value". It was an insignificant, short-lived disappointment for Alex and Annie. "That's one less thing to worry about," Annie mused.

When they were finished, all the numbers checked and totals verified, they deposited the monumental sum of fifty-two thousand dollars into Alex's Pensacola bank account. They added Annie to the account as *Mrs. Maryanne Throckmorton*, a life-event she didn't see coming. Alex put the deposit receipt in his wallet, and everyone had to thank everyone else as handshakes went around the room like party favors. Alex picked up a few good rubber bands off the desk, wrapped them around the Chinese money and stuck the bundle back in the bag. Alex was curious about one part of the transaction and asked the bank officer, "Tell me, Miss Ginny Lee, how were you able to make those telephone calls to Pensacola and Charlotte without getting a long-distance operator to connect you?"

"Cotton States Bank has a dedicated switchboard with our own operators, Mister Throckmorton." She spoke with aloof authority. Alex nodded and glanced over to Annie. She was ready to go. Miss Shrewsbury guided them out of the office and across the lobby. At the foyer, she shook their hands, and shared one last "goodbye and thank you" with them.

When they walked out of the bank and through the glass and brass doors, a peace of mind came over them. Once they were out on the sidewalk, the leather satchel was not actually all that much lighter. However, a weight was lifted up and off their shoulders. As they approached the Packard, Alex realized what a relief the hand-written deposit receipt in his back pocket was. They felt the satisfaction of a burden removed. Alex unlocked the passenger side for Annie.

Alex slid into the car and said, "I think it was a stroke of luck that we found that bank. A stroke of luck, that's what it was."

Notwithstanding, there was a thick wad of cash in his wallet and another in Annie's pocketbook. Combined, it was the five thousand from his mother's estate and the little cash he had left from Florida. They sat for a moment, thought about what happened inside the bank and digested what they had just accomplished.

"It's a little bit of a shame about that Chinese money, but if we ever buy a Monopoly game, we got some realistic looking cash to play with, Annie."

After sharing a laugh, and with a load off their minds, cleaned and fueled up, it was time to drive the Packard to East Chestnut Street.

# 5. NORTH CAROLINA

*Straighten Up And Fly Right*

### Friday, June 4, East Chestnut Street, Asheville, North Carolina, 2:30 PM

They parked at the curb, three doors down from their destination. It was the second house from the corner on Highland, a yellow Cape Cod, 1920's Bungalow style. A full front porch, with brick pillars wide at the bottom, narrowing as they rose upward. There was a two-tone black and yellow 1952 DeSoto in the driveway. A garage too small for the car sat at the back end of the concrete drive with the swing-up door stuck half open. Annie and Alex sat in the Packard with the engine running; like two cops on stakeout duty in a *Dragnet* episode.

"There it is. It's right there. The address written on the back of an old Stroh's beer coaster actually exists." He tapped his shirt pocket; the pocket with the coaster and the army photograph tucked inside.

They studied the house at 14 East Chestnut. The place looked well kept, with a groomed lawn and trimmed privets. Well-shaped evergreen yews stood on each side of the porch steps.

Alex put the car in gear and drove into the driveway. "You're going to come in with me, Annie, aren't you?"

"Absolutely … of course I'm coming in. I'm not going to miss this." She spoke as she cautiously maneuvered her hips, legs and taut green skirt to exit the car.

They walked up the three steps. Alex tapped the brass pineapple doorknocker three quick times. Annie moved her eyes up to look at him, smiled and down to the door again. It opened and a friendly "Good morning" came from inside. A pleasant looking man with black hair graying at the temples, stood back in the doorway. He looked to be in his mid-thirties with a thick black mustache covering his top lip. He spoke again, "May I help you?"

Alex started, "My name is Alexander Throckmorton, and this is my wife Annie..." He was interrupted.

"Throckmorton? Throckmorton ... come in, come on in! I knew a Nicholas Throckmorton in the Army. I flew with him in the Pacific. You must be his son, Alex. Come on in!" He was excited, animated and spoke rapidly. He stepped aside and showed them to the living room. A woman in a colorful floral print housedress stood at a doorway inside.

There was a fireplace, a pair of end tables and two Queen Anne upholstered armchairs. Two landscape paintings were on either side of the mantel. The home was well furnished, neat and inviting.

"I'm Bob McElvoy and this is my wife, Amy," he said. He reached out, shook Alex and Annie's hands in turn and stood by one of the chairs. "Come in, folks, and sit down here. And Amy, you come and sit with us, as well. We're going to be jaw wagging for a while!" Annie and Alex sat down on an overstuffed sofa behind a long coffee table.

Amy was also animated. "I will Bob, I'll join you, but I think I'll go put a pot of coffee on. You folks want some coffee?" she asked. Not only nodding their heads in the affirmative, but they also answered aloud in unison. Bob sat across from them on the edge of his seat. He was smiling, looking them over. He appeared anxious to begin the conversation. His wife had disappeared into the hallway and toward the kitchen. Annie sat with her hands folded on her lap and Alex was trying his very best to look comfortably relaxed. He didn't know what to expect. Annie was apprehensive.

"So you must be Nick's son. He told me all about you. You were a lad of ten or twelve, I think, when we were flying around in Southeast Asia. How's your father doing?"

Alex was silent for a split second and said quietly, "My father went back to China and was lost on a mission in 1946."

Bob sat motionless across from them, quickly blinked his eyes a few times and, "Wow, I didn't know that ... oh, I'm sorry. Your father was one hell of a pilot ... one hell of a good flyer and friend." Bob's gaze drifted somewhere beyond the walls of the home.

Amy McElvoy came out of the kitchen carrying a tray full of cups, a box of *Nabisco* vanilla wafers and a large pot of coffee. There was the proverbial, small, pointless talk about missed opportunities for keeping in touch and the lack of communication among separated friends.

The conversation started with Alex explaining that his mother had just passed away and that he found a beer coaster among her belongings. He explained further that he and Annie were newly married and decided to check out the address on the coaster while driving home to Florida. Alex showed him the picture of two men standing by the fighter plane.

Bob said, "Yep, that's me and your father. That was my bucket of bolts. I called her *Miss Chang*, as if she was Chinese, like one airstrip we flew in and out of. She was a brand-new Curtiss P-40 Warhawk, fresh off the boat. Our flight group just returned from Changsha, Hunan Province in China, I think, when that picture was taken. I think that was early 1942, maybe."

"It was. It says so here on the back," Alex spoke as he flipped the photograph over.

Robert McElvoy continued with his story. He went on to say how he and Nicholas Throckmorton served in the same squadron, and how everyone called Nick "the old man" because he was about ten years older than any of the other pilots. Nicholas and Robert had joined up together in 1938 back in Detroit. The Spanish were busy fighting their civil war and Hitler's Germany was starting to raise havoc in Europe. Most folks knew the inevitable would happen. They received subsequent assignment to the First American Volunteer Group. After months of training in Corpus Christi, Texas and then shipping off to Burma, the AVG became known as the Flying

Tigers, the elite crack unit of the Army Air Corps. The original name, AVG, was lost and forgotten. Their reputation was exaggerated and perhaps justifiably so. The AVG was made up of all volunteer pilots and ground crew. They were mostly Americans: Army, Navy and Marines along with some assorted civilian riff-raff and hotshots from across the globe. The pay was above all the other enlisted and officer pay grades at the time and some squadron leaders were eventually paid more than generals.

Robert McElvoy was rambling non-stop with his war stories and explanations. Alexander and Annie listened closely as the tales unfolded. Bob's wife, Amy, was all ears, perhaps finding out things she never knew. Nobody interrupted the veteran pilot.

He explained that they were part of a clandestine operation prior to the American entry into the War. It started out as a unit to protect the Chinese from the invading Japanese. There was a great deal of corruption and graft going on that was recognized but conveniently ignored. Some of the Chinese Nationalists were siphoning off American aid intended for airfields and roads. Quite a lot of free-lance trading and swapping of services began and continued for the duration of the war. The cheating and looting lingered on as the American commanders diplomatically forced themselves to look the other way.

"I want you to understand, Alexander. I want you to know that us pilots didn't have our hands in the till. Nicholas, me and the rest of us pilots were not involved. We weren't on the take. No, sir. It was that gang of hoodlums behind Chiang Kai-shek and his generals stealing all the American aid. It was clear to all us guys that money was being thrown down a bottomless pit called China. The new airfields never got built and roads for the new supply lines only existed on maps drawn up by the Chinese." Bob reached into his pocket, pulled out a pack of Camel and lit one. "It went on all during the war; us guys were landing in fields that were nothing more than rice paddies filled in with sand and gravel. We never saw any improvements to the situation at all."

He continued with his story and explained how the Army pilots would get along with whatever resources they could get their hands on. Moreover, American ingenuity and bravery saved the unit, the mission and the men. Admittedly, some of the pilots and mechanics saw the opportunity to make a quick buck smuggling jade, sapphires and semi-precious garnets. Some pilots hid the stones in their flak jackets for flights between Rangoon, Burma and the makeshift airfields in Southeast China.

Bob was silent for a minute. "Alex, your father and I made more than a few bucks doing that. It wasn't easy and I don't imagine it was legal, we thought of it as an insurance policy or something. We gave the stones to a Royal Air Force officer in Hunan, and there was another Limey colonel in Guangxi. If I remember correctly, his name was Fitzsimmons. Percival Fitzsimmons. He had quite a name. Your father called him Percy. He's the Brit who told us the gems would eventually end up in Hong Kong. We didn't get rich, but the cash added up. And it wasn't that worthless military script, either. The Chinese paid out in good old Yankee greenbacks."

Annie looked over at Alex and then to McElvoy, "It sounds to me that you men worked for your living. I think you did your job well. They lost and we won."

Alex reached out and held Annie's hand. He ran his finger around the jade ring. Annie noticed the connection and smiled at her husband.

Robert McElvoy was not finished. He explained about the unofficial five-hundred-dollar bonus pay. The Chinese confidentially paid the pilots for every confirmed Japanese aircraft destroyed either in the air or on the ground. The Army denied the pay, but it was a rumor never proven wrong. Bob explained that in 1942, the Air Corps officially disbanded the American Volunteer Group. It became the China Air Task Force; a part of the 14th Army Air Force and it remained until

163

1945. As the war ended, Nicholas went to the Philippines for some training that he never explained. Bob recalled he was gone about six or more months.

He went on, "Nick never said what that was all about, and I never asked. By the time he got back from Manila, the Japs had surrendered, and the war was over. He told me that he considered staying in the service, but not necessarily in the Army. I think he was talking to the guys at Central Intelligence Group off and on. That was the rumor going around. I couldn't swear to it in court, but I have a feeling that's what he had been doing. He would go to hush-hush meetings with the higher-ups, the field-grade officers, all during the war. He sometimes carried a fancy camera in the cockpit. And he had a radio that was different than mine or any of the others in our flight wing."

That line of conversation caught Alex's ear. He looked over to Annie and back to Robert McElvoy. Alex was intrigued and Annie, as well as Alex, was intently listening.

Bob continued, "As it was, our unit was broken up. Pilots and ground crew were scattered all over the Pacific theater. Nick stayed in the Philippines, and I ended up stationed on Okinawa with the Eighth Army Air Force. Two or three months later, I was sitting in the Officer's Mess at Kadena Airfield, Okinawa, when Nick walked in. That was early 1946; February or March, I think. What a reunion that was. We were finally going home and going home together. They packed hundreds of us on board a troop ship to Seattle named the *USS General Bliss*, and man, did we joke about that name. Nick and me spent four weeks on that ship, but some of the GI's already onboard had sailed all the way from Calcutta, India. Poor bastards ... those guys were on that wreck for two months. What a trip; that tub bounced up and down in the water like a cork. After we made port back in Seattle, we got discharged and we mustered out at Fort Lewis, Washington. We got out on April Fool's day. I remember we laughed long and hard about that: good old General Bliss on April Fools. Sometimes the Army truly is a joke. We picked up our muster-out pay and

164

travel allowance and hopped the Milwaukee Road's *Olympian* to Chicago."

Alex was hanging onto every word. He was listening intently and trying to lock all this information into a memorable timeline.

McElvoy recollected further, "Four days later, when we got off the troop train in Chicago, we immediately found a bar. I remember Nick wanted a Stroh's beer. He wanted a beer from Detroit. Well, the young barmaid was a looker, I remember. And I'm telling you, she was built; built like a brick shithouse. Nick said she had those firm, Betty Grable, headlamp boobs and she had a Cuban or Puerto Rican accent and like I said, she was a real looker. A young one, too, she was, with soft, smooth, bronze skin that glistened like it was rubbed with olive oil. She brought us the Stroh's and kept bringing them. That's where that beer coaster came from, Alex. It came from that bar in Chicago. We sat there and got half drunk on Stroh's and *Johnnie Walker* Scotch. We both figured on meeting up again someday. He wrote my address down on one of those coasters and Nick put a bunch of those beer coasters in his pockets. I think that barmaid's name was Joey. I remember most her beautiful skin tone and me and Nick couldn't get over a babe with a boy's name. She sure was one good looker." Bob suddenly realized he might have said a little too much. He looked over to his wife Amy and sheepishly shrugged his shoulders. She looked annoyed. Bob stopped talking for a minute and changed the direction of the conversation.

"Nick was genuinely looking forward to seeing you again, Alex. He really was. He was happy to be going back to Detroit. He talked about you a lot back in them Burma New Guinea jungles. But that night we were two ex-Army pilots drinking and celebrating. We told stories back and forth and how damn glad we were to be home. Well, we parted that night, and I never saw Nick again. I was drunk: knee-walking drunk. I'm pretty sure I left before Nick. Maybe I left him there in that bar. Somehow, I got on a train to Memphis the

165

next day and from there I caught a bus back here to Asheville. I think I had a hangover that lasted a month. Then I found out my high school sweetheart was pregnant with some other guy's baby. This here was my Mama and Daddy's home, and I got my job with the Post Office Department, got married to Amy here, and we lived upstairs for years. My Mama got the cancer, and that was it. So here we are: me and Amy." Bob looked over to his wife, who was smiling back at him.

Amy made the invitation, "You folks have to stay for supper."

Alex immediately answered, "No … no thank you. My wife and I are down here on our honeymoon, so I think we'll be taking you both out to dinner. I'm so glad to have met you, Robert. You've told me more things about my father and his Air Corps service than I ever knew. We were planning to overnight in Asheville anyhow, and we insist on treating you to dinner."

Bob and Amy looked at each other and Bob replied, "Sure, why not. It sounds like fun. We can talk some more." He looked over to a large cuckoo clock on the fireplace wall. It was nearing five o'clock. "Why don't Amy and I change, get freshened up, and you folks can too, get freshened up if you need to. There's a small bathroom right off the kitchen. Right there, first door on the left. How's that sound? We'll go upstairs and be back right after we change, okay?" Bob sounded eager for a night out.

"That's sounds like a good plan, Bob," Alex answered.

Bob and Amy stood up. Bob said, "We can go to the Hillside. The Hillside Hotel has good food, a fantastic restaurant, and nice rooms, too, I hear. We'll go to the Hillside, okay?"

Annie chimed in. "Okey dokey. That's what we'll do."

After Bob and Amy disappeared upstairs, Annie looked around the room once again, closely. "I don't think they have any children. There's no sign of children."

Alex glanced around too. With all the talk, he didn't take notice. "Probably no children, Annie. You're right. I'll go splash some water on my face and check out the bathroom for you. Be right back."

Annie stood up, smoothed her skirt and stretched. She grabbed two vanilla wafers out of the box and began walking around the living room, stretching her legs. When Alex returned from the bathroom, she was on her fourth cookie. It was her turn in the tiny bathroom. She touched up her hair, lipstick and rouge.


*It's Tight Like That*

**Friday, June 4, US Route 23, Asheville, North Carolina, 5:40 PM**

Bob and Amy came down the stairs, one behind the other. Bob started, "Do you have a tie, Alex? You have to wear a tie at the Hillside." Bob was wearing a wide, navy blue tie.

Alex answered that, yes, he did have a tie in the trunk of his car, and immediately guessed that Bob was likely wearing one of his Post Office Department ties. Robert and Amy seemed excited to be going out.

"Good," said Bob, "you can follow me."

Outside in the driveway, Alex opened his suitcase in the trunk and grabbed his only tie, the black one. He looked in Annie's small bag and found her little red silk neck scarf right on top, along with her dainties. Alex brought both, tossed them across the front seat to his wife and threw his sport coat onto the back seat. Annie gave her husband a coy smile, took off her pearl necklace and tied on her little red silk scarf. She moved the knot to one side and slipped her necklace into her purse. Alex backed the Packard out onto Chestnut Street, waited a minute, and followed the Desoto, Robert and Amy to the Hillside Hotel in downtown Asheville.

167

Bob and Amy pulled into the parking lot next to the Hotel, but Alex parked at the curb. It was busy in Asheville; shoppers and folks heading home from work filled the sidewalks. Inside, Alex said he would catch up to them in the dining room. He walked over to the front desk and checked in. He put on his tie and coat, standing in front of the check-in desk as he got the room key. It was clear to him that it was not necessary for Annie to pre-approve the room. The Hillside was, without a doubt, an upscale hotel.

The maitre d' met Alex at the dining room entrance. "I'm with a good-looking lady wearing a red silk scarf," Alex said.

The young man in the red jacket escorted Alex to the table where Annie, Bob and Amy sat. He motioned for Alex to be seated, "Bon appétit, monsieur". Alex smiled, replied, "Merci beaucoup," and wondered how many French live in Asheville.

Alex stepped to the table wearing a foxy grin. Annie nodded in appreciation of the tease.

The wait staff was dressed in red jackets, white shirts, black bow ties and black slacks. The menus touted all sorts of fare, from fried fresh-caught catfish to filet mignon. Alex persuaded Annie to try the barbeque spareribs, collard greens and potato salad. Bob and Amy ordered T-bone steaks.

Alex ordered bourbon over ice and Bob duplicated the request. When the waiter asked Annie what she would like to drink, Annie simply said, "A white wine." The waiter countered by asking, "What type of white wine, Ma'am?" Annie was fearless with her reply, "Bring me something I can't pronounce. Some fancy French stuff. I'll drink that. A small bottle, with a cork, Okay?"

Amy looked over to her husband with a questioning glance, and quickly added, "Me, too, the same."

"Good choice, Ladies. I will bring a *Chanson* Sauvignon Blanc for you. I'm sure you will enjoy it."

Amy corrected her order, and added, bring one bottle. One that we can share. Not a real big one, though." The waiter smiled, turned, and walked away with his white towel over his arm and his nose only slightly up in the air.

Alex looked over to Annie and said, "Good one, Annie. That was beautiful. Nice job, Annie girl." Bob and Amy giggled as if Alex's remark just gave them the *okay*.

Dessert would be a first for Alex and Annie. They decided to try the sweet potato pie with freshly whipped cream. Overall, it was a fantastic experience. It was another pleasant introduction into Southern cooking for Annie.

After the meals, Bob continued with his recollections of Nicholas Throckmorton and their time together in Southeast Asia. When the cigar girl stepped tableside, Alex asked Bob if he'd like to try a *Monterrey Culebra*, and explained it was a small, twisted smoke he once enjoyed while crossing the Panama Canal. Bob quickly accepted the offer, and Alex bought two Cubans and ordered two glasses of *Early Times* Kentucky bourbon.

In short order, blue smoke blended with bourbon, histories, and revelations about Bob's World War II relationship with Nicholas Throckmorton. Bob moved his chair alongside Alex. It was Amy who said, "Go right ahead and gab away, fellows. Annie and me are just as interested in listening to this story as you.

Alex glanced to Bob and said, "Fine with me. Don't need any secrets held here."

Robert McElvoy said he felt somewhat uncomfortable about relaying some of the things Nick told him. Alex then reassured him that no feelings can be hurt, and no toes stepped on. Alex said he wanted to know everything. He wanted to hear all the truth as Bob knew it.

Bob resumed his tales again, and revealed that Nick often mentioned how much he missed being around his son Alex and wished that he could have spent more time with him.

"Your father told me on more than one occasion that he and your mother didn't see eye-to-eye on a lot of things and that the biggest problem was her Catholic faith."

That was a slight surprise to Alex, as he was only somewhat aware of it. It prompted Alex to think back and sort through the memories of youth while listening to Bob with one ear. He remembered his father never went to church and that his mother regularly went to Mass on Sundays, but never asked him or his father, nor did she ever insist Alex go with her. Now that Bob mentioned it, Alex remembered.

Bob continued and said Nick complained that he was married too young and that an early pregnancy forced his wife into maturity and the cold marriage that followed. Alex glanced at Annie and she, like him, seemed to be hanging on every word. Bob knew nearly as much about his family as he did. Bob certainly knew more about his father.

Bob got a far-away look in his eyes, "Nicholas was a decent man, Alex. He was a good friend. Your father and I both got out of Burma with a nice little pile of cash. Understand that we didn't steal anything or cheat anybody. Shooting up Jap planes and sneaking colored stones out of Burma and into China paid off for both of us. We each did all right for ourselves. I wasted most of what I had as soon as I got back to Asheville. I spent many nights at the poker tables of the Crystal Room with the Yankee tourists and a lot of my money ended up going back up North with them Yankees."

Bob looked across the table to his wife, and said, "But I saved some of it, didn't I, Amy? I did have a little nest egg left, and I ended up at the Post Office Department, like I said. It's dull, don't take much skill, and don't pay a hell of a lot, but I got a decent pension to look forward to."

Alex ordered another round of Early Times for Bob and himself. The cigars were half-gone and he was getting tired of the smoke burning his eyes. He crushed his out. Alex reached under the table and put his hand on Annie's thigh. He stroked her leg, moving his hand along her thigh and over her garter snaps. He had a glass of bourbon in his other hand and lifted it as a half-hearted toast to Annie. She raised her wine glass. Their glasses clinked. He whispered, "I love you."

170

Bob started again, "Well, I think Amy and I will go after this drink, Alex. We'll let you newlyweds be. I've enjoyed meeting you both." He paused and began again with a serious tone in his voice. "There is something more I have to show you, though. Two more things, actually." He reached into his shirt pocket and brought out another Stroh's beer coaster and another aged photograph. He pushed them across the table to Alex and pointed to them as he spoke.

"I dug these out of my top dresser drawer back at the house. I thought maybe you'd like to have these." Bob took a drink of the bourbon, leaned a little toward Alex and continued, "This is the coaster that I kept from that night in Chicago. Nick wrote his address on it, just like he did on the one you showed me. And this here is a picture of Nick and his Warhawk bucket of bolts, *Nippon Nellie* he called her, all painted up with a portrait of a half-naked babe stretched out on her back and boobies up in the air. That's your father there in the flight helmet and I'm the one sitting on the wheel. There's Babs, Mort, they were pilots; and some of the ground jockeys."

Alex looked at the picture closely and flipped the coaster over. "Thanks Bob. Thanks, a helluva lot. Yes, that's our old address in Mount Clemens. That's where I grew up, *12 East Second Street*." Alex sat back in his chair and took another drink of bourbon. "But I've got a question, Bob, and maybe you can answer it."

"Shoot. Go ahead. I'll see if I can help."

Alex put Bob's photo and beer coaster into his pocket and brought out his photo of Nick and Bob. They were standing next to Miss Chang, Bob's aircraft. "In this photograph, my father has a holstered pistol strapped to his leg. Did the Old Man have a reason to have a weapon? Did the other pilots carry pistols?"

McElvoy explained, "Captains and above could carry a side arm. Your father was a captain and flight leader. He always carried that revolver. He wasn't required to, and it wasn't regulation, but he always carried it with him. Always. He took that gun everywhere. Nobody ever said anything. You could wear a *Bozo the Clown* outfit, and nobody would care. As long as you killed Japs and brought the plane back home, nobody cared."

Alex insisted on one last round of bourbon with Bob. When their evening eventually ended, Bob and Amy thanked Alex heartily for treating them to dinner. Bob obviously lavished the Cuban cigar with the bourbon and Amy enjoyed the wine with the name Annie could not pronounce. Alex thanked Robert McElvoy for his company and all the information he provided about his father. He added that it was an eye-opening evening and that it was deeply appreciated. Annie and Amy shared a quick hug. Alex and Bob shook hands. The McElvoys turned and gave a little wave as they left. Alex knew he would not be seeing them again.

Alex ordered one last bourbon, and having rehearsed the pronunciation in her mind several times, Annie asked for a glass of Sauvignon Blanc. She said it perfectly. After the waiter left, Alex whispered to his wife, "Annie girl, that was absolutely beautiful. Perfect. I love it. You amaze me." She leaned over and kissed him on the lips.

Alex realized that nobody could pull the wool over Annie's eyes. She would not allow herself to be embarrassed. It was impossible to hijack her pride at any price.

The waiter brought their round of drinks, lit a single candle and placed it on the table. A jazz and blues band had started. Annie and Alex sat and nursed their drinks and went over the past two hours of conversation they had shared with Bob and Amy. They admitted to hearing things they could not affirm and having questions they could not ask. However, they found out things they would never have known, if they had not made this trip to Asheville.

Although they enjoyed a quiet and tranquil stay at the Lee Hotel back in Kingsport, Tennessee, here in Asheville, they felt a relief they had not yet known. Alex and Annie learned a lot. They learned about the meaning of at least one of the two beer

172

coasters. And without the need for Alex or Annie to reveal anything, Bob McElvoy explained the mystery of the large amount of cash and justified the presence of the revolver and shells in the bank boxes.

Without worry, they could listen to the music and enjoyed the band. Annie and Alex truly relaxed for the first time in days.

A riddle was solved while they experienced an informative, fun and entertaining evening. Alex laughed again about the wine's pronunciation. Annie laughed too. "Maybe I should have asked for a bottle of Blatz," she said. Alex broke out in laughter. "Alex, not so loud! This is a high-class joint!" They laughed a little quieter.

They got out on the dance floor only once. The band did a rendition of Leadbelly's number called *It's Tight Like That*. They did an enthusiastic Lindy and got a brief applause in appreciation.

When the band quit for the night, Alex handed Annie the room key. He told her that he was going to move the Packard into the lot and bring up the suitcases and leather satchel. He would see her upstairs in Room 414. She thought about it only for a second and decided to go with him and bring in her overnight bag.

*Can Anyone Explain*

**Saturday, June 5, US Route 23, Asheville, North Carolina, 12:05 AM**

When Alex and Annie walked back into the lobby with their bags, a bellhop came over and immediately took charge of the luggage. Alex held onto his shoulder bag. "What room, sir?"

"Four-fourteen, thank you," Alex stepped to the desk and asked the clerk to have Room Service bring up a split bottle of Sauvignon Blanc. He caught up with Annie and they walked to the elevator with the bellhop.

173

Inside their room, Alex asked the bellhop to set the luggage on the bed, tipped him two Franklin half dollars, and watched him exit with a grin. Alex set the satchel on a round table that was keeping company with two upholstered parlor chairs. A moment later, room service arrived with the wine, bucket of ice, and two glasses.

Alex grabbed the bottle of Jim Beam from his satchel, stepped to the table and said, "Come on, Honey. Let's sit awhile."

He poured three fingers of Beam for himself and three of the Sauvignon for Annie.

"Looking at those old photographs gave me an idea, Annie girl. Tomorrow, the first thing we are going to do is buy a camera. We don't have any pictures of us, and we need some. We're on our honeymoon for a fact."

"Great idea. I never thought of it."

Alex brought the three coasters and the photographs out of the satchel. They sat, continued to examine the items and went over the day's events yet again. Neither one of them mentioned anything about the Jacksonville coaster to Bob or Amy. They now agreed that it would have served no purpose. Bob clearly recalled the one with his address in Asheville and the one with Nick's address in Detroit.

They learned a lot today. The Asheville beer coaster turned out to be exactly as they guessed. It turned out to be the address of an Army Air Corps pilot, Robert McElvoy. The revolver proved to be a bona fide possession of Nicholas Throckmorton, Captain, US Army Air Corps. The box of twelve cartridges, with only six remaining, was still unresolved. An explanation for the ammunition was not likely to be forthcoming and would be nearly impossible to investigate.

The photograph of the two pilots was in fact, of Nicholas Throckmorton and Robert McElvoy: comrades-in-arms, friends and drinking partners in the Air Corps. They had enlisted in the Army Air Corps together in Detroit and mustered out after the war at Fort Lewis, Washington.

174

They also discovered that the cash was the legitimate property of Captain Throckmorton, obtained while in the service of his country. It was his cash in the deposit boxes of the Bank of Detroit.

There was never any doubt about the dog tags. Although he left the Army, it seems Nicholas turned himself around and went right back. Did he re-enlist after he returned to Detroit, or had he already signed up for another stretch of service? That question could only be answered by doing long and tedious research of the Army's records, wherever they might be. While Alex was satisfied with the days' revelations, some questions remained unanswered. Admittedly, some big pieces of the puzzle were now in place. The deposit boxes had been emptied, but some mystery still lurked in the dark corners of the 1940's.

Alex put his attention back onto the coasters and lined them up neatly in a row. "Look at these: the one with the Asheville address and the one with the Detroit address: Robert McElvoy's address in Asheville and Nick Throckmorton's in Michigan. Then look at the last one … this one here, with the Jacksonville address." He paused. "The Jacksonville address is written in the same hand, likely by the same individual, very likely, my father. But it's sloppy and not as neatly printed as the other two and it's obvious that he was either tired or drunk, or both, when he wrote this one."

Annie looked at all three coasters. "That's easy enough. He wrote the Jacksonville coaster later in the night, after Robert left. Like you said, your father was drinking and tired. That's why the handwriting is so sloppy. Your father wrote somebody else's address on this one. And we won't know who or what that is until we get to Jacksonville and find out."

Alex sat back into the chair and took a drink of Jim Beam from the tall wine glass. "Now the question is, why would my father put this coaster with the Jacksonville address in the deposit box? I know there is a large Naval Air Station in Jacksonville. But what on God's green Earth could this third

175

coaster be referring to? And if it's not for a person, what does the address mean?"

After a pause, he continued, "And why exactly did he lock his revolver in that safe deposit box? He locked his weapon up and went back to the Orient. That makes no sense to me at all. I understand the money, the coasters and the tags. I do not understand the Smith & Wesson. The Old Man is dead and gone. I will never know, will I?"

"I think you could be reading way too much into this. Let it be. Let the mystery be. I think we're both taking this a little too far. Maybe we'll find out when we get to Jacksonville. Sometimes a secret can be kind of like a bad onion; you need to keep peeling off the skin before you get down to the good part."

He lit a cigarette and exhaled the smoke up toward the tall ceiling. He didn't fully comprehend Annie's explanation with the onion.

"Tomorrow, like I said, we're going to buy a camera. First thing."

She got up and sat on her husband's lap. "You figure on taking a lot of pictures of me, are you?"

Alex had an arm around Annie's waist and a hand on her thigh. "Yes, I do. And if you happen to be naked, I may need to get more film."

"Alex!" and she jumped up. "I'm going to brush my teeth and get ready for bed."


*L'Hymne à L'Amour (The Song Of Love)*

**Saturday, June 5, US Route 23, Asheville, North Carolina, 8:10 AM**

Annie awoke and sat up suddenly in bed. The sound of rustling paper and her husband's laughter puzzled her. "What *are* you doing, Alex!?"

176

It was indeed Saturday morning. Earlier, Alex went down to the lobby and picked up a newspaper. He was sitting in the chair across the room looking through the *Asheville Times*, comfortable in his unbuttoned shirt, slacks and socks. Alex was reading the funny pages when he laughed aloud and realized that he had awakened Annie. He apologized, "Sorry, Annie. I was reading *Gasoline Alley* and *Lil' Abner* in the funnies."

Annie gave her husband an incredulous look. "Are you kidding me?"

Alex folded the paper in half, walked over to her, sat down on the bed and gave his wife a peck on the cheek. "How about I call room service for breakfast? How would that be?"

She looked at him and smiled, "Wait until I shower and get ready for the day, okay? Then we can call room service."

Alex jumped up and said, "I'll shower first and be right out."

In about five minutes, he came out of the shower wearing a terry cloth Hillside Hotel bath towel, holding it closed with his right hand. He let it fall to the floor. He climbed under the covers and said, "Hurry up, Annie. I'll be waiting right here for you."

An hour later room service brought up the breakfast cart. Alex had taken a chance and ordered eggs Benedict, something neither he nor Annie experienced before. He justified the decision to Annie, "What you don't know, you can't judge. What you don't try, you don't know." He also suggested that it could be the proper choice in a hotel were French seems to be the second language. Annie appreciated that humor and agreed to his choice. As it turned out, they were happy with their breakfasts. Eggs Benedict didn't fall into the same category as grits.

Annie dressed in her pleated blue skirt and silk blouse while Alex sat at the table, with the satchel opened and papers spread out like playing cards. It seemed her husband was obsessed with the satchel's contents. She was sitting on the edge of the bed, snapping her stockings onto her garter. "What are you looking at now, Alex?" Annie slipped into her pumps and walked over to her husband.

"I was sitting here looking at my birth certificate. Bob was right. My mother married young. Very young. She was sixteen when I was born, and my father was eighteen. And my father's place of birth was Buffalo, New York. I never knew that. He must have left Buffalo when he was eighteen, maybe seventeen. No wonder I never knew anything about grandparents or other relatives on his side. The Old Man never talked about his family. No aunts, no uncles. I may have a whole flock of relatives living in Buffalo. And, quite possibly, I could have relatives that I don't know exist. That's wild, Annie. Absolutely, off-the-radar wild. I bought you that little ring back in Appleton, the jade. You have a jade that maybe my father carried with him into China.

And The Old Man might have been flying an airplane made by some of my relatives. I have even worked on those engines myself; Curtis Aircraft made the P-40 in Buffalo. There is so much here, so much we just found out. This is wild, Annie. There is just so much. So much information. So many possibilities."

Annie stood near her husband and put a hand on his shoulder. "You are flooding your brains with all this stuff, Alex. Time to knock it off. All that matters is what is going on now. You and me. We are what matters. So, let's check out of here and go get a camera." She went on to tease him, "I might get in the mood for some artful photography later."

"Well, Annie, I was thinking we could spend a full day and stay another night here in Asheville. We can arrange that. Right? There is no rush to hit the two-lane again, is there?"

"Aren't you in a hurry to get down to Florida; to your farm and horse and things?"

Alex spoke in broken, short sentences, thinking and planning as he went along. "We are on our honeymoon, Annie … I can call my neighbor Louis. He is boarding my horse now, anyway, and I can call him and let him know what's going on.

178

Keeping an eye on my place, that's not an issue, it's right up the driveway. There's no problem; I just have to let him know so I'll telephone him tonight, after dark, when he'll be done for the day. I originally told him that I could be gone three or four weeks so we can stay one more day."

Alex put the papers back in the satchel between the canvas holster and bottle of Jim Beam. He turned to Annie and put his hands on her hips. He placed a kiss on her fresh red lips and asked, "Okey dokey, Annie girl?"

She giggled and jokingly teased her husband, "See that, Alex? Don't you know? I learned some French in the restaurant last night, and now you're learning how to speak Wisconsin."


## *Bewitched, Bothered, and Bewildered*

### **Saturday, June 5, US Route 23, Asheville, North Carolina, 12:00 PM**

Alex and Annie were at the front desk checking in for another night at the Hillside. Alex set his leather bag on the counter and filled in the forms again. The clerk mentioned in an aloof tone that telephone requests for weekend stays were coming in heavily, and they were very fortunate to be able to lengthen their stay. The desk clerk explained with certainty that Asheville was an extremely popular weekend destination for people up and down the East Coast.

Alex finished filling in the register and reservedly said, "I'm not on the telephone. I'm standing right here in front of you, with cash in my hand."

The next comment from the desk clerk was, "Yes, sir."

Annie's heels clicked across the polished hardwood floor of the lobby. She held onto her husband's arm as they walked out through the large oak and glass doors of the hotel. Once they were on the sidewalk, they turned to make the corner from

Westmoreland Street to Broadway. They were walking on the sunny side of the street and in Carolina, that can warm you to your soul.

"I think you should do some shopping today, Annie. We are staying another night anyway. It's Saturday, and I want to have an enjoyable evening of dining and even some dancing, yes dancing, with my wife. We can think of it as a wedding gift to ourselves. We haven't had any of those have we? You go and get yourself a nice new dress, blouse, slacks, or whatever. My wife deserves a little pampering. What do you say?"

"Are you sure, Alex? We will need money to set up our household, won't we?"

"We have that, Annie. We have that in the bank."

Downtown Asheville had all the shops anyone would want within a block or two. They walked and talked, in and out of some retail storefronts until Annie discovered Henderson's Ladies Fashions. She decided she would spend some time there and mentioned to Alex that perhaps he could go off on his own for a while. Alex agreed and said he would be back as soon as he got a camera. If Annie didn't suggest that he leave her alone, the camera could have wound up being an oversight.

Alex left Annie at Henderson's and walked down along Broadway Street. He ducked into Dubury's, a men's store, and picked up two pair of linen summer-weight slacks. One was tan, the other black, his size, and right off the rack. He added two silk ties to replace the only one he had, three white cotton shirts and some argyle socks. Alex remembered that the last time he went shopping; he was in Sasebo, Japan on temporary assignment from the Valley Forge. But that was another story from the past. He paid for his items and asked the clerk for a few hangers and perhaps a strong piece of twine. The clerk obliged by putting a half dozen wire hangers and a good-sized roll of stout cotton twine in his parcel. He was good to go.

Two doors down at a Rexall Drug store, he picked up a *Kodak* Reflex II camera kit, with the six-inch reflective *Kodamatic* flash attachment. Three rolls of *Verichrome* six-twenty film completed his purchase. It added up to be a little pricey at a hundred and sixty-five dollars, but he justified the purchase as an investment in memories for years to come. Stamped into the bottom of the camera's chrome frame was: *Made by Kodak, Rochester, New York, USA*. He put all his items into one glossy grey paper bag with twisted jute handles.

Alex was extremely satisfied with his shopping experience. Directly in and out of a store: that was Alex's idea of a successful shopping trip. He walked out of the drug store and down the street toward Henderson's. Inside, he spotted the saleswoman whom he had left helping his wife earlier. He smiled and found an upholstered chair near the mirrored walls of the dress department and fitting rooms. He noticed the magazine table next to a stand ashtray. Alex set down his shopping bag and lit one of his Lucky Strikes. Annie just then exited the dressing room across the aisle, smiled and nodded at him. A few more trips into and out of the little room were in order. The instruction booklet for the new Kodak kept Alex busy for the next forty-five minutes. He was able to insert a roll of film and figure out which lever to push, which knob to turn, and when to turn it.

When they left Henderson's, Annie, too, was extremely pleased with how successful her shopping trip was and carried two large shopping bags. She rambled on to Alex about her new black silk chiffon cocktail dress with silk taffeta and shoulder straps of silk rope. Alex listened and smiled as she told him about her herringbone twill shorts for the warm Florida summer, her pale-yellow pencil skirt, black silk neck scarf, light blue slacks, and calico shirt. Annie thought a minute and started again, "And I got something maybe I shouldn't have. I can take them back."

Alex grinned and took the opportunity to make an attempt at dry humor. "What would that be, Annie? A couple of parakeets?"

"No, silly. I got another pair of shoes: black open-toed pumps with a double T-strap. Only twelve dollars and they will go perfect with my new dress and with the dancing tonight. I needed another pair of shoes. Is that okay? I need to paint my toes, though. I bought a pair of sheer toe nylons."

They stopped walking and Alex bent down a little. He gave his wife a loving kiss on the lips. "It's perfectly okay, Annie. Perfectly okay. A pair of black heels will make your great looking legs even greater. And I'm looking forward to seeing you in that black dress tonight."

They walked back to the hotel smiling, their steps in unison and carrying three bags. It was a wonderful morning. When they got inside, they set their bags by the desk. A bellhop came over to assist, and Alex asked if he would take a few snapshots of them. He happily obliged, and they even ended up posing for three snapshots outside the Hillside Hotel. Alex took one of the bellhop and Annie together. Annie stood on one leg, bent up the other at the knee and gave the young man a kiss on the cheek. "I hope that one turns out. If it does, I want to send it to Beth. She will get a kick out of his hat. And maybe one to Mama too."


*Work With Me, Annie*


**Saturday, June 5, US Route 23, Asheville, North Carolina, 8:10 PM**

Alex said "good-bye and thank you" to his friend and neighbor, Louis. He placed the black telephone headpiece back in the cradle and it clunked down with its weight. He stood and began to tell Annie about his conversation.

"I don't know if you heard me or not, Annie, but I told Louis we should be back in Santa Rosa County by Wednesday or Thursday of next week. Friday at the absolute latest."

"Uh huh. That's exactly what I heard." Annie was sitting on the edge of the big bed. She was near the nightstand, with the table lamp shining on her hands. She just finished painting her toes.  She spoke quietly, paying more attention to her nail polishing job than her husband.  She picked up her left hand, blew across the nails and proudly displayed them for Alex.  "What do you think?  It's Revlon's Coral Pink."

Alex looked across the room and said, "They are just super, Annie.  Just super," and sat back down in the chair by the phone.

Annie screwed the lid back on the nail polish and walked over to her husband.  "I heard every word, Alex.  I was not ignoring you.  I got lost in my lacquer job, that's all."

"It's not an issue.  I'm sorry," and he pulled her to his lap.  "Let me see those nails, Annie girl."

She put them out in front, on the table and asked, "How's that, Mister Alex?"

"Like I said: super, just super.  You always look better than I deserve, Annie."  He playfully pulled at the top of her robe and peeked inside to see her pert nipples pushing out against the terry.  They held each other a moment and Alex started again, "You know, we got lucky yesterday.  While you were in the shower, I was sitting here thinking how fortunate we have been.  And we got lucky at the bank."

"Really?"  Annie adjusted the front of her terry cloth wrap.

"We walked into the Cotton States National Bank with a satchel full of money and papers.  Also inside that satchel was a pistol.  It would not have been very far from impossible for you and me to have been arrested for attempted robbery or something, either at the bank or right here at the hotel."

"I didn't think of that.  Good golly.  I guess so."

"From now on, that weapon stays in the trunk … in the trunk and out of the satchel.  I'm going to pack that revolver, the holster and the shells in the back of the trunk behind the spare tire and forget them until I park the Patrician at my place.  I'm not trying to be funny or anything, but we dodged a bullet yesterday, Annie.  It could have been a front-page story: *Newlyweds locked up trying to rob bank in downtown*

*Asheville.* Can you imagine? We'll keep the gun in the trunk. From now on."

With Annie still on his lap, he asked, "It's about time we get ready for the dining room and dance floor, isn't it?"

Annie stood up and told Alex she would be ready in fifteen minutes. "So, you better be ready when I am, or I'll be leaving without you!"

In half an hour, they were downstairs and seated in the dining room. They enjoyed each other's company exclusively that evening. There were no suppositions to hash over or any unresolved mysteries. It was their first relaxed evening since Appleton: five days and nine hundred miles ago. Alex asked for and the Hillside Hotel had, Great Western Champagne. Annie relished the fact that her husband romantically asked for the same brand they enjoyed back in Wisconsin. Instead of the Fox River, it was a bucket of ice that kept it nicely chilled at their table.

The music started at nine o'clock with a mix of swing, jazz and Memphis blues. The six-piece band was from Charlotte, the Carl P. Farnsworth Hokum String & Brass Band. Carl, the guitar player, had an unlit cigar with a nasty wet end clamped between his stained teeth, and wore a low, wide-brimmed straw hat. Seated on a wooden stool, he was a big man, with fingers as large as sausages. When Alex heard a blues version of a song he first heard in port at Sasebo, Japan, he was surprised. With amazement, Alex watched him pick Blind Boy Fuller's *Meat Shakin' Woman* flawlessly without skipping a note, sliding over a fret or mashing a string. When the band took a break between sets, Alex walked to the small stage and requested a song dedicated to his new wife, Annie. He pushed a five-dollar bill into the guitar player's big hands.

As it turned out, that night at the Hillside Hotel gave them a distinctive memory that would surely last the rest of their lives. They were on the dance floor and just finished swinging to Duke Ellington's *That Lindy Hop*. The guitar player stood at the large chrome microphone and dedicated the next song to the honeymoon couple, *'Alex and Annie'*. They were surprised at the candid announcement. Applause came from every corner and table in the room. The band performed a praiseworthy version of Hank Ballard and the Moonlighters' popular new hit, *Work With Me Annie*.

Alex and Annie danced like Astaire and Rogers. They moved effortlessly together. Annie's new black chiffon and taffeta dress gently swirled across the floor like an autumn breeze pushing leaves. When the song ended and the applause started up again, Annie felt like she was a Hollywood star. She gave her husband a soul-deep kiss. The moment would be forever emblazoned on their lives. Alex also knew that some others in the room might not soon forget the song's evocative lyrics. The band ended their five-song set after that number, and Alex escorted Annie back to their table.

The soft resplendent light of a full moon washed into the ballroom through the tall windows. They danced until the band went home, well past midnight. It was a fantastic time.

*Carolina Moon*

## Sunday, June 6, US Route 23, Asheville, North Carolina, 10:10 AM

Annie looked across the room and saw the clothes had been scattered every which way by the previous night's raucous chaos. Her silky black dress was across a chair with her husband's tie and socks lying over it. Her taupe stockings were hiding under his shirt. Their shoes were all in different quadrants of the room. Annie's opened-toed heels lay skewed against the wall and Alex's wingtips by the door.

Alex inhaled the smoke, handed the cigarette to Annie and exhaled out into the expanse of the room. She took a quick puff and crushed it out in the ashtray. She gently laid her head back down to rest on his shoulder. Her auburn locks spread softly across the pillow and around the side of his face.

"I have a question, Alex."

"Go ahead. Ask away."

"How come a cigarette tastes so gosh darn good after making whoopee?"

"I honestly don't know. But I got a feeling it could be the Devil's way of getting his share of that bliss, that slice of Heaven on Earth that God created for us mere mortal men and women."

"Maybe. But I can tell you one thing. I can tell you, it sure ain't no Devil making my toes curl, Alex. You're the one doing that, by golly." She was twirling her pink nails in the tufts of hair over and around his ears. "You need a haircut, Mister Alex." She quickly forgot her grooming suggestion and asked, "How far are we driving today?"

"The last I looked at the map, I figured we can easily make it to Atlanta. That's right around two hundred miles if I estimated right. And we stay straight on Route 23. We continue along on US 23 all the way to Jacksonville now. I'll take another look at the map when we get in the car, but I think we can make Atlanta well before dark. He turned and faced her, Annie resting her head on his arm. Alex put a hand around her buttocks and pulled her to him. Annie slowly and steadily moved a leg over his and placed a full kiss on his lips. They held each other closely, cuddled and playfully pushed into each other. "Like the song from last night, you need to work with me, Annie. We really should get up."

Softly, she released him and whispered in disappointment, "Okey dokey, then."

When they checked out of the Hillside, they asked the bellhop to take another photograph of them standing next to the Packard. Annie asked Alex to wear his fedora. He agreed, provided she wore her new little black silk scarf. The bellhop took two snapshots that would certainly turn out to be quite the picture in black and white: scarf and hat. After the trunk was loaded, Alex took the cotton twine the salesman back at Dubury's gave him and stretched it across the back seat of the Packard. He tied each end to the small hooks above each of the rear side windows and created a makeshift clothesline for the coat hangers. Annie helped him put some of their things on the wire hangers and onto the newly fashioned clothesline. She was kidding with her husband, "It looks like we almost know what we are doing, Mister Alex. The Packard looks like a *Fuller Brush* traveling salesman's car!"

High thin and wispy clouds were overhead. The street was as quiet as they had ever seen it. Only an occasional car drove past them on Broadway Street as they left the city. Annie turned and looked behind them a few times. It was the very first time Alex noticed his wife doing that. He looked in the rear-view mirror.

"That was a helluva nice hotel, wasn't it, Annie?"

"Yes, it was, Alex. Yes, it was." She slid a little closer to her husband. They started down Route 23 again, heading south to Atlanta.

The clouds started to thicken an hour or so outside of Asheville. They were nearing the Georgia state line, south of Franklin, North Carolina. Another set of Burma Shave signs stood crooked and bent along the roadside. It was as if they were standing guard duty on the far side of the ditch, a never-ending advertising vigil in the knee-high grass along the road.

Annie read aloud again, *No use ... Knowing ... How to pick them ... If your half shaved ... Whiskers stick them. ... Burma Shave.*

Annie got excited about half a mile down the road. "Alex! We're in Georgia!"

# 6. GEORGIA

*I Don't Care If The Sun Don't Shine*

## Sunday, June 6, US Route 23, Rabun Gap, Georgia, 12:45 PM

The radio was silent since they left Asheville. What Sunday radio programming there was not the kind that Annie or Alex preferred. There certainly was no dance music. In fact, there was no music at all anywhere on the dial. Annie was able to find one station when they were about thirty miles inside the Georgia state line. Some blue grass mountain gospel tunes were barely audible through the static.

Traffic was almost nonexistent, with exceptionally few trucks and only the occasional car with its occupants dressed for church. Around Cornelia, north of Gainesville, the landscape changed from the high rolling hills of Carolina to the easily tillable and level country needed for farming. Here and there, a small grove of pecan or peach trees speckled the landscape. Areas of barren, dark red Georgia clay appeared as patchwork in some of the meadows and pastureland. They would pass the occasional sadly sparse and struggling cotton field. The meager remnants of cotton boll clung to some of the dried branches of last year's crop.

Annie asked Alex to stop the Packard as they passed one such cotton field. Outside of Lula, Alex pulled the car onto a wide section of the shoulder. It was a driveway of sorts, probably used as a machinery entrance or turn-around for the crops planted in the field. Annie hustled into the field, right off the road, and stood bending at the knees holding in her hand a half-open, spent cotton boll with a few puffs of raw cottonseed remaining. Alex snapped the shutter and motioned to his wife he was finished. "I'm sending that picture to my Mama! That is exactly what I'm going to do! I'll tell her you turned me into a cotton-pickin' housewife!"

188

Alex walked back to the unlocked trunk, held it open with an outstretched arm and pulled out one of the four remaining bottles of Blatz. The opener from the Appleton Woolworth lifted the cap off the bottle with a pop, fizzle, and whoosh. The warm beer spewed foam out, around, and down onto the gravel shoulder. They laughed and shared what was left of the warm brew. The partially blurred sun was under high clouds, but it was still getting warm. Annie needed to take off her cardigan; it became a victim of the spewing beer. Underneath she was wearing a dark blue, long sleeve cotton jersey-knit shirt. It hung low on her shoulders and Annie had it tucked into her blue jeans. When she dressed that morning, she felt she would not need her brassiere. Alex noticed her form and asked her to pose by the door of the Packard. They took two or three snapshots there on the side of the road as they finished the bottle of Blatz. After the pictures, they privately took a turn behind an open door on the other side of the car, watering the Georgia clay.

Standing at the back of the Packard, Alex started, "We are going to need to stop soon and get lunch somewhere along this stretch of road, Annie." He was looking away, down the road already traveled. "You're about done there?"

"Almost! Good golly! I'm not built like you, I need to pull my pants all the way down, or I'd pee all over them!" After the words came out, she realized that he already knew all about her anatomy.

They settled back in the car without saying a word. "Keep your eyes open for a diner or something, okay, Annie?"

"Okey dokey." Their little tussle was forgotten. She slid to the left and sat closer to him.

As they approached Gainesville, many newer poultry barns were standing near the roadside. The long, rather narrow structures spread their lengths through converted cotton fields. Family farms had been broken into smaller and more economically sustainable chicken ranches.

As they drove into Gainesville, many large Victorian homes in the classic Southern Antebellum style lined the road on both sides. Huge homes with large, looming front porches and towering columns painted impeccably white stood proudly on neatly mowed lawns. Lazy, low hanging Catalpa trees grew alongside the brick sidewalks leading to covered gazebos and pergolas. The city was quiet with sparse traffic. There were no businesses open, no storefronts with shoppers and only an occasional pedestrian. Clutches of finely dressed men and women were walking together in a grassy park outside of the city. One woman with a large, wide, floppy brimmed, light blue sun hat was walking a pure white French Poodle. Another walked a fuzzy little Pomeranian with its tiny legs moving fast and struggling to keep up. The scene was like a moving piece of fireplace art. The heavy, sweet smell of white Confederate Jasmine was unmistakable. The calls of grey mockingbirds broke the quiet of the afternoon. They were darting up and down from the trees, onto the lawns and back up again, chasing mole crickets.

They drove through Gainesville, continuing toward Buford and Atlanta. The railroad tracks in Buford ran right down the middle of Main Street, dividing the city center in half. There was diagonal parking on each side, with only a few cars. The thick smell of tannin was lying heavily in town. There was in fact, a large tannery in the small city, tucked behind a railroad spur and next to several large homes. A large, aging, shoe factory was nearby, and a sprawling Victorian style hotel was visible down the street lined with large arching Live Oak trees.

Annie thought aloud about the dilapidated factory, "It's a shame that shoe factory is in such poor stand. I wonder why."

She suggested that they drive further down the road and away from the smell of curing animal hides. Atlanta was about an hour down the road.

"As we get closer to Atlanta, Annie, there's bound to be a place where we can get something to eat and find a room.

There has to be. Atlanta is a big, big place. Not as big as Detroit, but still big."

*Honeysuckle Rose*

## Sunday, June 6, US Route 23, Lawrenceville, Georgia, 4:05 PM

Alex spotted an *Atlantic* service station up the road off on the right-hand side. He could see puffs of smoke rounding the corner of the building. As the Packard approached the service station, the smell of an oak hardwood fire wafted into the car. A rough-looking Oldsmobile stood parked at the pumps and a short, sinewy old man stood filling the gas tank. This was the first service station since Asheville with any activity and Alex saw it as an ideal opportunity to gas up and at least try to find somewhere to eat.

He pulled to the vacant side of the single pump. A long extension jutted from the roof, out and away from the building, fully covering the service island. The smoke was coming from a homemade barbeque smoker and grill, crafted from a recycled fifty-five-gallon oil drum, with blackened galvanized stovepipe pointed outward at angles that made no sense. A large wooden tomato crate displayed words painted in black letters: *Hot Boilt P-nuts*. Another crate had a message scrawled in red: *Pult Barb-A-Q Pork*. Two large wooden doors for the service bay hung wide open and an old blue-tick hunting dog was sprawled belly-down on the oil-soaked, packed dirt entryway.

The wiry old man at the service island finished wiping the windows on the beat-up Olds. He walked around and greeted Alex, "How ya'll doing, buddy? Fill 'er up?" He wore a grease-stained, frayed, lopsided, denim engineer's hat on his head and sported bib coveralls without a shirt with long grey chest hairs curled over the top.  A red bulbous nose adorned the middle of his weathered face.  Alex could smell alcohol.

"Yes, sir.  Fill it up.  Is there any place around here where we could get a meal?"  Alex spotted an old, rusty *Royal Crown Cola* ice chest against the outside wall with *Live Bate* painted on the lid in green.

"Nothing around here close by.  Inside we gots some darn tasty pulled pork to make samwiches from though.  We gots burgers and dogs, too."  He gazed inside the Patrician, with one hand on the gas nozzle and the other on the top of the pump.

Annie was sitting close to Alex.  She gently tugged at her husband's shirtsleeve, invoked caution, and whispered, "Check it out first, Alex."

Alex got out of the Packard, stretched and walked inside the station.  There was a short lunch counter, five plastic upholstered stools, a Sunbeam coffee machine and all the small necessities for a little diner.  Napkin holders, a pie and muffin case, all on a neat checkerboard pattern, red and white linoleum floor.  Behind the counter hung an assortment of fan belts, oil filters, work gloves, light bulbs, fuses, road maps and even a few fishing rods.  Odd boxes of shotgun shells, all gauges, were next to the register.  A pinball machine was stuck against the wall, next to the entrance door for the service bay.  A black leather bullwhip hung above the front door.  A young blonde woman, perhaps eighteen, sat on a stool behind the counter.  She put down her *Screen Stars* magazine and greeted Alex, "Howdy, mister.  Ya'll want somethin'?"  She was wearing over-sized blue jeans and a short sleeve t-shirt that was too small.  Her unrestrained breasts stood firm with dime-sized nipples pointing proudly skyward through the cotton fabric.

"Yes, my wife and I could have a bite to eat.  We'll be back in."  Alex nodded his head.  He walked out the door to the passenger side of the car and stuck his head inside.  He spoke quietly, "Come on in, Annie.  You really need to come in.  This will be worth the trouble.  You'll see."

Annie got out and followed her husband inside. They sat next to one another at the counter. Annie was looking around and taking it all in. When the old man came in from outside, Alex said, "You have quite the set-up here, buddy."

"Ain't too much we can't do here, young man. Gots everything from soup to nuts, just about."

"You do engine work and oil changes, do you?" Alex asked on a whim.

"Yep. Sure do."

That was all he needed to hear. "That Packard has about two thousand miles on it now. New miles ... break-in miles. Can you change the motor oil for me?"

"Yep. Sure enough. Keys in the ignition, are they?"

Alex answered *yes*, and in a flash, the old man pulled Alex's car into the open pit service bay. The oil was draining out of the crankcase in a matter of minutes. Annie would not soon forget this experience. Neither would Alex, for that matter. There were some subtle encouraging knee-bumps from Alex and a couple of nudges from Annie. The young woman behind the counter was patient and extremely soft-spoken. "I'm Honeysuckle Pruitt, I am." She had a voice as soft and smooth as whipped cream.

Alex and Annie decided to try the pulled pork barbeque. Honeysuckle carefully piled the meat on some homemade biscuits, placed a little dish full of coleslaw and two glasses of iced tea next to their plates. The hearty meals were delicious, and barbeque sauce dripped off every bite. Annie was teasing her husband with constant napkin wipes on their chins. The old man climbed up from the service pit, walked over to the counter wiping his oily hands and asked Alex if he preferred *Quaker State* or *Atlantic Richfield* motor oil. Alex answered, "Whatever you recommend. Whatever you would use in your car."

The old man took off his hat, gazed outside and scratched his scalp heartily. "In that case, then, I'll be puttin' some Quaker State thirty weight in." He quickly disappeared back into the pit. Alex looked at Annie and they gave each other a *what was that?* expression. They continued with their pork and biscuits. Honeysuckle said, "My Grand Daddy knows his oil, I'll tell ya. He knows his stuff about everythin' that needs knowin' about."

They asked her if there was a decent motel around and she replied that she didn't know of any. Her exact words were, "I don't know nothing about any of that motel stuff. I ain't never been to one, so, ya'll need to ask Grand Daddy. He knows."

The old man told Alex there was a respectable motel about ten miles down the road in Snellville. The old fellow said, "Yep, there's a nice enough one down that way, with a decent little chop house right beside it. It's *Pappy Red's,* it's called, the place right at the junction of Athens Road and Route 23 … that's right where it is … pleasure to be of assistance ... friends call me the *North Georgia Snake Man.* I'm Dean Pruitt," he said, smiling big. "The North Georgia Snake Man, that's me." The few teeth he had were coffee brown.

Dean walked out of the service station with Annie and Alex right behind him. Alex looked at the man and graciously said, "Well, thank you, Dean. Thanks for letting us know about the motel. You have been extremely helpful with your oil change and service, Dean. Your granddaughter there, Honeysuckle, did an excellent job with our sandwiches. They were very good, and the coleslaw and iced tea, too."

"Oh, that's not my grand girl. She just thinks she is, since she ain't got a real one. I treats her good that way, that's all. You folks want some boiled peanuts? Here, I'll gets ya'll some for the road."

The man spoke without a break between thoughts. His words ran together like sorghum syrup. He went off around the side of the service station and came back with a half-wet paper sack filled with hot boiled nuts. He held out the bag for Alex and held onto it for a moment. Dean slowly leaned in toward Alex and spoke in a low, gruff tone, "Hey ... ya'll want a jug of moonshine? I gots the best here in North Georgia, I do. Damn good liquor."

Alex was surprised. "How much?"

"A dollar a quart jar. As a matter of facts, son, I got my drivin' license back 1928 by runnin' moonshine down Georgia Highway 9 from Dawsonville to Atlanta, I did. A hundred and fifty dollars a trunk-load I got. Had me a car with big tires, I did. A big old *Buick* that ran like a scared rabbit, it did. Cars with big wheels goes fast. Your car out there gots some big tires. Big wheels and big tires goes fast ... you bet."

Alex looked over at a nervously curious Annie and agreed. The old man went back inside the station, reached under the cash register and came out with a Ball one-quart canning jar full of clear liquid. "Don't you go runnin' off at the mouth, now, hear? Ya'll don't know where you got that. Right?"

Annie's eyes went to Alex. There was no response for what they just heard, so they simply thanked Dean Pruitt. Alex paid him twelve dollars and sixty cents for the gas, oil change, sandwiches, peanuts and the jar of moonshine. Alex put the liquor in the trunk and the peanuts on the floor by Annie's feet. He slowly and carefully backed the Packard over the pit and out of the service bay. As he pulled out and onto Route 23, Honeysuckle was in the doorway watching them leave. Dean was pulling the two large, wooden service-bay doors closed.

"Alex, can you explain what just happened back there?"

"We got some moonshine ... corn liquor, I imagine."

"No, I mean, what just happened? I mean ... gas, food, shotgun bullets, fishing bait, fan belts, moonshine, oil change, pinball and pie for goodness' sake! Did you see the big black leather whip hanging above the door? What was that? The North Georgia Snake Man? I mean, good gosh! Honeysuckle, the girl, said she was Dean's granddaughter. And he denied it! What was that all about?"

"I don't know about that relationship. I do not even want to think about going down that road. They did share the same last name, I remember. But that business? Well, I think we're in Georgia. The Deep South. That's what I think."

Annie reached into the bag and pulled out a warm, wet, boiled peanut, squeezed off the soggy shell and tried it. Her nose wrinkled up, and she handed a couple to Alex. He tried them. "Tastes like warm half-baked navy beans. Okay if you're real fond of warm half-baked navy beans, I suppose."

Annie looked at her husband and threw the bag out the window. She looked out across the countryside and over a small grove of pecan trees. "They can keep their grits and boiled peanuts … are we going to try some of that moonshine tonight?"

"How about we save it for a special occasion?"

She teased her husband, "You mean the next time we have barbeque pork and biscuits?"

"That's exactly what I mean."

They found the motel in Snellville, Georgia, easily enough. Just as Dean told them, it sat prominently at the intersection of US 23 and US 78. Pappy Red's was a lot like Mrs. Murphy's back in Ohio. There were several neat, tidy detached cabins with a sense of privacy and at-home security. Each one was sitting as an independent little *home away from home* with white linen tieback curtains, white wainscot walls and shellacked Southern Pine floors. The air was thick. It was a very warm and muggy June afternoon. Annie had never before experienced that level of heat and humidity together. However, she affirmed that a Georgia spring breeze was definitely better than a January blizzard roaring into Appleton from the Canadian prairies.

The ceiling fan slowly and gently moved the air inside the room. Alex and Annie spent the evening watching television on channel 11 from Atlanta. It was the only station with a clear signal on the small *RCA* television. *The Colgate Comedy Hour* and *The Goodyear Television Playhouse* were their entertainment for the night. They shared a warm bottle of Blatz beer and snuggled into bed early. The crisp, clean, snow-white bed sheets were enough cover when they climbed into bed. The calls of katydids and cicadas in the tall oaks filtered through the screened windows into the two-room cottage. In the darkness of the early morning hours Annie awoke and gave Alex a little nudge.

"Could you get up and close the windows, Alex, please? I'm getting chilly."

A stiff northeast wind had picked up and a distinct, cool breeze off the Appalachian foothills was moving in. The brisk wind was announcing a change in the weather and was noisily brushing through the tall white pines and red oaks. Alex got up, closed the windows and spread the cotton blanket over them. They slept well for the rest of the night.

*Slow Poke*

**Monday, June 7, US Route 23, Snellville, Georgia, 8:15 AM**

Annie and Alex awoke to the sounds of trucks rumbling down the macadam and asphalt highway toward Atlanta. The big wheels moaned their fading song as they passed the motel. Mockingbirds and black crows rudely joined in the morning chaos. The smell of pitch pine and Georgia clay surrounded the cabin. It turned out to be a heavy overcast morning with a stubborn wind. An uncommon chill was in the spring air of Georgia, a stark contrast to yesterday's warmth and humidity.

Annie dressed in her new pencil skirt and white blouse with the scalloped trim. She needed her wool cardigan sweater. Alex wore his jacket to warm against the chilling dampness. They packed their bags back into the trunk of the large car and walked across the parking lot to the eatery. Alex held his arm around his wife, breaking the cold breeze.

Adjacent to the motel office was a café, named *Pappy Red Eats.* It was a small diner that carried a specialty fare Annie and Alex never before heard of.

A small, yellow and red neon sign read, *"Waffles -N-Chicken."* They understood it to mean waffles for breakfast and chicken for lunch and dinner. Their supposition was wrong.

With a little persuasion, Annie agreed to try the breakfast combination of waffles and fried chicken. Alex successfully argued his case to Annie and convinced her that it was no different than French toast and fried bacon. They enjoyed the breakfast, but Annie was not one to have it as a regular item. She asked for a souvenir menu from Pappy, and the owner gave it to her enthusiastically. She told him that she was going to send it to her old place of employment back in Appleton. Pappy rightfully took that as a compliment, and Annie meant it as such, but she did say something to Alex later. After they checked out of the motel and were driving south again, Annie giggled and started, "Alex, think of that waffle and chicken breakfast like it's a painted piece of that modern art stuff hanging on a wall. It's a bright and colorful picture and very pleasing to the eye. But no matter how many times you look at it and adjust it, it still looks a little crooked."

Alex added, "And I bet Pappy Red would think bratwurst and beer for breakfast would be strange too, Annie girl. How about we stop and get some boiled peanuts?" Alex was teasing her, and she playfully pushed her husband.

Driving south out of the Atlanta area, the country became more open, with vast grasslands, peanut plants pushing through the red clay, sprawling tilled cotton fields and groves of pecan trees with fresh, early summer foliage. Traffic was noticeably busier, a ten-fold busier than Sunday. There was a wide variety of homesteads along the way: small, unpainted or whitewashed houses with rusty tin roofs and broken screen doors were scattered and stuck in the middle of open fields. Just down the road would sit an impeccably kept large Antebellum or

Victorian home. Small towns like Lumber City and Hazelhurst had railroad tracks right down the middle of Main Street, just like Buford. The towns were oftentimes split in two with textile plants, sawmills, or granaries on one side of town and small homes on the other. Annie asked Alex how anyone could know which side was the *wrong side of the tracks*. He looked at her and answered in a deep tone, "That, my dear Annie, is a conundrum I need to ponder at much greater length that I am able to permit myself at this moment in time." They laughed at that.

While traveling down the two-lane asphalt highway under the heavily overcast sky, they shared life stories. They shared many of the same experiences, despite growing up in diverse environments. The biggest common thread they held was that they both lost their fathers in the World War. Annie and her younger sister Elisabeth were close throughout their childhood. Alex, on the other hand, had no siblings and no extended family whatsoever living in the Detroit area. His mother's family was all in Oshkosh, no small distance away. Alex supposed that could be the underlying reason why his mother turned so strongly to her faith and the Catholic Church. His mother never pushed him to go to church and the only time he was required to attend services was on Easter. When the notification of her husband's presumed death came, she withdrew into herself. As a young boy, Alex remembered staying outdoors until the streetlights came on. The streetlights were the curfew signal. There was strict discipline brought to bear by his mother when he strayed. Although he never gave it much thought, the conversation with Robert McElvoy brought it all back. He recalled the memories of the church and his mother's melancholy.

There was no way to know for sure, but the fact that his parents married extremely young and brought forth a child so early, could have been the underlying factor that drove his father to join the military. Alex told Annie perhaps his father had actually run away. Perhaps he *ran away to join the circus*, so to speak.  It was also highly plausible the same forces were at work in 1946.  His father was out of the Army and returned home to the realities of his married life.  He left all that behind in 1938, only to have it come to the forefront again.  Now that both parents were gone, there was no way to verify any of it.

Alex mused aloud, "It's a deep personal awakening when you remember things you experienced, but never paid any attention to, we really don't know some people until after they are dead and gone.  And when it's your parents, it can be a very unsettling feeling.  It's like your life went by without you noticing or paying any attention to it.  Like I said, it's a deep personal awakening."

Annie then recounted for her husband how her mother Irene so often talked down to her and made her feel like a schoolgirl.  When Annie called her mother and told her about Alex, Irene mercilessly played down Annie's news.  Her mother trivialized her eldest daughter's emotions down to snide wedding night advice.

Perhaps the cloudy skies brought on the heavyhearted conversation, but it didn't last long.  Alex recalled the few picnics on Belle Isle and the days spent at the Michigan State Fair alongside 8 Mile Road as wonderful memories.  Christmases and birthdays, Thanksgiving and Easter were all special.  He remembered that as a young boy of six or eight, he attended Sunday school at a Presbyterian church.  Cheerfully, Alex told Annie of the countless stories his father shared with him during his boyhood.  He paused, thought for a minute and decided he would go ahead and tell Annie his father's *Betty Grable - 1936 Ford* analogy from years ago.

He explained it all: the curved rear-end, smooth styling and the fender-mounted headlights.  Annie listened closely and considered what her husband was saying.  Her cheeks flushed a little.  After a brief moment of silence, she lifted up her sweater and jutted her breasts outward.  "Are these the headlamps you're talking about, Alex?"

"Yes, Ma'am. That's exactly what I'm talking about." It was a welcome wisp of humor. The serious discussion needed a breath of fresh air. It was still very overcast.

When it was Annie's turn, she told Alex how her father would cuss in Norwegian, and her mother would talk in Polish when she got upset with her or Beth. After the World War, raising them on her own, Irene Dahl spoke a good deal of Polish to her daughters. She made it very clear she had supreme authority. Annie continued with short stories about some of her father's Norwegian traditions. He was a non-practicing Lutheran and felt that God's green Earth was all the church anyone could ever need for worship. Christmas was the time when her father shared the old Norwegian customs: cakes, ginger cookies, doughnuts and Christmas carols were a vital part of the holiday season. She told Alex about lutefisk; the dried white fish cured with lye. It had the consistency of gelatin and was served with mashed peas, boiled potatoes and bacon. Annie shuddered at the rekindled thought. She explained it was like eating sardines coated in *Vaseline*. She remembered how awful she thought lutefisk was and realized that perhaps she was too harsh in her criticisms of some Southern foods. "From now on, Alex, I won't talk bad about boiled peanuts or waffles with fried chicken," she promised. "Grits, on the other hand, are still off-limits."

They pulled over in Hazelhurst, stopped at a small corner cafe and ordered a lunch of grilled cheese sandwiches and bottles of soda. When they returned to the highway, they intended to go as far as Waycross and stop for the day.

They were driving along the eastern limits of the great Okefenokee Swamp. Alex would turn the wipers on and off as the wind continued to push the drizzle from the east. Heavy with the weight of mist and fog, Spanish moss hung from the live oaks. Stands of dead and dying hardwoods and isolated, abandoned shacks stood as a testament to the unforgiving swamp. The stagnant water pools off the shoulders of the road were a silent confirmation of the presence of snakes and snapping turtles. American alligators were certainly lurking under the dead logs and between the cypress knees. The harsh call of crows and the occasional burp of a bullfrog gave warning to those who would dare to trespass. The smell of stagnant water and pine pitch lay as a heavy, wet blanket over the land.

This stretch of Route 23 was dark, dank and ominously dreary.

The dashboard radio was playing Hawkshaw Hawkins' *Slow Poke*. The drizzle and fog continued to force little droplets of water across the windshield. The world was chilly, soggy and grey.


*In The Jailhouse Now*

**Monday, June 7, US Route 23, Dillurd County, Georgia, 5:10 PM**

The mist, drizzle and light fog cast a gloom without shadows. The entire day was dark, dreary and damp. Alex had the headlamps turned on for the last twenty miles or so. He and Annie were tired of the road, their eyes heavy and their mood subdued. The next motel could not come soon enough. Annie was resting comfortably, leaning against her husband with her eyes closed. Just south of Alma, Georgia, directly off the unpaved shoulder, was a sign: *Wrightown Welcomes You. Speed limits enforced.* Fifty paces down the road there was another sign: *Obey or pay.*

Ten feet from a *Speed Limit 25* sign sat a blue and white Dillurd County Sheriff, Chevrolet Bel Air police cruiser. Alex hit the brakes and startled Annie, "What's that, Alex?"

"A cop. A damn cop." The single blue bubble-gum light came on. The siren belched two short, but piercing, wailing, bursts. Annie straightened up and Alex pulled the Packard to the shoulder of the road. "Damn it … the speed limit sign was there, right there. I mean *right* there. And the cop was parked right there, right behind it. He was in plain sight, hiding in plain sight, right behind the damn sign. In perfect disguise. The rat bastard."

"Alex, shushhh! He's coming." Annie was looking in the side mirror, watching, as the sheriff approached the Packard. Alex exhaled in exasperation and rolled down the window.

The officer stood at the door with one hand resting on his pistol and the other on the black nightstick. He was tall, with a big beer belly and had a day-old growth of beard. His shirt was too small and pulled at the buttons. He had a thin black mustache and wore a large brown campaign hat, like *Smokey the Bear*. Annie looked back to the side mirror again. Another officer had stepped out of the police cruiser, and was walking toward her side of the car. Her heart began to thump; harder and faster. This officer was shorter, thinner, his shirt almost fit, but he didn't have a waistline. An impressive, thick, black leather belt held up his trousers. Attached were a nightstick, pistol, handcuffs, and shiny bullets that looked like they were polished daily. His hat sat down on his head, pushing his ears out. Annie felt truly threatened for the first time in her life.

The sheriff directed his thunderous, rude voice at Alex, "Going kind of fast back there, boy ... didn't you see the big sign *Obey Or Pay*? And here ya'll go driving fast with Wisconsin tags on this big car. Ya'll need to bring out that license and registration, boy. Right now, boy!"

His eyes went all around the car, inside the back seat, over to Annie, to the floor and back to Alex. He smelled of cheap cigars. Alex pulled out his wallet and handed his driver's license out the window. The sheriff wrenched Alex's wallet out of his hand, and gruffly repeated, "Registration, boy." Alex reached over and clicked open the glove box. The bottle of Jim Beam bulged out. The sheriff immediately became visibly excited and extremely animated. His voice cracked with expectation, and he started to talk faster, "All right, now. We got something going on here, Kenny." The deputy on Annie's side pulled the car door wide open.

The words came out of the big sheriff's throat like a growl, "Get out of the car, boy. Ya'll get out too, girlie. Both of ya'll. Out of the car. Now, I tell ya!"

The orders spewed out of the burly man's mouth like vomit. He was wildly aflame and sprayed spittle as he barked out his instructions. He spread Alex on the front fender and frisked him. The other officer ordered Annie to put her hands on the fender, and then asked his boss for direction, "What now, Sheriff?"

"Use your stick, Kenny, not your hands. Use your stick."

The deputy cleared his throat, withdrew the nightstick from his belt, and gingerly brought it down and along Annie's nylon covered legs and back up, and down again, under and around her skirt. Annie heard him breathe heavily and closed her eyes tightly. Alex watched, seething with anxiety. The deputy grinned nervously. There were sweat droplets on his pink forehead. Alex called out, "Hey! That's a lady!" The sheriff acknowledged his complaint by crushing his elbow into the small of Alex's back. A cough erupted from Alex's lungs. He winced.

Then and there, they knew that this was going to be a long night. Annie could not imagine anything, anything at all, worse than this. The sheriff roughly pulled Alex's pack of Lucky Strikes and matches out of his shirt. He looked into the pack and put them into his own hip pocket.

The sheriff and his deputy handcuffed and shoved Alex and Annie mercilessly into the back of the patrol car. It smelled like gasoline, cigars, shoe polish and *Brasso*. They watched helplessly as their belongings were tossed and piled onto the damp ground. They threw Annie's party dress from Appleton and the black taffeta from Asheville out onto the red clay and weeds. The sheriff dumped the contents of the satchel onto the shoulder of the road without regard. His eyes bulged when he discovered the roll of colorful Chinese Yuan. He briefly studied Alex's checkbook and the other papers that fell to the ground. He roughly pushed everything back into the black leather bag, wrinkled and crushed. Annie shook her head and could only gasp as she watched her underclothes thrown about. Alex looked over at Annie. Tears ran down her cheeks. She was sobbing softly and gasped as the Dillurd County Sheriff found the pistol behind the spare tire. He slowly pulled the Smith and Wesson 38 out of the trunk and displayed it to his deputy Kenny. They had ear-to-ear grins like two raccoons in a picnic basket. His deputy discovered the moonshine, picked up the quart-canning jar and laughed. Both officers looked back to Alex and Annie in the back of the police cruiser.

"Damn it. We're in trouble, Annie girl." Another tear ran down Annie's cheek. She sat motionless and watched the two officers at the back of the Patrician.

The sheriff and his deputy jammed most of the items back into the trunk. They held out the jar of moonshine, the half-full bottle of Jim Beam, the holstered revolver, leather satchel and Annie's little overnight case. In handcuffs, Annie and Alex strained uncomfortably forward in the back seat of the patrol car; intently watching everything the two officers did.

Alex muttered, "Shit." They sat perfectly still. Like first graders in the principal's office, they knew they were about to face the music. They knew it would not be a children's song.

As soon as the officers got back inside the Chevy, the sheriff started the engine and at a snail's pace, drove down the shoulder of the road. His destination was no more than five hundred feet away; a tall, tin-roofed concrete block building. It had a large steel-barred window in front with three small glass block windows on the side. The big window had *Dillurd County Sheriff Department* painted in huge gold letters around a gold star. The building was only about fifteen feet off the pavement, with no grass whatsoever. There was a full-size flag at each end of the small porch: a Confederate battle flag and the Stars and Stripes. The flags hung like giant curtains on each side. A polished brass spittoon sat by the door.

The sheriff and his deputy frog-marched their prisoners into the jailhouse. Once their handcuffs had been removed, they were pushed into two of the three small jail cells inside. Inside each cell were cots with a thin straw mattresses and white porcelain toilets without seats. The water closets hung high up against the wall, and a single brass water faucet was in each cell with a three-inch covered drain directly underneath. The wood floorboards were smooth, white and had the pungent odor of bleach. There were so many different smells, that it was unsettling. Evidence of cigars, chlorine, pine pitch, wet wool, Aqua Velva men's cologne and body odor hung heavily in the cramped jailhouse.

The sheriff barked to Annie, "Ya'll gotta take off them stockings, honey pie. And your garter belt and brassiere too, if you gots one."

He snapped at Alex, "And your belt and shoelaces, mister, they needs to come off. Ya'll understand why we need to do this … it's not just to take potential weapons from ya'll, it's to prevent them suicides too. We don't want nobody hurting themselves."

Annie continued to sob. Her eyes burned. Neither she nor Alex said a word since they were pushed out of the patrol car. She stood in the corner of her cell, kicked off her pumps and turned her back to the officers. She reached up under her butter yellow skirt, pulled off her stockings and slid the garter belt down. She maneuvered her brassiere off one arm at a time down and out from underneath her blouse. She pushed them through the bars onto the floor outside and sat down heavily on the cot. Alex ripped off his belt and shoelaces, throwing them outside the cell. He stood at the door, red-faced and holding the bars. The deputy walked over to the cells. He picked up Alex's belt and laces and leered directly at Annie as he collected her stockings, brassiere and garter belt. He carried them across the room and put them on the smaller of the two desks. The deputy moved his hands slowly, rolled up the stockings, folded and carefully arranged Annie's garter belt and brassiere on the desktop.

Taking loud, heavy steps, the sheriff walked over to the cells. He coughed and stood with his hands on his hips. "I'm going to make this short and sweet for ya'll. Ya'll under arrest for excessive speed in a twenty-five-mile zone. Ya'll facing charges for hiding a firearm from law enforcement, suspicion of running bootleg liquor, suspicion of illegal exchange of foreign currency, having a open liquor bottle in a moving motor vehicle, and just plain suspicion. Ya'll understand?"

Alex and Annie looked at each other through the bars separating their cells. To them, this entire experience was beyond belief.

"How long do you intend to keep us here?" Alex was trying to steady his voice.

"Don't rightly know. Ya'll maybe see the judge tomorrow. I'll let him know in the morning that we got prisoners." The sheriff then pulled a packet of Swisher Sweets out of his breast pocket and lit one. He stood outside the cells, moving his eyes from Alex to Annie and back again. The deputy stood with folded arms, leaning his backside against his desk, and glaring toward the cells.

Annie whispered under her breath, "Oh, my gosh. Oh, my gosh."

There were no interior walls. A tiny lavatory stood tucked in the corner. A four-foot-high louvered partition separated it from the rest of the room. Three bare light bulbs in single porcelain fixtures hung from the ceiling. A large four-blade fan was twirling slowly in the center of the room. The sheriff had small eyes set close to one another and thick black hair hanging over his collar; shiny and slicked back with too much *Brylcreem*. The deputy was blonde, younger, and with a crew cut. His uniform was a size or more too large.

The sheriff walked back to his desk, just three yards away from the cells. He plopped into his wooden swivel chair and gave his attention to the items in front of him. Looking down at them, he began, "I'm Henry Parker, the Sheriff of Dillurd County and this here is my deputy, Kenny Barrett." He was thumbing through Alex's wallet and fingering through the contents of Annie's purse. He had a South Georgia accent as thick as blackstrap molasses and seemed to enjoy pouring it freely all over the jailhouse. "Mister Alexander Throckmorton. And we have a Miss Maryanne Dahl. Ya'll both traveling together, are ya'll? Ya'll living in sin? Ya'll just driving down the road thumbing your nose at decent living and traditional value?"

Alex and Annie protested in near-perfect unison, "We were married this last Tuesday in Detroit."

The sheriff questioned aloud, "And the Mister's got a Florida driver license? And Missy Annie Doll here got herself a Wisconsin one. Hmmm."

Alex answered, speaking quickly, in affirmation, "Yes, sir. I got out of the Navy nearly four months ago now, and I can explain that revolver. It belonged to my father. That Chinese money was an inheritance from my father and it's worthless. I'm keeping it as a souvenir, that's all." Alex considered it best not to answer for his wife.

The sheriff did not budge and did not look up. He evidently forgot about Annie's driver license. He gruffly responded, "Don't ya'll start, save it all for the judge. Not me. I arrest ya'll and jail ya'll. Judge Bevins is the one that judges ya'll." He was looking over every little item in Annie's purse and overnight bag.

The Southern Bell pay telephone hanging on the wall rang harshly. Sheriff Parker got up and answered it. "Yep, two prisoners. Alright. Tell Lee Roy he got a big yellow car to tow up to the house. See ya'll in a short-short."

"That was Momma, Kenny. She be coming with our supper," and he sat back down at his desk. He began to put the items back into the purse, overnight bag and wallet. "Take that stuff ya'll got there, Kenny and puts it all in a paper sack. And mark it on the bag like *prisoner belongings*. Ya'll hear?"

"Yessir, Sheriff Henry, sir." The deputy looked over to the cells with a depraved grin. He got a paper *Piggly Wiggly* grocery sack out of one of his desk drawers, slid Annie's garter belt ever so slowly inside and one charcoal grey stocking at a time. The last to go in was Annie's brassiere.

Alex and Annie sat on their cots and looked at each other. They each knew what the other was thinking: *Unbelievable.* Annie was shivering. Alex spoke softly, "Cover up with the blanket, Annie. Throw it over your arms and back."

Kenny yelled, "Hush up in there!" Sheriff Parker looked up, grinned and grunted.

The next fifteen minutes seemed like hours. Alex and Annie watched and took it all in. None of it seemed real. Alex took this experience to be like a macabre, offbeat Vincent Price horror movie. The sheriff started putting Alex's wallet, Bulova wristwatch, and the contents of his satchel into a large grey floor safe. It stood next to an open gun case loaded with three shotguns.

The door opened and in walked what could be anyone's sweet soft-spoken grandmother. "Hey, Momma. Thank ya, these two prisoners thank ya'll too." Momma Parker set down a wicker picnic basket with hinged lids.

She looked to Sheriff Henry Parker and asked, "Y'all coming home pretty soon, Henry?"

"In a little bit, Momma, in a little bit." He put the last of Annie's items back into her purse and tossed it into the safe.

Momma Parker looked to the jail cells, smiled and nodded her head, "See ya'll for breakfast," and she was out the door as quickly as she came in.

Annie sat with her hands folded in her lap and the blanket around her shoulders. Alex sat with his hands at his side and open palms to the cot.

The sheriff opened the basket. He took out two waxed paper covered paper plates, two plastic forks and two brown paper napkins. He carried them over to the cells and pushed them through the enlarged opening at the floor of the barred doors.

Annie and Alex looked at each other. Alex nodded to Annie. They each got up and retrieved the flimsy plates. The plates had fried bologna sandwiches, cold scrambled eggs and cold green beans scattered on them. Annie looked at Alex as if she were going to break into a trembling sob. She set the plate down on the bed, put her head into her hands and started to cry.

"Eat something, Annie girl. I think it's going to be a long night." She looked at the plate and then over at her husband. Reluctantly, she picked up the sandwich, took a bite or two and recognized the lingering taste of pure *Crisco* shortening. Alex was slowly working on everything.

Deputy Kenny Barrett looked at his watch and announced it was seven o'clock. "Okay for me to call it a day, Sheriff?"

"Yeah, okay, Kenny. See ya'll at six." Deputy Kenny Barrett took a lascivious glance at Annie and was out the door. The sheriff announced, "I'll be going shortly. Ya'll better eat what ya'll going to eat. I'll be taking what's left with me for the hogs."

Ten minutes later, he pulled the chains and turned two of the three ceiling lights off. The room turned grim and dingy. The remaining bulb was dim, yellow from tobacco smoke and grime and not more than twenty watts. The sheriff walked to the cells and retrieved the remnants of the suppers, paper plates and plastic forks. He announced, "The outside door will be locked. There ain't no getting out. No getting out, ya'll hear? Me and Kenny will be back at six a-clock. Ya'll see the judge maybe about nine or so. And me? Well, I live just two houses down." He turned, put the trash into the picnic basket and walked to the door.

"What if there's a fire or we get sick or something?" Alex asked. Annie sat on her cot and looked like a lost waif.

"Take a long look around, boy! Study it real close, buddy-boy ... there ain't nothing here to burn, boy! And don't ya'll get sick and we'll be fine. Got it?" He slammed the door.

There was dead quiet. Annie stood up and walked to Alex. They held hands between the bars. Annie started, "Alex. This is so wrong ... so wrong."

"Shhhh, Annie. We'll be out of here tomorrow."

"This is so damn wrong. I mean, this is wrong every which way 'til Sunday. There just isn't anything that's not wrong with this. No matter how you look at it, this is just wrong. So wrong." Her eyes burned with tears.

"We will be out of here tomorrow, Annie."


*Far Away Places*

## Monday, June 7, US Route 23, Dillurd County Jail, Wrightown, Georgia, 7:30 PM

Alex took two steps over to the cot in his cell and gave it a push. When it didn't budge, he looked down. Heavy lag bolts secured the legs to the floor. "The cots won't move, Annie. If you throw your mattress on the floor, at least we can lie down and sleep close anyway. The bars won't go away, but we will be close."

They moved their hard straw mattresses and bedding to the floor against the bars that separated them. Annie reached her forearm through the bars. She held nervously onto her husband's hand. "We will get out of here tomorrow, won't we Alex?"

"I'm sure of it, Annie," he forced his voice to show confidence.

They sat for a few minutes and held hands between the bars. Annie asked in an uncomfortable voice, "I gotta pee. Can you turn around?"

Alex turned his back and tried to grant his wife a small sense of dignity. He could hear his wife sobbing again as the toilet flushed with a loud, deep sucking gurgle. "Annie, we will be out of here tomorrow," he reassured her again.

211

"This part of our honeymoon stinks, Alex. This is so wrong. Just plain wrong. And don't try to drink the water out of that faucet. I tried it and it tastes like turpentine and *Pine-Sol*."

"We will get out of here tomorrow, Annie."

Annie's intermittent tears slowed. Alex's brain ached with worry. He feared for his wife's well-being.

They spent the night lying close yet harshly separated by cold steel. They didn't sleep and barely nodded off. Outside an occasional car passed by or a loud, growling tractor-trailer huffed along. It felt cold, damp and grimly uncomfortable on the straw beds. The night crept slowly along.

A grueling eternity passed before it began to brighten up outside. It didn't matter, but Alex forced a guess as to what time it was. He speculated it was about five in the morning. There was not a clock anywhere in sight. Annie was aware of her husband stirring next to her, sat up and whispered to him, "What's going on?"

"Nothing. Morning is coming. I need to use that toilet over here, then we can put these mattresses back and lay down or sit up on the beds. Sheriff Henry and his right-hand-man Deputy Kenny will be coming before too long."

After she heard the flush, Annie opened her eyes and spoke, "That deputy is a creep, Alex. Did you see him touching and rubbing his skinny fingers all over my things? That guy just ain't normal. His eyes are stuck close together like a lizard's, and they don't focus. He ain't normal."

"Let's try to keep it together, Annie. We do not want to agitate these two men. We need to do exactly what we are told and when we are told to do it. We need to work on getting out of this damn place. We need to keep our mouths shut and only talk when spoken to."

It was a frustrating realization for Annie, "Okey dokey, Alex. Okey dokey ... dear God, how I hate this place."

Alex started to ramble in an angry tone, "And it's pretty damn obvious to me that this whole set-up is just a back-woods, money-making machine. I mean, they have this new, almost new, cinder block building and a new Chevy cop car. The two desks are almost new. And look over there, Annie. They don't have a regular phone, for goodness sake. That's a lousy pay telephone hanging on that wall. They don't have a real telephone. And they don't have a real cop radio, either. This entire deal is a joke. It's not funny, but this is a damn joke. It's almost like a strip of *Lil' Abner*. These two local hillbilly cops sit at the side of the road, waiting right at the speed limit sign to put the pinch on people passing through town. I can imagine what this judge is going to be like. This is one of those speed traps you hear about. Like I said, all we can do is shut up and pay the damn fine. But we can't take this too personal, Annie. This is how this little black-water, jackass town on the edge of this God-forsaken Okefenokee Swamp makes money. Out here on *God's Little Half Acre* there can't be too many ways to pay for a couple of cops, a new jail and a new cop car."

Annie knew her husband was upset. She had not seen this level of anger before. His strong emotions and everything he said helped ease her nervous tensions. They sat on their beds and waited.


*I'm Movin' On*

**Tuesday, June 8, US Route 23, Dillurd County Jail, Wrightown, Georgia, 5:50 AM**

The harsh sound of a key roughly opening the jailhouse door got their attention. A mere second later, Deputy Kenny Barrett walked in. He was carrying a beat-up metal lunch box and an oversized red thermos. He didn't say a word or look toward them. He walked to his desk, pulling the chains on the two single light bulb fixtures as he passed. He then dropped his lunch box into the bottom desk drawer with a clunk, and walked over to the file cabinet and turned on the red plastic tabletop radio. It cracked, popped, and hissed before the Farm Bureau report was heard.

Deputy Kenny spoke in a condescending, mocking tone, "Did ya'll have a comfortable night together here in the Dillurd County lock-up? Sure hope so." He grinned at them as he sat down.

"Are you going to be taking us to the courthouse to see the judge, Deputy?" asked Alex.

"This here *is* the courthouse. Judge Oscar Bevins, he'll come right here about nine a-clocks or so. I'm sure Sheriff Parker done called him on the telephone last night."

Sheriff and Momma Parker came in together just as the deputy finished speaking. The sheriff emptied the picnic basket and brought the paper plates and plastic forks over to the cells. Annie murmured, "Thank you." Fried bologna sandwiches were on the plate with a ladle-full of grits and pork gravy. From that point on, neither the deputy nor the sheriff said a single word to Annie or Alex.

Time dragged slowly by, and it seemed like an eternity before the Farm Bureau announcer gave the time as nine o'clock, and a newscaster began with the day's weather forecast. The outer door opened, and a very large man entered the Dillurd County Jail. Alex knew it had to be the judge. Deputy Barrett turned the radio off.

Sheriff Henry Parker stood up and spoke, "Good morning, Judge." He stood almost at attention. The door slammed shut.

Judge Oscar Bevins walked to the deputy's desk, wobbling side to side with his feet pointed outwards like a duck. He pulled the chair back from the desk and heavily set his weight down.

The chair went *whoosh,* the judge released a deep, guttural *uuff,* coughed harshly, and started, "What do we have here, Sheriff?"

Sheriff Parker cleared his throat with a deep gurgle, and said, "We got two individuals, husband and wife, Alexander Throckmorton of Florida, and his wife Maryanne, maiden

214

name Dahl, from Wisconsin. I wrote up the charges last night and have them written up right there on the papers there on the desk, judge."

The sheriff had spoken slowly and clearly. His pronounced South Georgia drawl disappeared in front of Judge Bevins.

Annie and Alex watched from their cells and gave their full attention to the judge.

The judge spent a minute or two shuffling and glancing through the papers on the desk and said, "Bring them two out here, Henry, and we'll get this thing started."

Alex was apprehensive. Annie felt her heart go to her throat. They stood watching and waiting behind steel bars.

The sheriff unlocked the cells with noisy, metallic, clinks, clanks, and a clunk. He motioned them out, stood behind them, put his hands on their shoulders, and led them out to the desk, stopping directly in front of Judge Bevins. Deputy Kenny sat in a small chair next to the file cabinet and safe. The paper bag with Annie's things sat resting at his feet, with *Prisoner Stuff* written in pencil across the top edge.

Judge Bevins' shirt and topcoat bulged at the buttons; his fleshy pink neck hanging over the shirt collar. He had bifocals, very thin grey hair and he was breathing heavily. He fixed his eyes back on the papers and items in front of him. Without looking up, and running his fingers across the papers, he asked in a low, measured, antiseptic voice, "You are husband and wife? And were married in Michigan? Is that correct?"

In an instant, Alex answered, "That is correct, Your Honor."

"You have the right to a trial in front of a jury or you may enter a plea of guilty. If you desire a trial, you will be either held in custody until trial, or post bond as directed by this court. If you enter a guilty plea, you agree to accept the judgment of this court. Do you understand, Mister Throckmorton? And do you understand as well, Missus Throckmorton?"

Annie immediately answered, "Yes, sir."

As if he was still in the Navy, Alex stood at attention, "Yes, sir."

Alex's words flipped a switch. The judge became noticeably more animated, his voice deeper and louder. "Since you two were traveling together, in the same vehicle, with the same intent, destination, and purpose, I will direct all my questions to you, Mister Throckmorton, and understand your answers will be taken as one.

"Do you agree Missus Throckmorton?"

Annie's voice was breaking, "Yes, Your Honor."

Judge Oscar Leroy Bevins wasted no time, "Are you guilty of speeding, son?"

"Yes, sir."

The judge raised his voice a notch, "Dillard County, Georgia is a dry county.

"Are you also guilty of possession of an open bottle of alcoholic spirits as well as a bottle of bootleg moonshine alcohol in Wrightown, Dillard County, Georgia?"

"Yes, Your Honor."

"And are you also guilty of the illegal distribution, or the exchange of a foreign paper money and concealing a firearm and ammunition from law enforcement officers?"

Alex quickly answered, "Yes, yes, no, and no, Your Honor, sir!"

Judge Bevins looked over his glasses at Alex. "What?"

"I inherited that money and that revolver from my father. The money isn't worth the paper it's printed on, because China is a Communist country now. And I simply had that weapon in the back of my trunk, and it's not loaded, and I'm transporting it to our home in Florida, sir."

Before Alex could fully complete his sentence, the judge asked, "What do you mean about this home in Florida? I see that car of yours has Wisconsin registration tags." The judge turned his head down to the desk and started studying the papers again. His fat fingers roughly pushed the papers around.

Alex knew he had to make his case short. It had to be polite and exactly on point. First, he explained his trip to Wisconsin, for his mother's funeral, then declared that it was his father's

216

pistol, with his father's service number engraved on it. He finished by saying he and Annie were married last week in Detroit and were on their way to his home in Florida.

In the next few minutes, the judge allowed Alex to present his father's dog tags, photograph of his father with the pistol on his belt, the estate papers, deeds and Will. The judge asked the sheriff to show him the revolver and verify Alex's serial number defense. He looked over the estate transfer documents and began to speak between heavy breaths, with a pause between every five words or so. "These papers show your story to be true as far as you explained it. Your mother's Will seems to be proper. You have the bill of sale and title for the automobile you purchased in Milwaukee. The money is from the old China, so-to-speak, like you said. The Smith and Wesson is a fine weapon and without a doubt, in my mind anyhow, it's your father's as you just testified. Your marriage certificate is a genuine document. You and your wife need to be on your way. You say you two are going to Florida. Where in Florida?"

"Santa Rosa County, sir. Near Pensacola, Your Honor, sir."

The judge looked over at Annie. She was trembling and looking straight ahead, her eyes focused on the far wall of the jailhouse.

Judge Bevins began, "Miss Dahl ... Missus Throckmorton ... do you want to go to your new home to Florida?"

Annie moved her eyes down from the wall and looked directly at the judge. She answered with her voice cracking, "Yes, sir, Your Honor, sir." Annie was still trembling. Judge Bevins noticed.

The judge looked at Annie closely, his eyes moving slowly up from her beige pumps to her messy curls. He gazed directly into her eyes. "Calm down, miss. Your eyes are bloodshot, young lady. You have been crying so much they look like roadmaps of this great state of Georgia. You got little red lines all over your eyeballs. You can stop your crying now, my dear. We're almost finished here."

217

He pounded a brawny fist on the desk. Annie jumped. The deputy and the sheriff as well, were surprised at the noise. Alex was watching the judge and saw it coming. The judge took a deep breath. He began speaking again in a deep and booming tone. "You are guilty of speeding at forty miles in a twenty-five mile-an-hour zone, boy. You are guilty of possession of an open liquor container in a motorized vehicle. And you are guilty of possession of an illegal concoction of moonshine alcohol. The fine for these offenses is fifty dollars, fifty dollars and fifty dollars, Mister Throckmorton."

The judge labored with his words and took another deep breath, "The Dillurd County Sheriff needed to have your motor vehicle towed and stored for another charge of fifty dollars. You understand that the towing and storage charge is a fee. It's not a fine."

There was another moment of silence and another deep breath before the judge continued. "Therefore, the total due the County of Dillurd, State of Georgia, this eighth day of June, nineteen-hundred and fifty-four is two-hundred dollars. You are to pay me directly, Mister Throckmorton, acting as an Officer of the Court. Are you able to pay me, son?"

"Yes, sir. Thank you, Your Honor, sir."

"Give this man and his wife their possessions, Sheriff Parker. We can get this over and done with. Young lady, Miss Maryanne, I want you to take yourself a seat and calm down. Deputy Barrett, bring this lady a chair."

In ten minutes, Alex had his wallet and satchel back in his custody. He packed the Smith and Wesson, his documents and the Yuan into the leather bag. He counted the cash in his wallet, and he was satisfied it was all there: two-thousand five-hundred from Oshkosh and perhaps a hundred more. Alex paid the two hundred dollars in fines and the judge scribbled a receipt for him. Annie had the paper bag with her things sitting at her feet. She sat with her legs held tightly together and hands on her knees. When the deputy carried Annie's purse and cosmetic bag over to her, she took them and placed them squarely on her lap. She didn't look up at the deputy, but paid full attention to Alex. The judge sat at the sheriff's desk and closely watched it all.

The sheriff lit a little cigar and blew the smoke in Alex's direction. "Your car is in storage two houses down on the right. It's in my driveway. If ya'll want it brought up here, it's another fifty dollars." His thick drawl had returned.

Alex felt the back of his neck prickle with nerve bumps, "We will walk down and get it, thank you, Sheriff."

Sheriff Henry Parker handed the keys to Alex. "Now, ya'll drive safe the rest of the way, hear?"

"Thank you, Sheriff. We will. Ready, Annie?"

Judge Oscar Bevins stood up, folded the one hundred and fifty dollars he received from Alex, stuffed it into his pant pocket and handed a fifty-dollar bill to Sheriff Parker. The quart jar of moonshine went in the outside pocket of Judge Bevins' topcoat. He bellowed, "I think I'm done here, Sheriff." Turning to Alex and Annie he said, "You folks have a good trip." He waddled and walked away as the words spilled out into the jailhouse. The jar of liquor bulged from his pocket and bounced with every step he took. Annie and Alex followed slowly behind him and didn't look back.

Neither the Sheriff nor the Deputy spoke. Annie felt goose bumps dancing down her arms and legs as she walked outside. The Packard was sitting about a half-mile down the road on the packed red clay and stone of the sheriff's front yard. They didn't utter one word as they walked to the car. The sun was shining warmly, yet Annie felt the skin crawl on the back of her head and neck as they approached the Packard. Alex held her hand.

When they got to the car, Alex unlocked the passenger door and helped Annie inside with her purse and the paper bag with her clothing items. He walked around to the trunk and put the satchel inside, removed the revolver from the satchel and packed it behind the spare tire where it had been. There were clothes strewn out of the suitcases and all over the interior of the trunk. The clothes that were hanging across the back seat were on the floor of the Packard; the twine clothesline had been broken. Alex closed the trunk lid in disgust, walked to the door and got inside. He looked over at Annie as she slid over to him. They held each other and Annie cried. Alex squeezed out a tear also.

"I'm sorry, Annie. I'm sorry this had to happen. God knows I'm sorry, Annie."

Her chest heaved as she sobbed. She sat back and looked at her husband. Thoughtfully and clearly, she spoke. "Alex, please drive carefully and slowly. Drive slowly and drive carefully, please. How much further is it to Florida, Alex?"

"About eighty miles. Two hours, maybe."

"Alex, let's get as far away from this God-forsaken place as we can. Then let's get something to eat other than a gosh darn Crisco-greasy fried bologna sandwich."

He gave his wife a little kiss on the cheek and started the Packard. Alex eased the Ultramatic into drive and they were on the highway again. To his relief there was no other vehicle behind him.

A few miles down the road, Alex shared a thought with his wife, "Annie, at least they didn't steal our money. The money out of my wallet and your purse, I mean. Sure, the fines were awfully hefty. But can you imagine if we still had that fifty thousand in the trunk? They would have locked us up for years. They stole our cigarettes and whiskey, but I'm pretty sure they left our money alone."

Annie was silent. She was watching the road ahead and leaning comfortably on her husband's shoulder. "Drive slowly and drive carefully, Alex." She shifted her hips on the seat and put her head against his shoulder.

# 7. FLORIDA

*I've Got The World On A String*

## Tuesday, June 8, US Route 23, Florida Stateline, Nassau County, Florida, 12:00 PM

Alex pressed his palm on the chrome bar of the steering wheel and held it down for about three seconds. The Packard's horn sounded, and he announced, "Were in Florida, Annie. Another forty-five minutes and we'll be in Jacksonville. Then we'll stop, get ourselves a warm, dry and clean hotel room, maybe right on the beach, what do you think about that?"

"Perfect," she said, "Just perfect. We are out of Georgia."

Alex slowed the car, spotting a *Conoco Gas* sign up the road. They were in Hilliard, Florida at the junction of County Road 108. The roadside advertisements and billboards touting beachfront hotels were everywhere. Alex wheeled the Packard into the service station at the intersection.

Annie spoke with urgency, "I'm going to the washroom, Alex. I haven't been since yesterday."

Alex parked away from the gas pumps and alongside the building. They got out of the car and went inside the station, where Annie stepped behind the short counter, hurriedly took the key from its hook, and exited again. Alex put a quarter in the cigarette machine and pulled the round handle under the column for Lucky Strike. The harsh mechanical sound of metal on metal and a loud clunk brought the pack dropping down onto the tray underneath. One more quarter, and he pulled out a pack of Chesterfield for Annie. He put his cigarettes in his shirt pocket, stuck the Chesterfields in his pants and waited for the attendant to come back inside.

Alex asked him, "My wife and I had a rough trip through Georgia, and we're looking for a top-notch hotel and restaurant nearby. We're wrung out like dirty dishcloths, and we need a decent hotel for at least one, maybe two nights. Any good ones nearby? One you would recommend?"

The attendant immediately reached under the counter and gave Alex a color brochure for the Atlantic Beach Hotel. "Top of the line hotel, mister. You can't get no better than this … drive down the County Road here no more than 20 miles and make a right on Fletcher. You can't miss it. It's right on the beach, right on Fernandina Beach. It's top-notch, like you want."

Annie came walking back inside, hung up the key, stood next to Alex and gazed down at the brochure. He handed it to her and said, "Take a look at this. I'm thinking we could go here and spend the night. We can check it out, anyhow." Annie stood close to her husband and gently pushed into him.

Alex continued, "Thanks buddy. Can you tell me if there is good dining around the place?"

The bell dinged as another car pulled in. Going out the door, the attendant looked over his shoulder and said, "Right there at the Atlantic, like I said, ain't none better around, mister."

Alex took his wife's hand, and walked to the car. After Annie got in, he walked around to the driver's side and handed a dollar to the attendant. "Thanks again, bud."

Once inside and behind the steering wheel, Annie slid over and held his arm. "Alex, I need things. Please, I need new under things. I cannot use any of the ones I have. I just can't. That creepy deputy touched everything I own. I would feel so dirty. And my clothes are dirty."

"When we get to the hotel, we'll get a room, then we'll grab something to eat, and go do some shopping. It's early. It's not quite noon."

In half an hour, they were in Fernandina Beach and sitting in front of the Atlantic Beach Resort Hotel. The valet parking attendant stood back from the door of the Packard and waited for Alex to exit. "Will you be checking in, sir?"

"Yes, we will." Alex got out and handed him the keys, offered his arm to Annie and they walked toward the large glass and aluminum doors into the lobby. He felt emotionally spent and physically tired. Annie walked slowly and gingerly on weak knees. Alex spoke softly to his wife on the way inside. "I need a shave, and both of us are wearing wrinkled, dirty clothes. But stay proud, Annie girl. Stay proud and smile. Hold your head high, Annie. Keep your pride."

She looked up at her husband and smiled. His reassuring voice put life back into her soul. "You're beautiful, Annie. You're brave and you're beautiful. Don't forget it, Annie. I'm proud of you, Annie girl." At the reception desk, she stood close and leaned against him.

Alex checked in and paid for two nights. He requested a room at beach level and on the beach side. There was a suite available with two full size beds, a kitchenette, bath with separate shower and a wet bar. After the experience they just had, he felt he owed this to his wife.

The desk clerk asked, "How much luggage needs to be brought into the Atlantic, sir?"

Alex said there were three bags and paused a moment. He then clarified his statement further. He explained that the contents of all the bags were, in fact, loose in the trunk, "Thanks to the professional efforts of the Dillurd County, Georgia, Sheriff and his loyal deputy."

The clerk looked surprised and perplexed. He graciously nodded and told Alex all the items would be brought to their room. Alex instructed the clerk that extra care was required for the leather satchel. The desk clerk handed the room key to Alex, nodded again and said, "Enjoy your stay here at the Atlantic, Mister and Missus Throckmorton. If you need anything at all, we are here to make your stay as enjoyable as possible."

Alex thanked the young man as he and Annie walked down the hall to Suite 141. Alex opened the door and stepped aside. Annie gave her husband a little kiss on the lips, walked inside and disappeared into the bath.

Alex surveyed the room. There was a Danish modern console television in the center of a seating group upholstered in turquoise *Naugahyde*. He gazed out toward the white sands of the beach and the low, breaking surf of the Atlantic Ocean. He stood looking at the azure, blue sky and gently breaking waves. He could hear the bath water running and pictured Annie lying back in the tub. The floors were thick, plush blonde carpeting and marble tile. Mirrors were on the ocean-facing wall, opposite large vertical blinds hung across multiple sets of sliding glass doors that opened to the beach. Three polished aluminum seagulls in flight were the artwork hanging on the far wall, with a large gold sunburst clock next to them. Alex found the bar. There were fifths of scotch, bourbon, gin and one bottle each of Sauvignon Blanc and Sherry. He smiled as he turned the Sauvignon, reading the label and knew that Annie would smile too. The refrigerator under the bar was the smallest he ever saw. Packed inside were quart bottles of tonic, soda, *7 Up*, six bottles of *Budweiser* and two small, covered plastic containers with green olives and maraschino cherries. The countertop and four bar stools were a subtle shade of flamingo pink. Alex opened the bourbon and poured himself two fingers. He walked back and sat on the sofa, facing the ocean. There was a knock on the door.

He set his glass down on the cocktail table, walked to the door, and opened it for two bellhops. They entered with a luggage cart loaded with the three suitcases from the Packard, his shaving kit, Annie's cosmetic case, overnight bag and the leather satchel. Alex directed them toward one of the two beds. They also carried a paper sack with the hotel's crest. The young men set all the items gently down on the bed. Alex handed the men a five-dollar bill and thanked them. They were not yet out the door when Alex started to open the suitcases. He discovered all the clothes folded and neatly packed inside. They were mixed up, wrinkled and miss-matched, but folded and neat, nonetheless. "Amazing," Alex muttered. Inside the paper bag were the two remaining bottles of Blatz he bought a week ago in Appleton. The Smith and Wesson, holster and belt were packed in his suitcase of clothes, on top. He walked back to the sofa and his bourbon. There was a sound of a muted electric motor coming from the bath. He suspected it was a hairdryer.

A quarter of an hour went by, and Annie came out wearing a sea-green pile robe and slippers. "Alex, they have an electric hand-held hair dryer in there. It's fabulous. All kinds of bath oil, soaps and skin cream. It's fantastic." She was walking toward her husband while she pushed and fluffed her hair upwards. Annie spotted the open suitcases and changed direction to the bed. "Oh, our things are here. And, my goodness, they got them all folded." Annie started looking through the bags and said, "I think I'll dig out my grey herringbone shorts and that calico shirt I bought back in Asheville. I'll wear those. I haven't worn those yet and I didn't see that Deputy Kenny guy touching and feeling all over them."

"You get yourself set there, Annie and when you're done, I'll go shave and shower."

She sprung over to her husband and kissed him on the lips and remarked, "This place is perfect. This must be how the Ritz is!"

She grabbed her things in one swipe and went into the bathroom. Alex walked back to the seating group, reached into his shirt pocket and pulled out his cigarettes. He finished his smoke and bourbon while watching the gentle waves breaking on the beach.

Annie stood between the beds in front of the large, mirrored wall in her new shorts and blouse. She was refreshed and her spirits lifted after her hot bath and a change of clothes. The Georgia nightmare was over, and the depression and melancholy of the past night vanished. "You look beautiful, Annie girl."

Annie finished her mascara, rouge, powder and put on her lipstick. She pursed her lips together and looked into the mirror

225

at her husband. "I'm feeling much better … still tired, but much, much better." Annie snapped on her pearl earrings. Alex stood looking through the suitcases. He was pushing things to the side and moving items in and out. He pulled out a pair of socks, slacks and a shirt. He laid them on the bed and said, "After I shave and shower, we can go get something to eat. I just picked out my cleanest dirty shirt."

*Anytime*

## Tuesday, June 8, South Fletcher Ave., Fernandina, Florida, 2:10 PM

Alex tucked his shirt into his slacks and walked to the nightstand between the beds. He picked up the telephone and dialed *"0"*. "This is Throckmorton in 141. Could you please send someone to pick up some laundry?" He paused, waiting for the response. "Yes, three suitcases worth. All of it." There was a slight pause and Alex added, "Thank you."

"They do that, Alex? They do your laundry here?"

"They said they were happy to help. That's a good deal. While I was in the shower, I wondered about it. And that's just great … we'll have clean clothes to wear."

Annie was sitting on the edge of the bed with her hands folded on her lap. "Alex, I'm not going to keep my under things. Undies, bras, garters, stockings. All of it. I'm throwing them all away. I told you that creepy deputy touched and fingered and felt my things, and I won't wear them. No way can I wear any of those things again. I think he was drooling."

Alex walked to his wife and sat down next to her. "Fine, Annie. We'll throw them all out right now. We'll throw out anything you cannot wear." They stood by the bed and made quick work of it. It all went into the trashcan by the bar.

In a matter of minutes, there was a knock on the door. A bellhop maneuvered a wheeled canvas laundry hamper across

226

the carpeted floor. The young man promised the laundry would return sorted, laundered, or dry-cleaned. As he was pushing the hamper back out, Alex gave him the trashcan, "And all these go in the garbage, okay?"

There was a firm "Yes, sir," and the bellboy, trash and hamper were gone. Annie picked up her purse and they started toward the door. They walked hand-in-hand down the carpeted hall to the entrance leading out to the beach boardwalk. The plantings around the Atlantic Hotel included palmetto and date palms with tall arching fronds. Along the edge of the beach were canvas and wooden slat chairs and colorful covered gazebos. A brightly painted sign hung over the boardwalk entrance and introduced *The Atlantic Beach Café & Bar.* It stood as a colorful beachside attraction. Woven wood latticework walls and large ceiling fans gave the outdoor eatery a distinct Florida feel with a direct connection to the beach. Planter boxes full of colorful tuberous begonias and ornamental grasses lined the walkways. The cafe was crowded with customers of all ages, couples and singles. A combination of wrought iron and wicker furnishings on weathered grey wood decking gave the place an unmistakable ocean-side feel. They sat at the beach entrance side of the cafe at a small glass-topped round table. It was to be something new and different for lunch. They decided to again try different tastes and experience as many new things as they could. They ordered piña coladas with their black beans, fried plantains and tuna steak. When Alex explained plantains to Annie, she decided without reluctance to try them. "Wait until I tell Beth that I had fried bananas! And I had tuna fish that didn't come out of a can! She will not believe it!"

Alex got serious and took Annie by the hand. "It's our anniversary, Missus Throckmorton. It was just about this time last week that we became husband and wife. And it was two weeks ago when I first met you, and I knew then, I knew that I wanted you to become my wife. I will never, ever, forget that evening when I walked into the diner. I fell head over heels in love with the most beautiful woman in the world right there in Appleton, Wisconsin. Happy Anniversary, Annie. I love you. I love you with all my soul."

"And I can truly say I fell in love that night too, Alex. When I got home from work that night, I told Beth that I had just met someone pretty darn special. I was right. I hoped you would ask me to go away with you right then and there. I think I would have. But, as it worked out, everything fell into place pretty darn nice. And other than yesterday, it has been the best couple of weeks in my life." Annie lifted her glass and clicked it against Alex's, "And I love you."

"After lunch we can go shopping and get those personal things you talked about earlier, okay?"

"That sounds good. And then I'm going to take a nap."

## Good Rockin' Tonight

### Tuesday, June 8, The Atlantic Beach Resort Hotel, South Fletcher Ave., Fernandina, Florida, 3:40 PM

Alex stood with his wife at the curbside under the hotel canopy. The parking valet drove the Packard around the circle and parked at the couple's feet. As he exited the car, he gave them a tip of his hat and chimed, "Have a great afternoon, sir," as Annie got in.

Alex sat behind the wheel and slowly ran his hand over the dashboard and steering wheel. His eyes glanced over the car's interior. "My goodness. Holy cow. This car is exactly as it was the day I drove it out of the dealership back in Milwaukee. It's in perfect showroom condition. This is remarkable. It even smells new. They did an incredible job on this car." He put the Patrician 400 in gear and slowly drove around the circular drive to the service road. He put the transmission in park at looked over to his wife. Alex was just as impressed as Annie was with Atlantic Hotel's level of service. Neither of them was accustomed to such amenities. Although they checked in only hours ago, the Packard was thoroughly clean inside and out. The service at the hotel was above and beyond what either of them had expected. There was quite a stark difference between the accommodations of the Dillurd County jailhouse and the Atlantic Hotel. They relished the much-needed change of circumstance.

"This is amazing, Alex. How much do you think this is going to cost?"

"I would guess the car service is part of the room rate, Annie, like the bellhops and room service are. Those fellows generally work for their tips. All in all, this place is only about five dollars more per day than the Hillside back in Asheville. And besides, this is our honeymoon, Annie. And we have a bank account in Pensacola full with a boat-load of money the Old Man brought back from Indochina." He playfully looked over the top of his grey aviators at his wife.

Alex relaxed behind the wheel and ran his hand over the dashboard and steering wheel one more time. He muttered, "Remarkable," and put the car in gear. He drove to the street and teased his wife, "Let's go find a ladies' apparel store that will take our money." He joked, "Maybe we can convince them to take some of our Chinese cash."

Annie knew he was kidding, but she thought she would give him a warning anyway, "Don't you even think about it, mister!"

Alex pulled the Packard to the curb on Atlantic Avenue and 14th Street. The entire block consisted of clothing, dry goods, variety and souvenir storefronts. Cafes, newsstands and restaurants were stuck in between. It was a busy scene with shoppers and tourists. Annie shopped for and purchased, without any hesitation, all of her intimate items and four new pair of stockings. They walked down the street close to one another, holding hands. Annie occasionally gave her husband one of her sideways hip bumps.

They slowly walked past a Kodak film and camera storefront. The photographs on display in the window caught their attention. They immediately decided to get their portrait taken for themselves and a copy each for Annie's mother and sister. The photographer assured them that the portrait would be ready by noon on Wednesday. Annie joked with Alex and the photographer and said she would be perfectly content with a week-old wedding-day portrait.

Before they returned to the hotel, Alex talked his wife into a pair of sunglasses without too much trouble. Walking into the *Walgreen's* drug store, he told her, "There are a few items that are required accessories in Florida, Annie: sandals, shorts, sunglasses and suntan oil."

Inside Walgreen's, Annie quickly picked up a pair of *Foster Grants* with bright white frames. "We'll get the other three things tomorrow, Alex. I want to go back to the room and lie down." With fifty steps down the sidewalk and a turn of the ignition key, they were on their way. In a mere six minutes, Alex was once again handing his car keys to the parking valet of the Atlantic Hotel.

*Mister Sandman*

**Tuesday, June 8, The Atlantic Beach Resort Hotel, South Fletcher Ave., Fernandina, Florida, 8:00 PM**

Annie opened her eyes and moved her head about on the plush pillows of the bed. The clean, fresh sheets surrounded her nude form like a luxurious, weightless, white cottony cloud. The room was larger than she remembered, and the ocean appeared to be closer. The skies outside were darkening with the oncoming sunset, with subtle brushstrokes of pink, yellow, and carmine over shades of blue. She felt as safe and secure as she ever was in her life. She was gratified. Her husband was between her and the multiple sliding glass doors

230

to the beach. He was sitting comfortably in an armchair inside the lounge area, with his head relaxed downward and into his chest. He was snoring ever so softly, stretched out in his stocking feet in front of the television. *The Red Skelton Show* had just started. She smiled to herself, satisfied with the knowledge that her situation in life was about as perfect as it could get. Yesterday's nightmare was over, and Annie had that memory tightly wrapped and put away. Two weeks ago, Alex walked into her life and ordered breaded pork chops. The food and service must have been excellent. He came back.

The phone rang on the bedside table. It was enough to wake Alex; he turned and watched as his wife answered it. Sitting upright and rubbing the sand from his eyes, "Who was that, Annie?"

"That was the front desk. They are bringing up most of our clothes, for goodness' sake. This place is simply unbelievable." Annie shook her head in disbelief. She sat on the bedside looking over to her husband. "I'll get dressed." There was a knock at the door. Annie sprang to the bathroom, pulling a sheet from the bed and wrapping it around herself.

A bellhop stood at the door with a wheeled clothes rack. Dresses, skirts, blouses, shirts, slacks and trousers were all on wire hangers draped with paper-sleeved, clear plastic covers.

A little extra effort was required over the carpeting. Alex pulled and the young man pushed. They stopped at the bed. "These have been laundered and pressed for you, Sir. Some of your items required dry cleaning, not just laundry and they will be ready tomorrow by noon."

Alex reached into his trousers, gave the fellow a handful of silver, and said, "Thank you, thank you so very much. This hotel has been so helpful to us. We really appreciate it.

Alex shut the door behind the young man and turned to see his wife peering from the bathroom.

"Is he gone, Alex?" Her husband nodded. He was pushing and sliding the clothes up and down the rack, looking them over. There was a cardboard bin on the bottom of the portable wardrobe with folded small items. Inside were Alex's t-shirts, boxers and all their bundled socks wrapped in paper bands. Annie was pushing through the clothes also and found her uniform from Maxine's diner. "Look at this, Alex. This thing is starched and ironed. I have never worn such a snappy uniform. If Maxine could see this, she would be totally flummoxed. This dress looks darn snappy all washed and pressed professional."

Alex looked at his wife and walked toward her. "Well, if you did wear such a snappy uniform back at Maxine's, maybe you could have snagged a much snappier husband, Annie girl," he teased. "Did you have a good rest?"

"Yes. Yes, I did. I needed it, Alex."

"How about we order sandwiches or something light from room service? We can sit and watch the television and chat. You know, a quiet evening?"

Annie thought a minute and answered, "I would prefer going down to the dining room for a short while. I cannot think of having a sandwich now. Sandwiches and especially greasy fried bologna sandwiches are certainly not going to be on any plate of mine for quite a while."

Alex agreed and acknowledged that his wife correctly selected the dining room as the preferable alternative to a room service sandwich. They discovered a snack bar and soda fountain right off the lobby, so things worked out well. It was late and the dining room could wait until tomorrow. A white paper sack with take-out fried chicken, gravy, biscuits and French fries was the perfect solution. It was almost like their picnic at Peabody Park back in Appleton. They went back to their room and got comfortable on the long turquoise sofa that was tucked between the chairs. Their carryout went on the coffee table, and they tuned in *The United States Steel Hour*. It was only the second time they sat together in front of a television set. Despite its novelty, the television did not completely draw their attention away from each other.

He began to describe his place in Santa Rosa County, telling Annie about his partner and neighbor's wife, Hedy. "She's a German woman whose proper name is Hedwig. I'm positive you will like her. Louis met her while he was stationed in Stuttgart, Germany. They were married and well, you know the rest." Talking about them led Alex to think about calling his friend tomorrow. He wanted to check on things again, anyway. He also needed to give Louis an update on his expected day of his arrival back in Pensacola. Alex explained to Annie how he first met Louis outside the Navy base at the engine shop. He and Louis immediately hit it off and they became close friends. It was with Louis' prodding and encouragement that he bought the small ranch in Santa Rosa County. He discovered a new sense of independence after he purchased the farm. There was a drive ignited within him, a desire to succeed. A need to prosper on his own, with his own sweat and physical labor, was pushing him on.

With his newly uncovered desire to make good and the help of his new friend, he was on his way to a new way of life. It took Alex a full week to rebuild the engine of an old Ford 9N tractor left out in a grassland pasture to rust. With another week's labor on the transmission, he had the most important implement on his new property running as new. It was running as well as it did back in 1942. The Ford was another victim of war; a mechanical casualty, the old grey tractor was a rusty relic whose owner left to fight in a distant conflict and never returned.

"And now you want to start raising horses, Alex?"

"I have started. It all starts with one. Soon I need to find a brood mare for Sebastian. I will be looking for a quarter horse with strong lines. I have a strong sense of peace when I'm around Sebastian." He got up, walked to the dresser and brought back a piece of writing paper and a ballpoint pen. He set both on the coffee table in front of him. The Atlantic Hotel logo was prominent on both. Alex reached over and held his wife's knee as he went on, "There's something about a horse,

Annie. I have a deep appreciation for those beautiful animals. I believe I discovered my life's purpose walking on four strong legs and eating grass in Florida."

He grinned and looked into Annie's eyes. "And I found my life's passion walking on two great-looking legs and serving coffee in Wisconsin."

They shared a laugh.

He picked up the pen and began drawing little squares and lines on the sheet of paper. "Here's how my little farm is laid out, Annie. The main house there, barn, hay barn, and the driveway trails over here and through it all. And out here, about a thousand feet from the house, is Chumuckla Highway. That's the road out to the rest of the world. And it's the road into my part of the world."

Annie mused, "*Chumuckla*. That sounds like something my grandfather Papa Dahl would say in Norwegian. My dad would talk in Norwegian too, when he cussed or got real upset. His favorite expression was *Uff Da*, and when I asked him what that meant, he said, *'whatever you want it to mean'* and just kept on talking. As it turned out, he was right. It can mean whatever you want. I asked Deacon Wilkerson and that's what he said, too. It's a Norwegian one-size-fits-all expression."

It was ten o'clock and *Life With Father* came on the television. They were not paying much attention to the shows and Alex turned the set off. The conversation continued back and forth. Annie was curious as to why Alex's strong hands didn't have the telltale black mechanic's dirt worn into them.

"Well, I use *Babo* cleanser when I clean up. I've always used it, and with the help of an old shoe brush around my fingernails, they stay clean. It takes a little work, that's all."

Annie nodded and didn't mention Jimmy Malone's dirty hands. She decided to keep that to herself. He was over a thousand miles and a lifetime behind. She was content with the knowledge that her husband would at least make an effort to keep his hands clean. "Keep them clean, Alex," she said.

They sat close to one another. His conversation drifted back to those nights about two weeks ago in Appleton, right off US Routes 10 and 41.

Alex tried his best to tell Annie how he felt when he first laid eyes on her. He explained he had a sense of expectation when he first saw her; like looking for the prize in a box of *Cracker Jacks*. Annie quickly caught that fastball, sat up in the sofa and looked Alex straight in the eye. He knew Annie was having fun, but thought he would play along, "Did I say something wrong?"

"Well, Mister Alex, I do not think it's fair to compare me to some plastic Cracker Jack toy. I mean: all wrapped up in a little envelope and jammed into a box of candied popcorn."

He teased her right back. "I'm sorry. And I see where this is going. Are you trying to tell me that you don't mind me playing with my toys as long as my hands are clean?"

"Yes ... That's exactly what I'm saying."


*Cuban Pete*

**Wednesday, June 9, The Atlantic Beach Resort Hotel, South Fletcher Ave., Fernandina, Florida, 7:25 AM**

The morning sun was flooding through the large windows. Dancing flecks of sparkling sunlight bounced off the sand. Annie could hear the breaking Atlantic surf. She opened her eyes and looked across the pillow to her husband. "You were snoring last night, Alex."

He tried to explain, "That was not snoring, Annie. Those were the gentle growls of desire." He smiled, playfully put a leg over hers and kissed her before his suggestion, "How about we get some breakfast and go find 537 Corinth Street?"

Annie was in and out of the bathroom as Alex shaved. She got dressed into her slimming green skirt, frilly blouse and little black neck scarf. Annie was sitting by the dresser putting the finishing coat of red lacquer on her nails, covering the coral pink of Asheville. She sat blowing on her hands and turned her head sideways to look at her husband. "We might as well see if there is a restaurant open for breakfast near Corinth Street, right?"

"That sounds good, I think we are about a half hour away from Jacksonville." Alex stepped into his loafers and watched Annie sitting on the chair, legs crossed. He noticed she was sliding on a pair of patent leather black heels. "This is the first I've seen you wearing those."

"I bought these in Appleton before we went to Babe's." She stood by the mirrored wall checking the seam at the back of her hose and the shine of her shoes. Annie changed the direction of the conversation, "Today should be the day we finally fit the last pieces of the puzzle together, Alex. And I have been thinking about calling Mama and Beth today, too. I should let them know we are safe and finally in Florida." She turned and looked away from the mirror. She stood with a hand on her hip and gave her attention to Alex. "But I'm not going to say a word to Mama or Beth about our night in Georgia. Do you realize that was our most expensive motel room if you look at it that way? Two hundred bucks; I mean, we spent good money for that live-audience-participation horror theatre. Maybe it was not actually a horror show, but I sure didn't enjoy one bit of that presentation. I will never forget what happened to us in Georgia. You know, it seems like you always remember the bad people you meet and the bad things you experience. And that is a stinking, rotten shame."

Alex picked up his wife's handbag and handed it to her, "But I think we are making a helluva lot of good memories, too." They started out of the room and down the hall to the lobby. Alex continued, "And take a look at all the excitement we are having. I mean, it's like we're on a treasure hunt or something. We have been uncovering all kinds of fascinating little tidbits along the way. And we've had a good deal of fun traveling down this Hillbilly Highway, too."

Annie shrugged her shoulders. "Maybe someday we will be able to laugh about Wrightown, Georgia. Maybe someday we will."

Outside on the semi-circle driveway, the valet parked the Packard at the curb and tipped his red pillbox hat to Annie and Alex. He watched from the rear of the car as the hemline of Annie's skirt crept upward when she slid into the front seat. The pronounced bongo beat and Caribbean sound of Desi Arnaz's *Cuban Pete* was pouring out of the car radio. "What in the world is that about? Chic-chicky-boom-chic-chicky-boom?"

"That was *I Love Lucy's* TV husband, you know, Desi, that Cuban band leader. And this is Florida. This is definitely not the last time you will hear Spanish, Annie. Or chic-chicky-boom, for that matter." Alex drove right along the coastal road toward Jacksonville. Once he was in the city itself, he pulled into a Mobilgas, had the Packard fueled, windows wiped, and oil checked. They discovered that Corinth Street was about ten blocks away. Alex was curiously intrigued when the gas jockey told him that Corinth Street was a few blocks west of the Jacksonville Naval Air Station. When they were on their way again, Annie took a deep breath and looked over to her husband. "We are getting close, Mister Alex. We are getting close."

Corinth Street was a mixture of storefronts and vacant buildings. Looking for street numbers was no easy task. Most places, on both sides of the street, had none whatsoever. After elimination, they could only assume that number 537 was sitting between a vacant storefront and a butcher shop. Alex parked on the street directly in front of it.

537 Corinth Street was home to *Fernando's Havana Hideaway*. It was a lengthy sign, neatly painted all along the front of the building, just above the windows, in large red letters. Six floodlights with formed, bent necks stood above the lettering. An arching palm tree decorated each end of the sign. Unlit neon beer signs were in each of the four yellow-tint

237

windows and a small menu was thumb-tacked to the wall by the door. Cigarette butts littered the sidewalk and gutter. "It's a bar, Alex. That's what this is ... a bar!"

"And it doesn't seem to be open. Let's take a closer look." They hurried to get out and onto the sidewalk. At the door, Alex tried the knob. It didn't turn. They looked through the windows and into the dark interior. A sign on the door read: *Open Monday thru Saturday 1 - 12mid.*

Alex and Annie looked at each other with disappointment; like two kids who got only underwear and socks from Santa. "Looks like we will be coming back later, Annie. We can grab breakfast and go pick up our portrait. We can even make our telephone calls and come back, that's all." They felt disappointment as they walked back to the Patrician.

Annie knew better, but decided to tease her husband a little anyway, "We could easily say the heck with it, Alex, and simply let the sleeping dog lie and just walk away."

He started the car and shook his head. "I don't think so. We need to find out what's *inside* that bar."

The remaining hours of the morning dragged by. They forced themselves into working hard at being busy. Alex told his wife, "We are killing ourselves just killing time, Annie."

They fit in a brunch buffet at the hotel restaurant and returned to Room 141 to make their telephone calls. Alex let his friend and neighbor Louis know that they should be back in Santa Rosa County by Saturday. Annie was not able to get an answer at her mother's number in Vermont, but she did connect with Beth in Appleton. She had fun with her sister and told her about everything from the fried plantains and tuna steak to the bellhops and their red pillbox hats. Beth had told her some good news: Laura Wilkerson was moving in as her roommate. Annie welcomed that piece of news. When she left Appleton, she knew Beth would get along fine without her, but it was calming to know Beth would not be alone in the apartment.

After she ended the telephone call, Annie felt an odd sense of relief at the inability to complete the other telephone call to Vermont. Her day was going so well. It would have been a shame to topple her apple cart.

About half past noon, they left the hotel and drove back to the photographer on Atlantic Avenue and 14th Street to pick up their portraits. They were extremely pleased with the result. When they were back out on the sidewalk, Alex reminded Annie about the sandals she could enjoy. He explained, "Now that you are a bona-fide resident of Florida, owning a pair of sandals is an absolute requirement." No extra persuasion was required before his wife made that purchase. Annie rarely turned down an opportunity to visit a shoe store.

The time finally came for them to proceed to Corinth Street once again. After they settled into the front seat of the Packard, With the turn of the key, the big engine rumbled to life. They turned and looked at one another. Annie smiled. Alex put the car in gear.


*Come On-a My House*

**Wednesday, June 9, 537 Corinth Street, Jacksonville, Florida, 1:20 PM**

Alex was able to park directly in front of Fernando's again. A brick was propped against the front door, holding it open. The neon signs were on, brandishing *Viking, Falstaff, Miller High Life,* and *Pabst Blue Ribbon.* As Alex turned the car off, Annie looked over to her husband, and asked, "Are we ready for this?"

"I think we are. It's been a week since we looked at those beer coasters. It's time to put the last question to bed."

They walked slowly inside and studied their surroundings as they went. It certainly was a bar in every sense of the word. The heels of Annie's patent leather pumps clicked across the tile floor. Long, dark, polished wood planks went the length of the room. Five square tables, each with four chairs, lined the opposite wall. Three men at the bar turned and watched Annie and Alex walk in. They were sitting with their hands around glasses of beer and looked as if they were a permanent fixture, like mannequins in a store window. A *Brunswick* coin-operated bowling machine was in the far corner with its bright lights flashing away at random. A large ceiling fan churned the thick smell of stale beer, cigarettes, and *Spic and Span*.

"Let's sit right at the bar, Annie."

His wife answered him softly as they approached, "Okey dokey." Annie carefully maneuvered her hips, thighs and taut pencil skirt onto the barstool. She sat gracefully with her heels hanging on the chair rails. Annie flicked her curls off her shoulders and kept her white framed Ray-Bans on. With her arms and elbows on the bar, Annie looked down to the men seated at the other end. She smiled, "A beer's good."

Alex loosened his tie, pulled off his sunglasses and dropped his hat on the bar. "We've been waiting for this moment. It has all built up to this."

"Yes, it has."

Around the corner, out from a narrow door at the end of the bar, came a tall, gorgeous, bronze-skinned woman. She had coal black hair, red lips, polished ruby red nails, and was wearing a brown skirt, three-inch red heels, and a white blouse. She reached under the bar and brought out two coasters and two little napkins.

She looked to Alex, and asked, "Hello, there. Are we having lunch today?" She spoke with a thick, heavy Latin accent and appeared to be about the same age as Alex and Annie.

"What do you think, Annie? Anything to eat?"

"A beer and pretzels or potato chips are fine. I'm not hungry."

Alex looked around for beer signage and spotted one for a local Pensacola brew. "Bring a couple of Viking lagers, please, and a bag of chips, or pretzels, or peanuts. Thanks."

"All right, two Vikings and a bowl of pretzels coming up." She walked toward the far end of the bar to the half-round glass door of a *Bevador* beer cooler, reached inside and turned the Lazy-Susan shelf to the Vikings.

Along the mirrored wall behind the bar, there were two-gallon jars of pickled eggs, pigs feet, and sausage at the far end of the rows of liquor bottles. Little foil packs of *Alka Seltzer* hung from a cardboard cutout of the company mascot, *Speedy*. Wire racks with red pistachios and little bags of Spanish peanuts stood tucked next to the large brass, mechanical *National* cash register. Annie watched the barmaid closely as she came back with both bottles in one hand. She turned, grabbed a wooden bowl off a small stack and shoved it into a large cardboard box of pretzel sticks. As she placed the bottles and bowl down on the bar she said, "There you go, folks. I'll get you a glass, Miss. Anything else?"

"Thanks, I don't need a glass, I'm fine," Annie replied.

"I think we're good for now, thanks." Alex picked up his bottle and took a swallow.

Annie had a flash of thought and did not want the barmaid to walk away. She quickly decided to take the conversation down a new road. "I see this bar is called the *Havana Hideaway*. Are you Cuban, like that Ricky Ricardo fellow, Desi whats-his-name?" Alex looked over to his wife. He was surprised and amused. Annie was being Annie. He had realized what she was doing and wondered why he didn't think of it.

The barmaid replied, "*Si*. I came to United States when I was ten years old with *mi madre* and *pappa*. My pappa, he's Fernando, he owns this bar. But he's getting much older now and doesn't work the bar much anymore. We live upstairs. I run it mostly by myself and with some help from my very close friend, my darling man, *mi hombre querido*. And *mi madre*, my mother, she helps with the food."

Annie nodded and took a drink of beer. "That is a delightful story. You have a nice place here."

The barmaid nodded, "*Si, gracias*. Thank you." She walked away. Annie and Alex exchanged glances.

"Well, Alex, what do you think? Are you thinking what I'm thinking?"

"I don't believe it. I'm not sure, but there is definitely, most definitely, something going on here. I'm going to call her back here." Alex raised his voice a notch and motioned to her, "Can I get a shot of Jim Beam, please?" He reached into his shirt pocket and brought out his pack of cigarettes and book of matches. In one smooth motion, he lit a Lucky.

Annie and Alex were nibbling on the pretzels as she brought the bourbon.

"What's your name?" Annie complimented, "You look so beautiful."

"Oh, no. I am not so beautiful." She was being overly modest and flushed with the flattery. She was indeed a beauty. "But, *gracias*. It's just the dim light in here, that's all. My name is Jovita. Jovita Maria Vasquello. They call me *Joey* for short."

For a split second, the world stood still. The bar and everyone in it stood locked in time. There was not a sound anywhere else in the universe. Annie and Alex realized what just happened. Alex took a deep breath. Annie was the first to escape the vacuum. She picked up the conversation anew.

"That's cute," Annie said, "That's a cute nickname: *Joey*." She lowered her head a little and looked over the top of her sunglasses at her husband. Alex was looking straight across the bar at the Latin beauty. He downed the shot of Beam, put it back on the bar with a tap and wiped the back of his hand across his lips.

Alex picked up his cigarette from the ashtray, took a puff and flicked the ashes. He slowly exhaled the smoke from the corner of his mouth, and asked, "Have you ever been to Chicago, Joey? It sounds to me that there is a touch of Chicago in your accent."

Joey took the bait; she was hooked. She played with the bar rag hanging at her waist and looked puzzled, gazing back and forth at them. "Yes, seven or eight, maybe nine, years ago. I was going to the University of Illinois at Chicago. It didn't do me too much good, did it? I mean ... here I am working in a bar. Being a barmaid isn't exactly what you would expect out of a college education is it?" She leaned a hand on the bar and stood directly in front of them. "But wait a minute. You and your lady don't know me from Chicago. I don't remember you. I went to university, and I worked a bar job at night. How do you know about me and my accent?" Alex took a swallow of lager and Annie did the same.

Alex was direct, "Joey, did you know a man by the name of Nicholas Throckmorton back in Chicago?" Annie reached into her purse and pulled out her pack of Chesterfields. She kept her eyes on the barmaid.

Jovita's eyes grew wide with surprise. "*Si*. Yes, that's my Nicky. He is my man. He lives upstairs here and helps around the place when he is not out of town or out of the country. He was an Army pilot in the war and now he is a salesman for a large airplane company. Either *Boeing* or *Lockheed*, I'm not sure, it does not matter. He does work for them and travels to different places. You know him?"

Annie was holding her Ronson to her cigarette as she spoke. "Is Nicholas here now?" The Chesterfield moved with her red lips.

The barmaid looked nervous, not threatened, but curiously nervous. "No, he is out of the country on business now, in Panama. He has been gone a month already. He usually comes back every few weeks, but sometimes he stays away longer. There was one time last year, he was in my home country, Cuba, for two months: June and July. He was lucky and got the chance to meet our new national patriot, Fidel, who is fighting for our freedom."

Alex asked, "He must sell a lot of airplanes or airplane parts, to Panama and Cuba, then?"

"I don't exactly know. He goes away and comes back. He sells things, not just airplanes. That is all I know. It's not my business and he does not talk about it. What is this all about, then? Why do you ask so many questions?" She was still tugging nervously at the bar rag hanging from her apron.

Alex asked, "Do you have a pen handy, Joey? I need to borrow your pen."

Joey reached into her pocket and handed a gold-tone *Papermate* ballpoint to Alex. Annie took another swallow of beer and started watching her husband intently. She wondered where all this would end and how much the cornbread would crumble before it was all over. Annie drew on the cigarette, watching every move her husband made and all the curiosity and bewilderment of Joey's expression.

Alex started writing on the back of his Pabst Blue Ribbon beer coaster. He wrote: *Alex. RD 2, Chumuckla Hwy, Pensacola, Fla.* With a sigh and a nod, Annie exhaled a cloud of smoke.

"Joey, the next time you see Nicholas, give this to him," Alex spoke as he pushed the coaster across the bar to Jovita. He laid a five-dollar bill down, got up and offered his hand to Annie. She gingerly slid sideways off the barstool. The barmaid was watching them intently and didn't understand what was happening. "Thanks for the beer and pretzels, Joey." He put on his aviators and fedora and gave Annie his arm; ready to leave. "Let's go home. Now we know. It's time for us to go home, Annie girl."

Joey looked at the coaster, and back up to Alex and Annie. They were on their way out the door. Annie's heels clicked on the tile floor as she swayed her form and walked toward the door. Alex walked alongside his wife, his arm around her and his hand resting on the side of her hip. Two of the three men at the far end of the bar watched as Annie and Alex exited. The third was still staring into his beer. The barmaid had her eyes locked on the young couple walking out the door.

Outside, Alex stood next to the car and held Annie. He kissed his wife briefly and paused. He gazed into her green eyes and had a thought.

"Your birthday is next month, isn't it, Annie? What would you like?" He spoke as he opened the passenger door for her.

Annie sat inside the Patrician, with one foot on the curb. She looked up at her husband and said, "I love you, Alex. And for my birthday, I want what every little girl wants. A pony. But a brood mare will do just perfectly."

She had that smile. She shifted her hips and settled herself into the cream Packard.

Two men in blue denim coveralls walked along the sidewalk and past the Packard.

Back inside the Hideaway, Joey was fingering the coaster. She looked down at it one more time and suddenly realized aloud, "*Mi dios.* That was Alexander." She reached out and steadied herself, holding onto the bar with her free hand.

## *(Fade to black.)*

The story continues with:

# The Katydid Effect

# THE CHAPTER MUSIC

| | |
|---|---|
| Falling In Love Again | Marlene Dietrich |
| Shake, Rattle, and Roll | Big Joe Turner |
| Secret Love | Doris Day |
| 'Till I Waltz Again With You | Teresa Brewer |
| Goodnight, Irene | Les Paul, Mary Ford |
| Don't Let The Stars Get In Your Eyes | Perry Como |
| Let's Go Steady | Davis Sisters |
| Don't Sit Under The Apple Tree | Andrews Sisters |
| You Belong To Me | Jo Stafford |
| Heart And Soul | The Four Aces |
| I Still Get A Thrill | Joni James |
| Wishing Ring | Joni James |
| Hold Me, Thrill Me, Kiss Me | Karen Chandler |
| Sh-Boom; (Life Would Be A Dream) | The Chords |
| Be My Life's Companion | The Mills Bros |
| Botch-a Me | Rosemary Clooney |
| Young At Heart | Frank Sinatra |
| Honeymoon On A Rocket Ship | Hank Snow |
| Wanted | Perry Como |

| | |
|---|---|
| Among My Souvenirs | Connie Francis |
| Moonlight Bay | The Mills Bros |
| Thank You For The Boogie Ride | Anita O'Day |
| Let Me Be The One | Hank Locklin |
| Happy Trails | Roy Rogers |
| Rags To Riches | Tony Bennett |
| Little Things Mean A Lot | Kitty Kallen |
| That's Amoré | Dean Martin |
| Baby We're Really In Love | Hank Williams |
| Make Love To Me | Jo Stafford |
| Ricochet | Teresa Brewer |
| Good Lovin' | The Clovers |
| Walkin' My Baby Back Home | Johnny Ray |
| I Won't Be Home No More | Hank Williams |
| You, You, You | The Ames Bros |
| Sixteen Tons | Merle Travis |
| Kiss Of Fire | Georgia Gibbs |
| Straighten Up And Fly Right | Andrews Sisters |

| | |
|---|---|
| It's Tight Like That | Lead Belly |
| Can Anyone Explain | The Ames Bros |
| L'Hymne à L'Amour | Edith Piaf |
| Bewitched, Bothered, & Bewildered | Rita Hayworth |
| Work With Me, Annie | Hank Ballard |
| Carolina Moon | Annette Hanshaw |
| Don't Care If The Sun Don't Shine | Georgia Gibbs |
| Honeysuckle Rose | Fats Waller |
| Slow Poke | Hawkshaw Hawkins |
| In The Jailhouse Now | Webb Pierce |
| Far Away Places | Margaret Whitting |
| I'm Movin' On | Hank Snow |
| I've Got The World On A String | Frank Sinatra |
| Anytime | Eddy Arnold |
| Good Rockin' Tonight | Wynonie Harris |
| Mister Sandman | The Chordettes |
| Cuban Pete | Desi Arnaz |
| Come On-a My House | Rosemary Clooney |

# Post Script

**The title spring:**

(from Chapter 7, Florida, "Come On-a My House") Annie sat inside the Patrician, with her feet on the curb and looked up at her husband. "I love you, Alex. And for my birthday, I want what every little girl wants. A pony. But a brood mare will do just perfectly." She had that smile. She shifted her hips and swung her legs into the cream Packard.

This novel contains genuine 100% recycled and rearranged alphabetic symbols, words and post-consumer thought.

You can find me on Facebook, Amazon, or Goodreads.

# THE LAST PAGE

*Some words are written in stone.*

6½ x 11 inch
Carved Fieldstone
Crafted in Pigeon Forge, Tennessee, USA, at
*The Sandman's Workshop*

Kilroy was here

*As a self-published author, my readers are my best advocates.
Please consider a simple rating or brief review
on Amazon or Goodreads.
It is appreciated.*

Made in the USA
Monee, IL
09 June 2025

12f0e742-75f2-460a-9dbe-de3a75ebee80R01